Spire Publishing

www.spirepublishing.com

Going Nowhere

by
Malcolm Taylor

Spire Publishing
www.spirepublishing.com

First published in Great Britain 2005 by Malcolm Taylor.
This edition first published in Canada 2007 by Spire Publishing.
Spire Publishing is a trademark of Adlibbed Ltd.

Note to Librarians: A cataloguing record for this book is available from the Library and Archives Canada. Visit www.collectionscanada.ca/amicus/index-e.html

Designed in Toronto, Canada
by Adlibbed Ltd.
Set in Baskerville and Baskerville Italics.
Printed and bound in the US or the UK
by Lightningsource Ltd.

ISBN: 1-897312-57-1

Spire Publishing
www.spirepublishing.com

To Siân.

*I wrote this for your father
when he was your age.
How time flies.*

GOING NOWHERE

O N THE NIGHT BEFORE THE DAY IT STARTED NIMROD woke suddenly an hour after midnight and sat bolt upright in bed.

Something was wrong.

He scoured the room, which glowed yellow from the light of the moon. Everything was in its place.

He sniffed the air. Nothing to disturb the special smell that belonged only to his room and nobody else's.

He tasted the warmth rising like baked bread from his bed. As deliciously marshmallowy as ever.

He listened intently to the night silence. Nothing. Yet … after a pause he cocked his head to one side and cranked up his ears. Something was still not quite right. Then he caught it. A metallic after-clang trembling in the night air. The town hall clock had struck early. And oddly.

A moment later he heard the machinery wind itself up, take a deep breath and release the coiled spring that swung the hammer that struck the bell with its familiar coppery chime.

One o'clock. Twice.

Tucking his perplexity to one side he returned his head into the warmth of his six pillows and burrowed back into his interrupted sleep.

Down the sleeping lane, across the narrow wooded valley, up in the slumbering town square, a shadow plucked itself from the cobbles. It shook its leathery head and fluttered dopily back into the night sky, blinking. This bird of the night was just on its way back to the dark lands beyond the woods when the moon came out from behind the clouds and flooded its eyes, causing it to collide with the clock, its horny beak creating an off-key chime.

Nobody else in the village heard it.

Nobody – not even Nimrod – picked up the creak of its leathery wings as it heaved itself back into the sky, heading back towards where the air was thicker and darker and kinder to its light-sensitive eyes.

Nothing but a small hiccup in the clockwork regularity of just another night.

But the uneasy clang had tweaked something in Nimrod's unconscious mind, and turned a rusty key in a long unused lock.

So, in the morning, when the seventh chime of eight of clock roused him, as always, from his night's sleep, the mischief was already simmering.

On the surface of this bright day all was familiar. The sun streamed like melting butter through the gap between the yellow curtains. The cosy smell of yesterday's clothes tangled with the aroma of six breakfasts from six neighbouring houses. These were what Nimrod knew best and they filled him – as predictable things do – with a sense of peace and comfort. No surprises to jolt a brain clambering out of muddy slumber.

Except – and the thought sent an electric tremor through him – today was his Final Youngday.

It was the last day he could run like a wild thing through the centre of the town without being taken for a thief … the last day he could clatter sticks against the railings of strangers' houses and then stick his tongue out at them when they yelled at him … the last day he could bark at dogs and meow at cats and spread both honey and peanut butter on the same hunk of bread … the last glorious day of Not Being Responsible.

Final Youngdays were ordained by law to be days of unreserved frivolity, and you were expected to devote yourself seriously to silliness.

Final Youngdays were days when you played the giddy goat with grave parents.

But what if you had no parents?

What then?

What now?

What is *now?*

When is *now?*

How could you describe it?

He tried, a bit, on his own.

Now, he decided, wasn't something you could delay until later. Now was, well, *now.* Unless he'd missed something, *now* meant … no procrastinating. It fitted into the tiny crack between *then* and *soon.* It was either about to appear … or it had just vanished. It was a fleeting moment. A firefly you could never catch. A trick of the light.

So why did it matter? It made no sense.

Suddenly it became the single most important challenge of his Final Youngday. He had woken up not knowing the meaning of one of the most used words in the English language. Well then, when his head hit the pillow this evening, he would know all there was to know about it. *Now.*

As he pulled on his boots and wondered what he could whip up for breakfast he thought some more about it.

Why did people say *now then* to you when the words had opposite meanings?

If it wasn't history and it wasn't the future, what exactly was it?

His head hurt.

He was going nowhere.

But the Library would know.

And it might also produce the answer to the other question tapping at the inside of his head like a woodpecker:

Why?

He wasn't sure why *why* was so insistent. He knew the word well enough – it had driven him into many a deep-thinking session that sometimes went on so long they made his brain hurt.

Why are girl's buttons on the wrong side?

Why does a bath wrinkle fingertips but not toes?

Why isn't it tea time yet?

But this *why* wasn't that kind of why.

After a hearty breakfast he tried to unravel the uneasy curiosity that not even a plate of buttered fluffcakes could banish.

It stayed with him, nudging him, as he steered his trusty wheelboard along his garden path, skidded down the valley path, squealed through the waking village, across the town square, screeching to a halt only to greet Crandall, the town tidier-upperer, who was studying a handful of bedraggled objects in his hand so intently he never even noticed Nimrod.

Funny, he was saying to himself, *funny. Never seen feathers like these, not in all my countless years. Who ever heard of leather feathers? They rhymed, but there was no reason to them. What kind of curious bird could have shed leather feathers?*

Across the valley and up the hill Nimrod's curiosity kept nagging him. Perplexing questions could usually be solved during a good hard skidding session with the plank of wood and the armchair wheels his father had crafted into the fastest vehicle in World's End; but this time, when he performed his famous double-spinback and braked to a stop just inches from the great oaken doors of the World's End Library, he was no wiser than when he'd set out.

He loved libraries. Standing there waiting for it to open, his hands thrust deep into his pockets as he kicked at pebbles, he thought there could be no place on earth so full of adventures. Walking through these doors he could visit faraway lands, meet people of every shade and shape, roar down raging rivers, hack his way through thick jungles, hear the ticking of the very Clock of Life.

When he heard the grate of the key in the door, the old excitement rose inside him again.

Something was going to happen in there today. It always did!

The door opened on a lean and lofty woman whose nose was weighed down by spectacles so thick her features seemed all dragged down towards the tip of her chin. It gave her a stern, forbidding air - but you mustn't allow yourself to be deluded by such first impressions. Miss Tillery was all dreams, everything she believed in lived inside her, sailing along, propelled by the warm breezes in her head, and she had no time for building expressions on her face.

"Why, good morning, Nimrod. You're up early today."

"Well you see, Miss Tillery, I had this sudden urge to be surrounded by books today. Does that sound odd to you?"

"If that's odd," replied the librarian, making a circular sweeping gesture encompassing the entire contents of her dominion, "then I must be a very peculiar kettle of fish. Now step forward and tell me the real reason."

"The real reason. Ah." He'd never been one for getting straight to the point. Particularly when the point was, well, there wasn't really a point, more a sort of nagging curiosity. He assembled his most inquisitive face - he had a whole private library of expressions to choose from - and puckered up his eyebrows impishly.

"Do you perhaps have any books on now?"

Miss Tillery rolled her eyes in her head and tasted the word. It had a nutty kind of flavour, like almonds.

"By now, I presume you mean Now? With a capital letter?"

"Sorry," said Nimrod, "did I pronounce it wrong?"

"*Now*. As opposed to *Then*."

"Exactly." Nimrod gazed expectantly up at the Guardian of the Books, who studied him from her lofty position.

"May I ask why?"

"Well, I'm not sure, exactly. It's just that, today being my Final Youngday and all, I woke up and asked myself: what now? Or should that be Now – with a capital letter?"

There was a loud, echoing creak as Miss Tillery unwound herself and turned round. It wasn't the floor: Miss Tillery had been born with creaky bones, a comfortable sort of sound, like a boat at rest in the tides.

"I have just the book, Nimrod. Follow me."

She creaked down an aisle of old leather-bound books, muttering to herself.

"Artichokes … Bull's-eyes … Cotton wool and Dalmatians … let's see… Eiderdowns … Fluff … Gobstoppers and HB Pencils … Ice cream … Jonquils … King Penguins … Liquorice … and Mist… here we are … the very book … all you ever need to know about Now."

She reached out and withdrew a heavy volume from the shelves, savouring the cloud of brown dust. "I love book dust," she once said; "book dust is clean dust, it tastes of words and hyphens and has the sherbetty zing of exclamation marks. Sometimes I collect it in little terracotta jars and sprinkle it on my soup…"

Alphabet soup probably, surmised Nimrod. He craned his head to read the title on the side of the big old book, a difficult task, for he didn't have much of a neck to crane.

The Great Curiosity Chest it read. *Open when Baffled*.

Taking it over to a table she laid it down gently, and as her hands lifted away, Nimrod noticed how she allowed them to briefly caress the surface of the book.

"I think you'll find what you're looking for in there."

Nimrod pulled up a chair and reverently parted the great volume. The pink parchment pages were brittle with age, crackling warmly as he turned them.

Miss Tillery returned to her desk where she sat sucking at lemon lozenges and working her way for the eleven and a halfth time through every volume on the shelf.

Above her dangled the sign that had hung there (rather crookedly) since the library first opened its doors. It read:

Books Must Enlighten.
Books Must Lift the Spirit.
Let no Ill Tidings Bring Despair to Those who Seek Wisdom.

What this really meant that only happy books were permitted in this library. Books written to make you feel good. Books on war, books with tragic endings, grumpy books, miserable books – none of them were allowed shelf space here in the World's End Central Lending Library (Closed Sundays and during Feasts). Books on politics were especially unwelcome.

Now.

The word leaped out of the page at him. He leaned forward to read what it had to say, which was:

If I describe the correct meaning of the word today, by the time you read this it will already be "then" – so I can only urge you to grab now with both hands and enjoy it for all it's worth.

Eagerly his eyes darted over to the next page, where the entry continued:

Readers can only be advised to stay clear of this dark and dismal place, and think no more of it.

Grab it with both hands? Stay clear and think no more of it? This didn't add up!

He looked up at Miss Tillery. She was lost in a world of *Caves of Coral and Other Curiosities.*

He peered back at the book again. No question about it. On the left page he was being encouraged to make the most of *now*, on the right

12

page he was being warned to stay well clear of it. What had made the compiler change his mind when he changed his page?

And then he noticed it. A slight unevenness halfway up where the two pages joined. Blinking, he leaned in closer to inspect the binding. Running his eyes up and down he could see where someone had carefully snipped a single page out of the book.

He checked the page numbers.

On the left, page 356. On the right, page 359.

Why?

He slid the book across the table and sat back to address this riddle. Perhaps Miss Tillery knew the answer? He looked up: she was buried deep in a coral cave, a lemon lozenge clicking in her mouth.

The way the entry on *now* was written, it didn't seem likely the compiler had much more to add to it. The implication was that *now* was something to take part in rather than to read about – so what was this *dark and dismal place* that didn't bear thinking about?

After this, the next entry was:

Noxious*: (nok-shus), adj. describing an offensive act which cannot be excused by even the most forgiving, such as tearing pages out of library books.*

So what could the missing word be? What fitted between *now* and *noxious?* He could think of none; his mind was a complete blank.

But one person would know the answer.

"Excuse me – Miss Tillery?"

He stood before her desk, chin tucked in, eyes looking up, waiting until she reached out for a fresh lemon lozenge to pop into her mouth, watching her eyes closely to pounce on the next ever-so-slight lapse of concentration.

"Sorry to disturb you, Miss Tillery, but can you think of any words that fit between *now* and *noxious?*

Hardly pausing she peered over her spectacles at him.

"Of course. The word you're looking for is *nowhere.*" Her eyes darted down to the page again.

"Er, no, I don't think so. The word I'm looking for is probably the name of a place. "

The book on coral caves slammed shut as if it had collapsed under a marine avalanche. She made a great show of stretching out her arm to uncover her wristwatch under her blouse and studying it closely.

"My goodness, that time already? Sorry, Nimrod. Closing time. Must rush." And up she stood.

"But … but you've only just opened!"

"Open, close, life is but a procession of openings and closings. Pack up your things, Nimrod. Time to be on your way…"

Nimrod was still watching her eyes closely. Was he mistaken, or had she cast an almost imperceptible glance up the E-F aisle?

Under the guise of reaching down to do up his bootlaces, he followed her line of vision up the aisle, to the nethermost shadows, where he could just make out an old leather trunk.

She clapped her palms together, and book dust rose up into the air. "Leave the book. I'll put it away. Off we go."

Nimrod decided to put her to the test, just to be sure.

"Are you sure nowhere isn't a place?"

"Of course it's not. Places have to be somewhere, and *nowhere* can't be *somewhere*, by definition. Do hurry up, Nimrod; I don't have all day."

He was right. On the mention of nowhere, her nervous eyes had flicked momentarily towards the leather trunk and back. Whatever had been written on the missing page, Nimrod was willing to bet he'd find it in the trunk.

"Very well, Miss B. Thanks for your help. Sorry to have troubled you." With a skip and a jump he was at the front door, where he stopped and looked back.

"Oh, Miss Tillery?"

"What is it, boy?" She stood up so suddenly, her head collided with the corner of the sign that banned ill tidings from the library.

"I only wanted to say, watch your head on that sign…"

She raised her eyes reproachfully. Nimrod took his opportunity to duck down the first aisle to the left of the door, the longest aisle in the library, the *Cookery* section.

Huddled in the top corner, he heard the librarian tutting and sighing and whatever-nexting and that-was-a-damn-close-thinging… then he heard the leather volume sliding up off the table and slithering back between its familiar neighbours on the shelf. Moments later her shoes click-clacked briskly past him, the door shut, the key grated in the lock, and her indignant footsteps crunched up the gravel and disappeared.

Alone in the Library.

Under normal circumstances Nimrod would have been giddy with joy. But the scent of conspiracy amongst those he trusted most – books and the Chief Librarian – threw him into an uneasy state.

Dust danced in the beams of light piercing the darkness from high windows. Skirting these spotlights, he moved alphabetically across to the E-F aisle where he had seen the trunk; the softer he trod, the louder the creaks seemed to echo across the room.

For a long time, he stood looking down at it.

What else could be hidden away in this trunk, so important a librarian was prepared to damage the books placed in her care?

He reached down and grasped the lid, heaving upwards.

Stubbornly it stayed shut.

Locked. He should have guessed.

Thrusting his hands into his pocket in frustration, he fiddled nervously with the bits and pieces that had gathered amidst the fluff. Small coins, a rounded pebble he liked to rub with his thumb, candy wrappings, a stick of chalk, a twirl of wire…

Wire!

Once, long ago, he had watched his father fiddle open the cake cupboard when his mother still hadn't arrived back from her cookery lesson. His dear mother and father. He sniffed as he remembered the figure of his father trudging off into the distance. Then, a year later, the Mayor standing at their door, hat in hand. Your Mother … a terrible accident … a runaway train … no survivors…

Shaking both unhappy memory from his thoughts, he drew the curl of wire from his pocket and knelt to feed it into the lock. Two tiny spiders ran out and gave him dirty looks. Easy on! That's our home you're invading there, pal!

Turning his head to one side so he could listen (what he expected to hear Nimrod couldn't say) he worried away at the mechanism inside until, suddenly, he heard a satisfying mechanical click.

This time the lid opened easily.

Inside was a small pile of very old books – and the missing pink parchment sheet from the *Great Curiosity Chest.*

Not daring to touch it, he leaned closer and read:

Nowhere: (Noh-ware), *a dark, sinister land, half in this world and half   out of it. Travellers should avoid this place like inns that do   not served cooked meals. Lying just sixty one miles as*
  the crow flies from the North Gate of World's End
  (see: World's End) the land is home to the unspeakable Nowarts and...

Click. Rattle. Scrape.

Nimrod looked up. What was that.

Groan. Creak. Slollop.

He'd recognise that slollop anywhere. It was one of Miss Tillery's lemon lozenges connecting with her teeth.

He pressed the lid back and it clicked into place. Back into the shadows he stepped, until they had wrapped coolly round him.

Voices were drawing closer. He recognised Miss Tillery, and – goodness, wasn't that Mr Coolper, the Mayor himself?

"How much did he see?" Mayor Coolper was asking, in an unusually hushed and secretive voice. (Nimrod had never heard the Mayor speaking softly; this was a man who spoke in Speeches, even a passing Hello Nimrod would be declaimed as if to a large, restless audience.)

"I think I managed to stop him in time. He was getting very close."

"Nice work, Verbena." So that was Miss Tillery's first name. The things you learn in libraries. "I mean, he's only a boy. Next year he receives The Knowledge; this year, youth must prevail. We can't go darkening his innocence with such threatening shadows."

"Indeed not, Mr Mayor. Indeed not. Boys must be boys..."

As they drew closer Nimrod scampered back along the rear aisle, clinging to the shadows near the wall.

"Rufus! Enoch! Grab one end each and follow me."

Peering through the shadows Nimrod saw two shapes step forward to grab the chest.

This was his chance. Scampering forward, he darted through the door and out into the crisp World's End morning, where even the sparrows seemed to be whispering secrets about him to each other.

One foot on the wheelboard and the other scooting nineteen to the dozen along the path he gathered his thoughts together.

Nowhere.

Why was it the name echoed in his head like a voice speaking into an empty biscuit tin?

Nowhere. Don't talk to me of Nowhere.

The voice in his head swirled around like a tiny whirling wind, lifting up little rustling leaves of memory. This wasn't the usual voice that blew through the inner corridors of his head, the voice that said annoying things like:

"You've already eaten enough of those."

"Get up - it's already gone eleven o'clock."

"No you can't. Hand it in to the Lost Property Office."

"Green vegetables are good for you."

There was something - yes, familiar about the voice. He drew a deep breath as he tried to locate it, and, as he did, in rushed a torrent of familiar scents ... new-baked bread, flour on aprons, warmth rising off a soft plump body, freshly soaped skin ... the unique, wonderful smell of ... his mother.

His eyes misted over as he remembered in perfect detail the little procession carrying the box along the winding path under the flowering jacaranda trees towards the cemetery planted with a thousand buddleias swarming with ten times as many butterflies. He remembered as if it were yesterday the little popping collisions of silk on air as the wings flapped and fluttered and hovered in the air to fan the funeral procession through ... he remembered (would he ever forget) the thumping grief deep inside him as he watched the box being lowered into the wet earth and the groan of the ropes and the trickles of soil on the lid of the coffin...

No. No that memory. Earlier, Nimrod, dig down earlier...

And then it came back to him.

He saw - and smelt - the Laughing Room of his family house with the silly drawings on the wall and the three Mimic-Mice on the mantelpiece watching so that when their time came (just before bedtime, usually) they would perform their mimes of the high points of the day, one mouse per

17

family member, exaggerating their characteristics like little live action cartoons, deflating their pomposity...

In the corner. Look in the corner.

In his memory, Nimrod turned his face immediately to the corner and saw, with a jolt of memory, a little man with dark serious eyes and glistening grey eyes crouched over a little pile of parchment which crackled in his nervous fingers.

Father!

It had started a week before, when his father - Lemli - had brought home a packet of papers that seemed to Nimrod at least a million years old.

Just after suppertime was always Games Time. But, for seven days his father had sat there, tucking the crackled papers deep into the shadows so that neither he nor his mother could read what was on them, his eyebrows arched and the twinkle in his eyes turned briefly off to save electricity.

"Where's Father gone?" he asked his mother one night, looking through the window at the silhouette of the thought-bowed man black against the circle of yellow moon.

"Nowhere, little Nimrod. You're father's gone ... Nowhere."

"But I can see him, mother, look, out the window, look..." He remembered tugging on her apron like an enthusiastic bell-ringer - and the pressure of her floury hand on his tousled hair.

"Shh, my son. Marriage does that to men sometimes. They look like they're sitting there but they've really gone ... Nowhere."

Then, flashing forward through his memories, he recalled the evening when the muttering of his parents' voices had gone on long into the night ... how he had risen from his bed at midnight and seen not one but two silhouettes in front of the moon, joined by the hands ... then the sad, faraway look in his mother's eyes when she set the places for breakfast the next morning and how he had trembled when he saw not three but just two bowls laid out on the table.

"Today, Nimrod, you sit in your father's place."

"But where's Father gone?"

She went over to the window and looked out.

"Nowhere. He's gone Nowhere."

18

And that was where his treasured memories of his father ceased.

Later, when his mother was out, he searched the house high and low for the old crackled parchment for a clue to where old Lemli might have gone, but found nothing.

Somehow he could never bring himself to ask his mother the question again. He knew she was coming up with different answers to her own questions every time she went over to the window and stared out.

Now it all came flooding back. That's what Final Youngdays did for you; you drew the same memories up from your well, but when you looked into them you saw deeper, you understood better, and the face reflected in them ... your face ... was an older, wiser face.

The pink parchment pages his father had crouched over all those evenings so long ago.

So that's where he had gone.

His mother had been telling him the truth all along.

Nowhere.

He'd gone off to find Nowhere.

Had he made it? Had he eventually got there? Was he, even now, sitting in some dark cold dungeon, a prisoner of those unspeakable Nowarts, thinking of his family the way they did of him, silently, night after night?

If that was where he was, he wasn't far.

Sixty one miles as the crow flies.

Above him there was a loud caw; a pitch black crow flew self-importantly overhead, in a hurry. Was he on his way to Nowhere – or was he on his way back? What tales could he tell?

The knowledge of this mysterious place had tarnished him for ever. From now on he could never *un*know what he had just learned; like the discovery that people died - ("a terrible accident, Nimrod. Hate to be the bearer of this tragic news...") – it would always be with him. Why did it always come from the Mayor? Is that what Mayors were for? Is that why they wore chains – to weigh them down like sadness?

How could he have lived all his life in World's End without even suspecting the existence of its enigmatic neighbour? What was so dreadful about it that children had to be kept from knowing of it?

And then, suddenly, it all fell into place.

Everything was meant.

He had climbed out of bed this Final Youngday asking the question: What now? And the library had led him to the answer.

First your father. First the brave Lemli tried. Now, young Nimrod, now you must find out all you can about Nowhere. Your time has come.

Like bathwater crashing into a tub Nimrod felt hot and cold streams splash together inside him and rise up from his boots until he didn't know if he was quivering from fever or shivering from cold.

This wouldn't do. Today he would learn what there was to be learned about Nowhere. Even – and he had to gulp bravely as the thought presented itself – even if he had to up sticks and actually go there.

"Two bags of flour. Six walnut shells full of honey. The dew from a hundred gooseberries. A sprinkle of clover…"

This muttered recipe came from the other side of the feather-duster flowers that divided the path in two. Lost in his dream world Nimrod crashed straight through them - and squealed to a halt slap bang in front of a powdery old man coming from the other direction, making notes as he walked. Nimrod immediately recognised the World's End baker.

The younger inhabitants of the town usually tried to avoid The Oastman, as he was known, for he spoke little (and gruffly when he did), and his eyes were buried so deeply under a forest of eyebrows they disappeared into the shadows, like small forest creatures. But today…

"Good day, Mr Oastman," Nimrod called out as he stepped forward. "And what a glorious day it is to be alive."

"What are you trying to say, Nimrod?" asked the Oastman, his eyes emerging briefly to reveal an ability to twinkle Nimrod had never heard commented on. "Are you suggesting there are other days when it's glorious to be dead?"

Nimrod gulped, and gazed around him, pretending he had just noticed the weather. Start again.

"Nice sort of day, wouldn't you say?"

The Oastman sniffed. "Nice enough." He wasn't one for long chats, and although his nose pointed towards Nimrod, both his feet were aimed away, towards a path leading to his house.

"It's the sort of day," continued Nimrod, "the sort of day one is awfully pleased to be Somewhere." He pointedly pronounced Somewhere with a capital S. "I mean, as opposed to being nowhere." Nowhere in this case was only afforded a small n.

"Eh?" The Oastman raised his puzzled head.

"Er, by nowhere, I mean Nowhere."

At the very mention of Nowhere, The Oastman's eyebrows dropped with a loud crash.

"*What* did you say?"

Nimrod decided it was time to be bold. "I was speaking about Nowhere, Mr Oastman. Have you ever visited it? Perhaps you baked someone there a cake once? They say it's not that far away, and you being such a famous baker in the area and all ..."

The baker did a living impression of one of his jam tarts in an oven, starting white and doughy, turning hot and brown, and then puffing out and glowing purple.

"The cheek of it!" he muttered in the direction of some invisible friend on his left, "How dare, how *dare* he talk to me of *that* place. And on his Final Youngday too - a year before he's meant to know!! What *is* today's youth coming to? Next thing you know he'll be gallivanting off to consult Kabil in his forest. Young people today. I ask you. No manners. No sense of civic responsibility."

With a snort he set off along the path leading to his house, muttering. Nimrod caught the expression: "Children. Thank fate and fortune I was never one of those."

So he wasn't dreaming. *Nowhere* did exist.

There were only two options. One was: remind himself this was his Final Youngday, forget the whole silly mystery, and trot off for a celebratory mid-morning sleep. The other was: pursue the clue the baker had just dropped, and visit Kabil in his lair. Nimrod had heard talk of the mysterious wizard who - it was whispered – had struck a dark deal with the Grey Forces.

By now, the mystery of Nowhere was the biggest *why* ever to buzz over the surface of his curiosity like a fly on a window pane. Even if he could sleep – which he doubted – the puzzle wouldn't go away; it would be there, laughing at him through its fingers when he woke up.

Anyway, visiting Kabil wasn't exactly a trip to Nowhere. He'd still be here, near his home, in his beloved World's End. And what was a stroll through the Lower Valley Forest, anyway?

Just thinking of the Lower Valley Forest made Nimrod's heart beat at twice its normal rate. Nobody in World's End ever ventured there. The first row of trees stood like sentries, branches linked like hands, knots like bulbous eyes peering out from under lumpy eyebrows of bark, their message clear: *stay out all who venture near!*

And behind, glimpses of a great brooding forest strangled with ivy, great twisted trees arching up to block out the sunlight. Winds whistled sinister music through the leaves, and strange birds and animals from times long past were said to flitter through the shadows. It was a forest even the owls avoided.

Only one thing for it.

To the North West lay the road that forked into the Lower Valley Forest on one side and the road out of World's End on the other, the very road his brave father had travelled all those years ago.

To the East, waited the friendly road that led down the Upper Valley and then up again, straight up to the bright yellow door of his home and the mat that said and meant Welcome.

If Nimrod had travelled East, this book would only have been 22 pages long, and you'd have been very displeased with him for cheating you out of an adventure.

So of course you'll be thrilled to learn that he tucked his wheelboard behind a bush, took a deep breath, pointed himself North West – and marched forward.

*

At the exact moment Nimrod's right boot made contact with the path, deep in the cavernous lungs of a sleeping mountain far, far away a crystal stirred on a bed of air.

It had always lived a trembling life, this crystal, it and the eight others which rested like partly separated orange segments on the fountain of air which flowed up from the floor of the cave. Sometimes they all stirred, each in its own different way, like sleepers troubled by dreams. But, at the exact moment Nimrod's right book struck the gravel, the tiniest of the crystals jerked and twitched and lost its balance and teetered on the edge before toppling off and crashing to the rocky floor of the cave, where it shattered into a starburst of tiny shiny fragments.

Deeper down in the same cave, where no light penetrated, the sound caused a matted lid to open - sideways, like sliding shutters – and a dark orb blinked out of the darkness.

What little air there was in the room clouded up with the fetid odour of sour breath. In the depths of the cave, a squat little creature shook its sleep-dulled brain (all three ounces of it) once, twice, three times and four, to rouse itself awake after its long sleep. It tasted the Bisto wisps of freshness that floated through, coughed, spluttered, and shook itself in disgust. In a while it drew itself up on its haunches, this thing, this tangled hairy thing, dully aware that it had been summoned from slumber to do what it was programmed to do.

The fragments of crystal were still rocking on the cave floor when the creature took its first step. With a swaying movement, like a spider alerted to prey by the plucking of its web, it extended its upper extremities in the gloom to scan the positions of everything in its lair and test them against the template in its memory, which was stored - like files - as odour-memories, in the sticky hairs at the back of its nasal cavity.

No doubt about it. Something was amiss.

Yesterday, there had been nine amber crystals. Today, there were only eight – eight and a hundred thousand broken splinters.

A complex, primitive reaction kicked in, one the creature was too brutish to understand but which it nonetheless knew it had been born to fulfil. It also seemed to sense that it would forfeit its life in the process, and despite its feral nature the knowledge caused it to wrinkle its brow and whimper.

Sharp talons scraped at the stony ground, clattering and twitching as it scuttled up the incline that wound its way around the air-fountain where the remaining crystals shimmered in the darkness. Up …up to where it was programmed to go.

Turning a corner too hastily, its lizardy tail struck a rock and snapped away from its body, squirming about on the foot of the cave, thrashing wildly. The creature scurried on, leaving its nether part behind. Unseen, the jagged edge writhed and wriggled - and bony shapes pressed out from within, like fingers sliding into a glove. In slow painful spasms the tail was growing a new body identical to the one already scuttling up the dark tunnel with its tidings.

The newly formed creature sniffed the foul air, storing the patterns of the eight rising and falling crystals in its memory, then dragged itself over to where its progenitor had slept all those years, and flopped down in a half-sleep to wait and listen and guard.

Upwards scurried its parent, on its first and last journey, its claws clutching at the rocks as its negotiated the sharp corners ... further ..., higher ... towards the fresh air (hateful taste) closer to the surface.

At their lowest station the Underguards heard it coming, that dreadful clittering clatter as the creature flexed every sinew in its body to carry its message instinctively to its destination. The sentries looked only briefly at each other, then – although no training had prepared them for this – as one man they stepped back and swung the gates wide open.

Leaving a rush of stinking air in its wake the creature scampered past them, its jowls pumping out sour enzymes to taste the message it bore, uselessly trying to make sense of it.

The tunnel spiralled upwards, onwards, outwards. Crashing into the jagged rock walls the creature sought the mountain peak, panting for breath, its nostrils rejecting the sour billows of fresh air starting to contaminate the foul cave-mist still stored inside it.

Out through the Surface Gate it sped, slashing out with its talons at the guards as it passed, clearing its path of all obstacles as it scuttled onwards, upwards, towards...

Gate after gate opened as the creature approached them. In the labyrinth of tunnels it instinctively knew just which to choose, which to disregard.

In the Great War Room a cloaked head rose from a battle-plan etched by the acid of a long bony fingertip into a flat rock.

The man – dare we call this a man? – rose to his full height and turned to the doors, the cloth of his cowl billowing out in the sudden movement.

Standing there where the double doors joined was a squat creature, dark green in colour, its trunk encased in a tortoise's shell, its head scarred and hairless like a reptile's but its arms and legs sinewy and hairy like a man's. It swivelled its head, cocking an ear-aperture to one side to catch any orders; it was swaying expectantly.

"Open!" The voice escaped from the hood like a sigh of despair.

Obediently the shelled guard turned and tapped a secret pattern on the vast double doors with its long horny finger-nails; they swung slowly open on hinges greased by the wax from the ears of slaves.

No sooner had they parted enough to permit the passage of a medium-sized warthog when the cave-creature hurled in through the gap and flung itself down on the grey marble floor at the feet of the hooded patriarch.

A frightful gasp – between a hiss of steam and a death-rattle – emerged from its nostrils. Too much fresh air up here. The cave-thing was slowly suffocating. Thirsty for breath it summoned together the last pockets of cave-mist within its slimy inner tubes and tunnels then, with a mighty effort, expelled them into the room, its beak of a mouth grimacing with pain as it formed the only three words it would ever speak.

"Ninth. Crystal. Fallen."

Then, with a long pained wheeze, it expelled the last of its life-breath from its body and lay twitching on the ground.

Kicking it out of the way, the hooded man stepped forward.

From within the darkness of the cowl came a howl, like a wolf baying at the moon …then a voice, a soft voice, gentle and persuasive, wistful almost.

The shelled sentry crept up and cocked its head to listen.

"I have long dreaded this moment. Sound the alarm. It has begun."

*

On the brow of the last hill before the narrow path leading down into the Lower Valley Forest, Nimrod turned to survey his town.

Off the main Village Square narrow cobbled roads wound off in all directions, daubed with houses painted pale peach, orange, lime, apple and rich damson plum. What a fruit salad of a town he lived in. Further out, the houses grew sparser, encircled by low myrtle fences and shaded by trees that blossomed eleven months of the year. Almost at the edge, under a quaint chimney just waiting for some small child to draw in a welcoming spiral of smoke, Nimrod picked out his own little house.

Shapes moved up and down the paths, his neighbours, going about their daily business, stopping to chat and ask after each other and pass the time of day without thinking up excuses to move on. A small knot moved through the square towards the Town Hall, two of them carrying a trunk. But it was too distant for him to recognize the mysterious chest from the library as it headed for its new hiding place.

As towns go there's not much of World's End - at the last census just seven hundred and eighteen people were counted. If the truth be known, this figure is not considered very accurate, because the Census Master was also the proud holder of the Fibber's Trophy for the fifth year in succession. (Six years ago the winner had lied to him about the date of the play-off.)

But this town meant everything to Nimrod, and his heart pumped a pint of pride through his system, though as he approached the forest he wished it had been a pint of courage.

The gnarled trees reached their branches out towards him like beggars. He regretted telling nobody where he was bound; if he disappeared now, no one would know where to even *start* looking. But the mystery of Nowhere overpowered his foreboding and in he stepped, along the dark wet path, whistling a happy tune that would have given the Census Master a run for his money in this year's Fibbing Championship.

The wind caressed the crisp dead-leaf branches like fingers trailing an out-of-tune harp, and a damp, festering smell rose up from the rotting forest leaves that squirmed as he trod on them.

For a moment Nimrod had second thoughts. Deciding that these were insufficient he summoned up third, fourth and fifth thoughts. But something in the forest seemed to draw him on, to beckon him in deeper.

Timorous insects scuttled out of the way of his boots, irritated at being disturbed, and not that far away a forest creature howled.

Beware! Unwelcome intruder!

Had he translated it right?

Could they mean him?

He drew his jerkin closer to his body; the air was wintry here where the sun was as much a stranger as him. And the silence … somehow the deathly hush broken only by the crackle of the dead leaves made the temperature feel many degrees colder.

He stopped. A rickety signpost had been hammered into a tree-trunk. Dim letters spelt out the words:

HOUSE OF KABIL
MASTER WIZARD/SORCERER
ALL VISITORS ARE TRESPASSERS.
NO TRESPASSERS.

There you go then. A clear command. The terminus for the obedient.

But while his reverse gear pleaded, so did Nowhere. And Nowhere won. Nimrod looked in the other direction, pretending he hadn't seen a thing, and pressed on.

Not much later he came to a second signpost, which read:

DIDN'T YOU READ THE FIRST SIGN?

On top of this one, glaring balefully through bloodshot eyes, perched a pitch-black raven, glowering down at Nimrod. It licked its lips.

"Ah well," he said out loud, to nobody in particular but just loud enough for the raven to hear every word, "such a pity I never learned to read."

First - out-and-out disobedience. Now - bare-faced lines. This wasn't the path to Kabil's dwelling … it was the road to ruin.

Onwards and downwards he went, whistling in the dark.

About fifty yards further, a third sign had been hammered into the ground. This one cautioned him thus:

ABSOLUTELY, POSITIVELY NO TRESPASSERS.
(AND THAT MEANS YOU!)

On top, buckling it with its weight, sat a Hunter Eagle, its tummy rumbling with hunger. Nimrod grinned timidly at it, but didn't even think of turning back. Well, a bit. Well, actually, he thought of little else until the next sign came into view, a dozen paces deeper. A menacing vulture guarded this one; its claws had gouged deep gashes into the wood. His personal sign said:

TRESPASSERS WILL BE CRUELLY TREATED.

"I can still turn back," thought Nimrod. "It's not too late yet, but it may very well be, before too long."

While he was still trying to make his mind up he came upon the last sign. There were no bones about its message:

TRESPASSERS WILL BE KILLED.

And guarding it was a huge black pterodactyl, preening its leathery wings.

Nimrod stepped up to it, his hands in his pocket and his heart in his throat. "One peck and you're history!" he warned the extinct Cretaceous bird, in words entirely free of saliva.

Two coal-black eyes pierced him, two deep pools in a haze of mist. He averted his eyes – and saw, at the far end of the path, a tumbledown wreck of a cottage, its right side sunk deeper into the forest bed than the left. What ever it was, welcoming it wasn't.

For a long time he stood weighing up the balance of things. Was Nowhere really worth the vultures, the prehistoric birds, the lop-sided cottages in dark forests, the ominous strangers concealed inside? He seriously considered calling off his stupid mission and returning home for tea and cakes. But … but no, dammit, he had vowed to learn about Nowhere and learn he would.

Casting one last look at the pterodactyl, which was now unfolding its wings like an umbrella, he hurried off towards the cottage.

A musty aroma floated up from the direction of the cottage, its origin a thin blue ribbon of smoke drifting out of a crooked chimney askew on the roof. Tangled shrubs encircled the cottage and a creeper clung to its walls, exploding into little black and yellow flowers as you watched, puff, puff, puff. There was a knocker in the shape of a skull on the front door, and, underneath, a notice in blood-red ink (Nimrod hoped it was ink) read:

KNOCK AT YOUR OWN PERIL.

Nimrod knocked. At his own peril.

From deep inside came angry muttering and the shuffle of slippered feet, then a rattling noise, a cry of "What fresh hell can this be!" - and the door opened, creaking like a rusty wheelbarrow.

Standing before Nimrod was the most fretful man he had ever seen. His eyebrows were curved into quote marks enclosing a nose which resembled a big inquisitive question mark. He was dressed in a black dinner jacket, with shiny patches that reflected Nimrod's eyes blinking back at him. Straining at the single thread mooring the last button his brightly coloured waistcoat was stained with honey and decorated with butterflies. Peering closer Nimrod saw that they were alive, fluttering their wings and giving the waistcoat an air of constant bustle. The wizard's hands were buried in a fluffy muff which a swarm of moths was busy dining on, and on top of a silver mop of uncombed hair a bowler hat with a nibbled brim was perched like an afterthought. Above his upper lip clung a droopy moustache which offered clues to his choice in breakfast, and from under a furrowed brow a pair of sad eyes peered out, expecting the worst. Around his neck a placard read:

I THOUGHT I SAID NO TRESPASSERS

But the old wizard contradicted his own counsel.

"How nice to have a visitor." said Kabil. "Nobody's dropped in for umpteen years. Step inside."

"Don't mind if I do," said Nimrod – and, suddenly, he didn't.

Inside, the wizard's house looked as if a bomb – no, worse, a small boy – had hit it. The floor was strewn with piles of books. Chairs swung from hooks on the wall. Pasted to the ceiling were faded newspaper clippings, one of which announced the invention of the press that had printed it.

A stuffed parrot dangled from a thin thread attached to a wooden beam and a swarm of moths of various shapes and sizes fluttered hither and thither, flirting with his gown. Kabil brushed them aside as he walked through.

"Blasted *Lepidoptera!*" he muttered, as you and I might carp at midges.

In the centre stood a large 'No Parking' sign, against which leaned a bicycle with only one wheel intact. Shelves lined the eastern wall, propping up bottles filled with coloured liquids and powders and little glass balls that shone and sparkled; one was filled to the stopper with shoelaces in every colour of the rainbow. In the corner a toy band kept churning out the first two lines of the World's End Anthem until the mechanism slowed down and ground to a moaning halt. A pair of false teeth smiled at Nimrod from inside a champagne glass. Seven hats of seven shapes hung from seven crooked nails. But the main attraction lay on a small table covered in magic symbols of light and darkness. A gen-u-ine Crystal Ball.

Over in one far corner a small fire warmed a flagon connected to a glass flask by a spaghetti of transparent rubber tubing held together by clothes pegs and paper clips. It emitted soft burping sounds as it coughed little black clouds a couple of feet up into the air. There was a tiny crash of thunder … more like a pop, really … and tiny drops of rain came drizzling down into a bucket.

Kabil noticed how Nimrod was gaping at it.

"That'll make my fortune, that will. Kabil's Incredible Ice Instigator. Nearly there. I'm just working on the right spell to accomplish the instant chilling." His face lit up. "I made it boil last Thursday. Imagine that. Boiling rain! Talking of boiling, what would you say to a nice cup of tea?"

Nimrod shrugged.

"Any particular blend?" asked Kabil, eyebrows arched. "Would you prefer Indian, China, Assam, Hemp, Earl Grey, English Breakfast, Orange Pekoe or Ceylon?"

"Ah," said Nimrod. "I really wouldn't mind a nice cup of Ceylon."

"Blast!" muttered Kabil, "now you've caught me out. All I have is coffee. Will coffee do?" With a sigh of weary defeat he added: "can't say I didn't give it my best shot. I mean, you *might* have said, actually, if you don't mind, I'd sooner have a cup of coffee, in which case I would have said, well there you go, it's already on the boil, and you would have thought highly of me. Still, as I keep saying, a bird in the bush is worth two in the hand. Now where's that kettle of mine?"

Nimrod was still busy trying to see where the bird - or even the bush - fitted in, when a big, steaming mug of coffee appeared before him. When he looked up, he found Kabil inspecting him closely as if he was an article up for sale.

"Is anything wrong?" Nimrod asked.

"Wrong? Oh my goodness me no. It's just that I haven't had visitors for so long I'd forgotten what they looked like."

"If I might suggest, " started Nimrod, "might it have something to do with all those notices outside?"

"Ah yes." Kabil looked mournful. "I put those up yonks ago. I kept flunking at the University of Wizardry. Thirty times, in fact. Some people just aren't good at written exams. So we came to a mutual agreement: they continued teaching, I left. Result? Two satisfied parties." He gave the kind of shrug that's meant to mean what do I care, but Nimrod could see that he did really, deeply.

Nimrod didn't know quite how to respond. So he returned to the original question. "But why did you put them up? All those scary notices?"

"It helps," Kabil explained with an air of authority. "All wizards have them, you know. Dire warnings to the interloper. *Admonitory Notices* was the last lesson I attended before they sacked me. I know sleeping during lessons is nothing to be proud of, but it was the snoring they couldn't come to terms with. It was their fault in the first place. Far too much homework."

Nimrod sought refuge in his coffee, then turned his steamed-up eyes back on Kabil. "You're a wizard, right? Then would you show me a trick, please?"

"A trick? Do you really want to see a trick?" Kabil was beside himself (or almost – that was another lesson he had missed).

"There's nothing I'd rather."

"Why, that's most considerate of you ... most considerate indeed."

31

Sorting through the debris on the floor and knocking over a scale model of a Bessemer Converter he rummaged like a mad thing through his junk, flinging the discards over his shoulder. Nimrod hopped from foot to foot to dodge the missiles. As he rummaged around the wizard muttered to himself. "Magic Wand ... now where is it ... I had it last Halloween ... damn wand ... where is it? Fiddlesticks. That's where I should have filed it. Sticks you fiddle with. Damn and blast it thrice times over. Make yourself known, wand ... Mr Wand ... the esteemed and *tres honorable* Monsieur Wand ... now get your act together and reveal yourself to your lord and master."

On and on he fussed, hunting absolutely everywhere. But try as he might, the wand refused to be found. Suddenly Kabil turned to Nimrod with a victorious expression hidden amongst his wizardly folds and crumples

"See? It's gone. Disappeared off the face of the earth. Look!" He peeled back the sleeves of his robe to reveal arms almost as gnarled as the oldest trees in the forest. "Nothing up North." Hoisting his wizard's skirt he revealed a pair of knobbly legs jammed into bright yellow socks. "Nothing down South." He smiled victoriously. "How's that for a bewildering trick? The Incredible Disappearing Wand. No springs. No elastic. All real magic."

Nimrod thought, well, perhaps, but he applauded loudly and said "Bravo. Bravo."

Kabil beamed. "Now of you go and tell everyone you meet: you should have seen him do the Disappearing Wand. I saw it for myself. Couldn't believe my eyes. One moment it ... it just wasn't there. You take it from me, that Kabil, what a sorcerer, a wizard of massive dimensions. You people ought to be proud of him!"

"Well I am," gushed Nimrod. "Really. As a wizard I think you're the bees knees."

Kabil clapped his hands. "Another coffee for the boy! I'll double the last one. Two spoons. Six sugars."

"Not right now, thanks. Now, about why I came to see you..."

Kabil looked even more perturbed. "Oh yes, my rent. I suppose it was inevitable. What is the world coming to, sending a boy to do a man's job. I hope they're paying you handsomely, though I doubt it. I know the City Treasurer, fingers like fly-paper. All right then, how much do I owe? I must be what, at least twenty years in arrears…" Plunging a bony hand into a pocket he withdrew some loose change and held it out.

"Nobody in World's End pays rent any more, don't you know?" explained Nimrod, waving away the offering. "Rent was abolished ages ago."

"My goodness, how time flies. Still," he said, dropping the money into a mechanical piggy bank which had opened its mouth when it heard the jingle, "it all goes to prove. All work and no play makes Jack a dull boy."

"Who's Jack?" Nimrod was about to ask, but thought better of it: if he was so dull he wasn't worth asking after. Instead he said: "Mr Kabil, I've come here to enquire about Nowhere."

"No, no, you've got my name wrong. It's not *Mister* Kabil; it's just Kabil. I don't approve of first names. Why have two when one will do equally well? It's like owning two houses and only living in one. I'm a wizard, not a politician. But I'm pleased to hear you asking about Nowhere. So few people do, these days."

"What is Nowhere like, Mr.. Er, I mean, Kabil?"

"Nowhere? Funny you should ask about Nowhere, I was just thinking about it myself. I can see you and me are going to get on famously. What's your name?"

Nimrod told him.

"I like it," Kabil said. "Two syllables. All the best names have two syllables. That's why I don't like people calling me Mister. Doubles the syllables. Nowhere's got two syllables too, did you notice? But that's the exception that proves the rule. Not a good place, Nowhere. The pits. Of course, I've never been there in person, but I know it all the same."

"Is it really as dark as everyone says?"

"Oh, I suppose as places go, Nowhere is fairly dark. In fact, it's pitch black. You can't see a thing. But never you worry. If you're planning on visiting Nowhere, I'll give you a pair of spectacles that will open your eyes. But remember, once you put them on, the Nowarts can see you as well."

"Nowarts?" said innocently. "What on earth are they?"

"That's exactly what they're not," said Kabil, "they're nothing on earth."

This only served to whet Nimrod's appetite. "Tell me more," he whispered breathlessly.

"Nowarts are the inhabitants of Nowhere, of course. Dark creatures, grey as the night. Don't involve yourself with the Nowarts my lad. They're not to be meddled with."

"More! Tell me more!" pleaded Nimrod in a hushed voice.

"You don't want to know too much, believe me. Suffice it to say that that the worst creature you ever dreamed about after eating smelly cheese too late at night is ten times more attractive than a Nowart. There. I've said quite enough. So you're planning to visit Nowhere, are you?"

"Well, not exactly visit…"

"Brave boy. I'm exceedingly proud of you. Wait there and I'll dig out those goggles."

He swam through the debris across to an oxidised copper kettle, removed the lid, and withdrew an ancient pair of glasses. "Here," he said, "keep them in a safe place for the journey."

Nimrod took them and inspected them. Engraved into the wide rims were words in a language he couldn't recognize. A pair of tiny lozenges, one attached to each arm, had been sealed up with red wax. The frames were formed from something purple, shiny like metal but slightly sticky to the touch. They were surprisingly light.

"Don't they have lenses?" Nimrod asked, turning them over in his hand.

"Lenses?" Kabil looked puzzled. "Oh shoot. Lenses."

He yanked open a cupboard door, releasing another swarm of butterflies and moths, and scrummaged through the contents. Out fell a battered top hat, a dead bat with a bandaged wing, a large dice with spots of different colours, and the lost magic wand. But no lenses.

Kabil looked crestfallen and bewildered, both at the same time.

"Spedangle it!" he exclaimed … daringly - for this was an expression he used only in direst need. "Now where could I have put the little beggars?" He stood, thinking hard, for a good five minutes, and not a muscle moved. Then his face dropped about six inches.

"Oh yes," he said, and so liked the way he said it that he repeated it over and over again. "Oh yes, oh yes, oh yes, oh yes, oh yes, OH YES."

With that he sat down in satisfaction.

"Oh yes what?" ventured Nimrod.

"I've remembered," he said proudly. "I've remembered where they are. I put them into my little sewing box, which I gave away. No one can say I haven't got a memory to die for. In fact, I've got the best memory in World's End."

"Who did you give the sewing box to?"

"I've forgotten, I'm afraid" Then he looked sideways at Nimrod. "But even people with the best memories forget things now and again. Stands to reason. It only happens to those whose heads are crammed so full of things to remember there's no space left for any more. Did you study the Science of the Mind at your school??"

"Certainly not!" said Nimrod.

"Good," he said, sounding immensely relieved. "Pleased to hear that. Waste of precious brain power. Well now you've had your first lesson. Store it away somewhere safe until you need it, like the glasses."

"The glasses," repeated Nimrod. "Or, more to the point, the lenses. Won't you please try to remember? It's there, somewhere, hiding. What if you were to sweep out an unwanted memory?"

"Forgetting's an impossible task for a sage like me. Goes against all my moral principles. I was only saying the same to my last visitor. What was his name again? Corkscrew of a man. The teacher ... somebody remind me ... Septimus ... Hepatitis ... Nepotist ... no, Crepitus, yes, that's it, Mister Crepitus." His eyebrows formed an upturned V. "I'm not adding syllables there, you understand. That's his first name. You're Nimrod – he's Mister. When they named him, his parents wanted to give him a good start in life, so they chose the forename *Mister* so people would treat him with respect right from day one. It was never easy to address a two week old baby as Mister, but there you are. He always looked old, that one. Have you met him?"

"Have I met him? He was my teacher. He taught me all I know. I can still hear the creak of his cane as he stood in front of the class, bending it menacingly. Oh yes, I know Mister Crepitus all right!"

"Ah!" said Kabil. "So you know him by his first name! Funny that.

35

Most children don't earn that privilege. Either you were a very advanced pupil, or he was a very enlightened teacher."

"Why did he consult you?"

Kabil frowned so deeply his hat tilted and fell off.

"Come now, little Nimrod. You know I can't tell you that. We wizards are sworn to safeguard our secrets. It's what we're famous for. It's in our Code of Practice. We take an oath, you know. Can't go spreading confidential information to all and sundry. Particularly Mister Crepitus. He wouldn't want the world to know he consulted me about mixing up a special spell to subdue a bossy wife, now would he? Sorry, Nimrod. But that must and will always remain a private matter between Crepitus and me."

"Old 'Whacker' Crepitus? A bossy wife? Now how about that!"

Kabil looked relieved.

"Ah, so he told you too. Well that's only to be expected. You and him being on first name terms…"

"So you gave him the sewing basket?" Nimrod didn't want to appear too eager, but time was running short. Final Youngdays only lasted one day a lifetime, after all.

"That was my Cunning Ploy." (He pronounced the words with a capital C and P.) "I coated the tip of a bodkin with 3.25cc of Potion Number 4. Women always prick themselves when they sew, it's all part of the spirit of martyrdom they adopt when they perform household chores. I believe they take secret oaths, like us wizards. When she pierces her thumb, in goes the anti-bossy mixture, and out goes the bullying element. Clever, what?"

"Brilliant!" exclaimed Nimrod. "You're a genius!"

Kabil blushed, bright pink. Then his head shot up so fast that he found himself looking behind his back. He quickly righted it, then exclaimed: "That's who."

"Who?"

"I gave the box to Mister Crepitus. See? My memory's even better than yours. You couldn't remember that."

Nimrod didn't bother to argue; he was too busy quaking in his boots. Of all the people in World's End, Crepitus was the person he most feared. Now he'd have to brave him – and run the risk of hearing the creaking of the cane again. Just when he had learned to forget it.

"D-do you think he might still have the sewing basket?"

"I don't see why not. You could always go and ask him."

Nimrod pulled himself out of the chair, making a rude pop with his nether regions like a cork sliding out of a bottle. He headed for the door but Kabil reached out and stayed him.

"Oh no you don't. Stay right where you are."

Nimrod nerve's returned. Maybe the old man wanted to practise spells on him. After all those years and his memory rusty ...

But Kabil held him gently by the forearm, and led him across the room. "Come – there's a thing I must show you."

When Nimrod saw where the wizard was taking him, his heart fluttered. They were headed straight for the crystal ball.

The globe – half the size of a football – swam with a sort of milky-marbleness, like a dolphin's eyes. Then, realising he had never seen a dolphin Nimrod decided it was more as if Kabil had scooped clouds out of the sky and imprisoned them inside it. Nimrod was mesmerised by the swirl; here now was real magic.

"My lad," said Kabil, and suddenly he stood tall and strong, suddenly Nimrod saw that this was a real wizard after all, a wizard with a mysterious force in his voice. "If you're planning to go to Nowhere, Nimrod, I'll see you right."

"How?" asked Nimrod, his eyes wide.

"Take a look at this here crystal ball," he said, running his fingers lovingly over the dome. "By using this here crystal ball, I'll be able to watch over every stage in your journey." His eyes narrowed and deepened. "Three times you'll be able to call on me for help. Three times only - then the power is spent. You must choose your occasions wisely."

He reached down and cranked a tiny handle in the platform. The clouds cleared as the sky does after a rainstorm - and Nimrod made out a twisting path winding between grotesque boulders.

"You see?" said Kabil, "I can keep tabs on you all the time. But I'm powerless to help unless you call for me."

"How do I do that?" enquired Nimrod, wishing his heart wouldn't thump so noisily.

"By calling out: *Kabil, Kabil, Kabil - by the powers of light and goodness I direct you to send aid.*"

"That will give me the power? Even though I'm so far away?"

"It will. Now come over here with me."

Kabil led him across to another cupboard and drew out a flask and a small leather casket.

"Take these," he said. "The flask contains a nectar the likes of which you've never tasted before. Just one drop on your lips will quench your thirst for a whole day or more. And the casket contains my own brand of diet wafers - half of one will still your hunger until the sun rises again."

Nimrod tucked them gratefully into his jerkin. But Kabil wasn't finished yet. He reached back into the depths of the cupboard and withdrew a small instrument with a grey strap, like a wristwatch.

"And this – go on, take it, it won't bite. That little arrow will direct you back to me no matter where you are. So if you get lost, just consult your Kabil Kompass."

Nimrod strapped it securely to his wrist. Kabil watched him like a father standing over a boy strapping on his sports boots before a big match, and draped a long spidery arm around his shoulders.

"Just a few more words of advice before you go. Whatever you do, make sure you find those lenses. They will be your most valuable allies. But without the frame, they are powerless. As I told you, they will render Nowhere and the Nowarts visible to you. But it will also render you visible to the Creatures of the Night, as the Nowarts like to be known, so beware.

"Also, whenever you find yourself in even a murmur of trouble, think good thoughts. Try to conjure up happy images. This often does the trick. And always remember that you have three opportunities to call on me. I will be watching your progress. Now be off - and may the powers of light and goodness form a ring around you."

Nimrod didn't know quite what to say. He could feel the tears of gratitude welling up in his eyes, and he didn't trust his own voice. He nodded a couple of times (but not too vehemently to dislodge the tears) and turned away.

"Oh no! Disaster has struck!"

Kabil sounded so pained Nimrod had to turn back. Had he lost something else? Had the pterodactyl come for his supper?

"It's the macaroons! They'll be spoiled!" He rushed madly off to a small oven set into the wall, out of which blue smoke was streaming. Nimrod decided that if any time was ripe to leave this was it, bang on the nose, so he clutched at the cask and flasket ... repeat ... the flask and casket and skipped out of the door. The last word he heard was a most unwizardly one, but he convinced himself it was a spelling error and not that one, and ran back up the path.

The return journey was not nearly so terrifying as the journey there. The trees no longer seemed so overshadowing and dark, the icy winds had settled and the birds had thought of something better to do than sitting all day long on stupid notice boards.

This gave Nimrod his chance. As he came to each one he grasped the posts and with every sinew he could summon uprooted them from the ground and tossed them deep into the scrub.

The first notice, though, deserved a different treatment. With the stick of chalk he always kept in his pocket for emergencies he changed the message to read:

HOUSE OF KABIL
MASTER WIZARD / SORCERER
ALL VISITORS VERY WELCOME INDEED
COFFEE GUARANTEED (DELICIOUS)

But in the forests of his mind, something dark stirred. What had started as a search for answers to the question *what now?* seemed to be turning into something far more sinister. Did Kabil really imagine he, Nimrod, was really planning to set out on an actual journey to Nowhere? Using *feet?* Him still in the bloom of youth? More to the point, if he wasn't, then why had he accepted the spectacles, the wristwatch, the wafers?

Wrapped up in these thoughts he was distracted by an aria from an opera delivered in a knee-trembling *basso profondo*. Looking up, he saw a figure coming from the opposite direction: Sam Quincetry.

Nimrod's heart leaped. Here was an opportunity not to be missed. Sam knew all there was to know about absolutely everyone. With so few inhabitants in the village it was hardly worth printing a newspaper, so one of the townsfolk was elected to spread the news. Bertha Quincetry had been the obvious choice. She wasn't exactly a gossip, but she did like to know who was doing what to whom. And when she found out, she couldn't wait to share the information with all and sundry, generous soul that she was.

Every morning she would sit in a large chair in the middle of the marketplace, and the people of World's End would come to whisper questions.

Is it true that Mr Elgrid is getting married?
How many times has Mrs Beltangle been on a diet?
Do you know anyone who wants a cat without a tail?
Why won't Mayor Coolper eat his greens?
Why did the chicken cross the road?

And so on.
And so forth.
Bertha charged nothing for this service, but expected a small gift in return. Any gift would do – as long is you could eat it. As a result her circumference unfolded, until one night, somewhere between midnight and one o'clock, while Sam was in the bathroom, he heard a pop. He rushed back – his wife was gone. All night he searched, in cupboards, under the bed, behind the fridge, in the fridge, but she was nowhere to be fund. The next morning Sam found a piece of wrinkled, shrivelled pink skin like a punctured balloon caught up in the bedclothes, and saw the hole in the ceiling. That was that. Flesh one moment, thin air the next. The World's End newspaper had burst.

So, after a suitable period of mourning, Sam took over.

"Good morning, Mr Quincetry," greeted Nimrod. "Just the man I wanted to see."

"That goes both ways, Nimrod," replied Mr Quincetry, and his face lit up with real pleasure. "I presume you have a morsel of goss ... er some interesting news to share?"

Nimrod hesitated. He could approach this two ways: the short way or the long way. "Er ... busy morning, Mr Quincetry?"

Sam Quincetry snorted. "Busy morning you ask me? I always have busy mornings, every morning of my life is a trial. Up before the sun, down after the last midnight chime. Ear to the ground. Nose to the grindstone. Fight the good fight, that's my lot in life. Spread the news, good or not. Fearlessness First, that's my catchphrase. I tell what needs to be told. That's the kind of man you see before you, Nimrod. Never shirk from the facts. What I know, I tell. There's not a person can scare me off the truth, not a soul, you hear me?"

Nimrod nodded, mutely, to let Quincetry know that he had indeed got the picture.

"Standing before you today, Nimrod, let me offer you some precious advice. Stand your ground, boy. Keep your chin up. Let courage be your watchword. Follow that advice and one day you can count yourself proud if you're even half the man I am. Fearless Sam, the Newspaper Man."

While Sam was busy talking, Nimrod was busy plucking up courage to ask the vital question.

"Er," he began, then decided that on his Final Youngday normal rules didn't apply, "er, exactly how far it is to Nowhere?"

Sam stopped halfway through the word *fearless* and went seven shades whiter, as if his face had suddenly been dipped in a patent brand of detergent.

"No-*what?*"

"No-*Where*, please," said Nimrod politely. "You know, where the Nowarts live."

Sam Quincetry apparently knew all too well.

"And where ... wh-where ha-have you just c-come from?"

Nimrod opened his eyes innocently. "Why, from Kabil, the Wizard. He's really had a terrible press, you know, you'd understand that, you being the Newspaper Man and all ..."

But he was cut off at a point precisely between the two *l*'s of *all* by Sam Quincetry, whose jaw suddenly gaped so wide that it creaked , the same kind of noise his late wife might have made lowering herself into a cane chair.

"D-do you seriously mean to t-tell me you've just visited K-kabil, and that y-you're thinking about ... *that* place?" As he spoke, his nose began to twitch like a rabbit in a lettuce patch.

"Got it in one," Nimrod congratulated him. "Smack on the nose. I wanted to find out more about Nowhere..."

Nimrod had no time to finish his explanation. When he looked up, the fearless Sam Quincetry was in the final stages of scarpering over the brow of the hill, whimpering.

"Oh dear," sighed Nimrod, not (on the spur of the moment) able to think up anything more original to say, and set off down the road. "Aren't people odd?"

*

They sat around the stone table, the Inner Circle, the five members of the Committee of War, looking across to where their leader stood, hands thrust behind his back, gazing out of the window into the dark of the day.

He turned suddenly and strode towards them, his cloak billowing out behind him.

"We must prepare ourselves for turmoil," he growled. "The ninth crystal has shattered."

There was a gasp from the Men of War. They looked at one another in disbelief, echoing their leader's words.

" The crystal!"

"Shattered!"

"Not the seventh. Not even the eighth. But the ninth!"

"There's turmoil afoot!"

"We'd better prepare ourselves!"

Each adopted his darkest, most quarrelsome expression, each secretly convinced he was the only member of the Inner Circle who didn't have the faintest idea what the Hooded One was on about.

"I see you tremble," continued their leader. "As well you might. Even now, great peril is approaching from beyond, in the form of a young knight who dreams of our destruction. He must be stopped in his tracks."

He spun round and pointed at the ugliest of his Least Mistrusted – not an easy choice, for they were, without exception, an unseemly lot.

"You – Xero. Send the most cunning of your men to locate him and follow him as he crosses the Plain. Go now. Don't gawp at me, you with that hideous purple tongue of yours lolloping about in that wet pink hole of a mouth. Every second wasted is – " he thought about it – "a waste of one sixtieth of a minute."

They all murmured in humble appreciation of their leader's great wisdom. He truly was a great and sagacious leader indeed.

"Now!" His voice grew shrill.

Xero bowed subserviently, contorting himself into the stoop of a gnarled tree. His head uncomfortably close to the ground he muttered obsequiously: "It is done. Now. Not then. Not later. Now. I will do it now. Note the present tense of my deed. Observe me as I obey at this very nowness in time…"

The Hooded One leaned forward.

"Oh shut up. As for the rest of you – I want a report on the readiness of your platoons to meet this Great Peril. Be assured – it will result in War. Limbs will doubtless be lost. There may be some blindness – and the odd case of deafness should the odd ear be excised. And disfigurement … terrible disfigurement … as you bravely defend me. Starting on the left – let's hear it loud and clear."

Each of them was thinking: bit of an over-reaction, surely? A crystal – not crystals, one lousy crystal – breaks, and a knight – not an army of knights but a single two-legged Beyonderling – trudges our way to pit his puny strength against the combined forces of Nowhere … do us a favour! Well, Leader knows best. If the Hooded One says they must fight down to the last wart, then that precious wart will have to be sacrificed.

The Captain of the Guard spoke first.

"I am well prepared, Great One. Six hundred and sixty five Nowarts, not including me. Spears for all. Sharp prodding sticks for two hundred and nine of them. Eleven packs of glue-puddles. One Anti-Sunlight Shield…"

Deep within his robes the Hooded One fiddled about, counting on his fingers as the Captain enumerated his arsenal, till he could contain himself no longer.

"Faster, or I'll snip out the tongue that impedes your words."

The catalogue of men and weapons and battle accessories continued round the table, each of the Inner Circle desperately trying to remember how many loyal subjects they'd had last time they'd counted ... and what weapons lay gathering dust on the shelves of the arsenal. What they didn't remember they made up – and because they could sense how important it was to their leader, they doubled, trebled their estimates to keep him from losing his temper, which was never a pleasant experience.

"Enough!"

The sleeve of the great cowl rose and a bony, pimpled hand emerged from the darkness to halt the proceedings.

"Even if some of you have exaggerated your estimates I am still satisfied that we have the resources to protect ourselves. Off you go now, off to your Command Stations to await my bidding. Your men must be whipped up into a frenzy. They must be prepared to sacrifice their very lives for my safety – or worse than death could befall them. And the same applies to you. On the command go, go. Ten ... nine ... eight ... seven ... go! What are you waiting for? Catch you by surprise, did I?"

They were in such a hurry to do his bidding they ran into each other and collided at the door.

Deep within the hood, their leader felt quietly satisfied. Fear, that was the trick. The more they feared you, the more they'd do to appease you.

Just as he turned to look out of the tall slit of a window a bird flapped wearily past, a bird with leathery wings, a crumpled beak and a bald patch on its chest.

He wasn't sure why, but the sight of it chilled him, like an omen.

*

A length of chalk hung from a slate nailed to the front of Mr Crepitus' front door. On it, in that spidery green ink beloved of loony letter-writers and teachers was written the question of the day:

ATTENTION VISITORS
To gain entry, add the final digit of the year the statue of Lord
Sagramort was erected to the first digit of the atomic number
of iron – and subtract the number of legs of a Worm Spider.
Tap the number on the   plate below the doorbell and wait
patiently until your answer has been marked.
Ignoramuses will be refused entry.
Wipe your feet if successful.

Nimrod's heart sunk. History had always been his weak point,
particularly dates. Atomic numbers – what were they, and why did a
lump of stupid iron need one – would it be softer or less grey without it?
Would it stop being magnetic? And as for the worm-spider, did it have
hundreds of little legs like a worm – or two banks of big curly ones like
a spider ? What a ridiculous door-knocker.

Then he thought – surely Crepitus wouldn't wire up his door to
recognise new numbers every day … he was too ham-fisted to change
the time on the school clock when someone forgot to wind it. The
questions might change, but chances were they always added up to the
same number every time.

He remembered Crepitus standing in front of the class, four red
buttons on his waistcoat, four licks of grey hair hanging over his
forehead, and the four sandwiches he always unwrapped during break.
His lucky number? A memory aid for his front door password?

He reached out and, knuckles trembling, tapped the fingerplate once
… twice … thrice … and then once again.

There was a long pause; nothing happened except Nimrod's tummy
became so agitated it made an embarrassing gurgling sound once …
twice … thrice … and then once again.

Then some mechanism buried in the door rattled once … twice …
thrice … and then once again – and the door swung slowly open.

"Well done, boy. You may approach if your nails are clean.!"

The voice rolled out from deep inside; it reminded Nimrod of chalky
knuckles, the smell of carbolic soap, the crackle of a sheaf of exam
results riffled by sadistic, delaying fingers.

Too late to retreat now. He stepped under a low beam into a narrow corridor which emptied into a gloomy cave of a room. At the far end, wrapped in a sagging armchair, a long bony figure, all coiled in on itself like a folded umbrella, extended a long bony finger to beckon him forward.

"Come closer, boy. My eyes aren't what they were."

Creaking down the narrow corridor Nimrod inspected the gallery of framed diplomas, most of which Mr Crepitus had designed himself. A diploma in Sternness, which Mr Crepitus had apparently passed with flying colours. No surprises there. A diploma in Cane Flexing, an action which Nimrod had seen him rehearse time and again. (It had been Crepitus's habit to proudly grasp *The Persuader* at both ends and flex it till it groaned, just before bringing it smartly down across the knuckles). There was even a Diploma in Designing Diplomas.

Nimrod nervously approached the chair, which had been woven out of discarded canes. There it was again. That lean, sad face, those pale eyes retreating into the shadows, those elephant ears sprouting tussocks of matted hair. Yes, and there were those thin, bloodless lips and the narrow nose with the dewdrop on its tip, the cheeks veined like smelly cheese, the expression of contempt for anyone not lucky enough to be him.

"It's good to see you again, Mr Crepitus…"

"Don't fib, boy. Never fib to a history teacher. Their lives are already too full of time's embellishments."

"Well it is. You're the only person in town who can help me now." Defiantly he anchored his heels on a scrap of what was more floor than rug.

Clearing the frog from his throat he continued, enunciating each word carefully, as he had been taught.

"Why I came here was … is … well, it's nothing to do with schoolwork exactly … nothing to do with any kind of work, really…."

"Get, to the point, boy. " Crepitus's watery eyes settled on his ex-pupil's feet. "When did those shoes last see polish? They're starving, boy, dying of malnutrition. Do you know what that word means? Do you even know how many syllables it has?"

Nimrod raised a leg and buffed a boot on the back of his breeches.

"Er, three sir," he said, counting on his fingers. "I mean, er, four…"

"Three or four? Make your mind up."

"Four, sir. Definitely four. Twice as many as Nowhere."

"Meaning? Out with it. Don't swallow your words."

"Er, a place where the Nowarts live. Nowhere, I mean. Not mal-new –whatsit..."

Crepitus settled back in his chair, which made a sound like a flexing cane.

"Now there's a thing. Nimrod and Nowhere. Two obnoxious N-words sharing the same sentence. This morning I would have said they didn't belong a hundred feet of each other,. But looking into your eyes, well, I'm not so sure."

Nimrod's dammed-up words cascaded out in a torrent.

"You see, sir, years ago my father went there. Nowhere, I mean. Just got up one morning and off he went, off to discover the secrets of a place people still won't speak of. This morning – my Final Youngday, by the way, but don't tell anybody – this morning I decided that the best possible gift a boy could get would be, well, to unwrap his own father. If you know what I mean."

"I see."

There was a long silence. Nimrod knew those silences.

"Was it my grammar, sir? Did I confuse my tenses?"

"You'd better sit down, boy. Nimrod. Nimrod the hunter. Well you've certainly tracked me down. And why? Not to thank me for all that wisdom I instilled into your cotton-wool brain, no chance of that, you ungrateful tick. Nobody thanks teachers. They blame them, boy, repeat after me, b-l-a-m-e. And let's hear no more about tenses. Not tenses nor past participles nor the cardinal sin of rubbing out with a wet finger. This is far more important than such things. Well? What are you waiting for? Borrow a seat. We'll start with a cup of tea." Crepitus never actually invited any guests to *take* a seat, not since somebody actually had, all the way down the road, across the village square and through the front door of his home. Chairs cost good money.

Nimrod located a cushion and sank down on it. It sighed like a martyr.

Crepitus moistened his lips again with that slithery tongue of his. "If you're considering a trip to ... *that* place, the least I can give you is a cup of cheer. You'll need it. " He called out: "Hildagonda! Tea! Two cups! Piping hot!" It was his classroom voice, exclamation marks everywhere.

He leaned forward, so close Nimrod could smell the indelible ink on his tongue.

"I'm surprised at you, boy. Off to that place indeed. You never struck me as that sort of boy."

"I can't help it, Mr Crepitus, sir," apologized Nimrod. "It's just that, well, you never taught us about Nowhere, and I only want to know..."

"BOY!" Crepitus exploded, "never dare mention that place again in my lounge. Talk about it if you have to, but never ever utter its name. Do I make myself clear?"

"Yes, Mr Crepitus," muttered Nimrod. "But I do wish you'd stop calling me that. I'm out of school now, and no longer a boy,"

"You'll always be a boy, boy, no matter how long you live. Just like I'll always be your teacher. That's something time will never change. Teacher and boy. Boy and teacher. Those are our lots in life."

Nimrod was just thinking up a suitable response to this when Mrs Crepitus shuffled in bearing two steaming mugs of tea.

"Crepitus!" she said sternly. "Stand up when I enter the room. Where did you leave your manners?"

Then stern Mr Crepitus, cantankerous Mr Crepitus, Crepitus of the Caning Diploma, sheepishly rose to his feet and lowered his eyes.

"Yes, dear. Sorry, dear."

"I should hope so too. Don't go making the same mistake in future or you can go and stand in the corner until you see the error of your ways."

Was this possible? The Scourge of Schoolboys scourged? Nimrod rose to his feet and dipped his eyes.

"Er, you must be Mrs Crepitus. Pleased to meet you, ma'am."

She creased her forehead. "And who might you be? Did I invite you? Do you have a card with your name on?"

"Er, Mr Crepitus invited me in," he managed to stammer.

"This is *not* Mr Crepitus's house," she replied in a voice that seemed to start life in her slippers. "I spend more time in it, so, by rights, it's more mine than his. Didn't you teach your boys reason, Crepitus?"

"I did my best, dear," he said.

She snorted. "Quiet, you. And as for you, boy, in this house you take your orders from me. And your first order is: drink your tea before it gets cold. If that tea isn't finished in ten minutes you'll be smirking on the other side of your face. No point owning a kettle if guests always drink their tea cold. Now get to it, the pair of you. I don't want to hear anything from the you but satisfied tea slurping. I hope I make myself clear?"

Out she shuffled out, introducing a note of menace into the flipping and flopping of cotton slippers.

Crepitus peeped through his fingers at Nimrod, who hid his own astonishment behind his teacup. Only when Crepitus was certain his wife was out of reach did he lower himself back down into his chair.

"Phew. Now we can have our little talk. And for pity's sake drink up – she's a terror when she's thwarted. When exactly did you plan to leave for ... that place?"

"I was thinking of tomorrow," replied Nimrod.

"Tomorrow?" exclaimed Crepitus. "Why, that's the day after today."

Quickly counting on his fingers, Nimrod agreed that it was.

"Tut, tut," said Crepitus, frowning. "Yes, I know that's strong language, something I don't normally encourage, but extreme cases call for extreme measures. You're a silly boy, Nimrod. Always were. That place you mentioned, it's not for the likes of *you*."

"Then who is it for the likes of?" inquired the would-be traveller.

"Patience, and you will learn." Crepitus shook his head very sadly. Then he began to speak.

"Many years ago, Nimrod, more years than a man can count, before the days of our grandfathers' grandfathers' grandfathers, a band of old men arrived and set up camp here where World's End now stands. The lands they left behind were beset by turmoil; wars raged and men wielded sword and hammer to beat their beliefs into the heads of others who thought differently. These pilgrims sought the farthest point from these conflicts and you can't get much further than this before the world runs out. They could have pressed on a little further, but the water here was sweet, the grass rich and green and nourishing for the cattle and sheep that accompanied them on their quest for a peaceful life.

"They brought few possessions with them … a change of clothing, some books, scrolls and quill pens to set down their thoughts, pictures of loved ones left behind - their needs were simple. But one old pilgrim – a grey bearded sage remembered only as Q - bore with him a locked chest of glowing amber, and two terra cotta jars which he guarded so jealously it was rumoured they contained treasures beyond counting.

"What was it they had salvaged from their threatened homelands? We'll never know what was so important to them they braved their old bones against barren plains, rocky mountains and raging rivers, but tradition has it that these artefacts were as old as time itself. The scrolls, it is said, were the original operating manuals for the world, entrusted, rather foolishly, to its first inhabitants. The amber chest – rumour has it they housed a set of crystals that measured the emotions of the planet, all its fears and potential, all the weight of its disappointments.

"The jars – well, they were burial urns. Burial urns for a lifetime of ancestral memories. How are you doing with all these long words, Nimrod? As I remember, you were always good at words. Words were to you what a ball is to a sportsman. I hope your fascination with them hasn't paled now that you've left school."

Nimrod made a gesture: go on. This was no time for flattery. This was a time for stories.

Crepitus leaned forward and his bones creaked like a ship at rest in an ebbing tide.

"Once they were settled the old pilgrim took himself off into the forest with his jars … to a deep glade where no trees grew, to contemplate and wrestle with his memories and those passed on by his ancestors. For days, weeks, months, probably years, he remained there, out of sight. Just him and his precious relics. Nobody went near him. Then, late one afternoon when the gloom was settling and the insects beginning their evening whispers, a small flickering flame was seen moving through the trees and out he came, a jar tucked under each arm and a flaming torch in his hand. Drink your tea, Nimrod, or we'll both be in for the high jump.

"He hobbled to the centre of the village which by now had risen from the plains. His fellow pilgrims fell in behind him in a long winding procession. He led them to the Speaking Rock. When everyone was settled he addressed them.

"'My friends', he said, 'thank you for your patience. During my long absence I have stared long and hard into our collective memories, struggling to make sense of our past lives. After a while it became clear that truth doesn't dwell in your navel button like a hermit in a cave. Bits of it lurk everywhere. Only by joining the dots in a particular order – not necessarily in the order they were formed – will a picture emerge to give shape to the random trail of our footprints from cradle to grave. My task has been one of sorting, weeding, shuffling, of isolating and separating.

"'Concentrate on anything long enough and hard enough and it will form a natural shape … a half-shape, I grant you, more like a haze, like a buzz of insects round a flame, but if you look hard enough with your inner eye you will find it, veiled within its trembling borders. That's what I've been studying, alone in the darkness of the forest. There in the half-light they paraded before me, decisions good and bad, turnings right and wrong. I plucked out those that made a difference … separated good from bad … wise from ignorant … captured them and sorted them into these two burial urns.'

"He held them up for all to see. The gathered pilgrims surged forward but he ordered them back: nobody was ready for them yet. The jars were identical in shape and size, even down to the flaws in the potter's glaze, though one was warm and the other icy cold to the touch. Strange, indecipherable characters had been carved into the jars, and everyone yearned to know what they contained, particularly as the plugs were jammed in deep, and secured with thick twine.'"

Strange, indecipherable characters. Nimrod thought of the spectacle frames in his sling bag. Should he dare fish them out and show them to his old teacher? No; those were his secret, his and Kabil's.

Instead he asked: "Did anyone ever get a good look inside them?"

Crepitus looked him up and down with an expression of contempt only available to schoolmasters. All in good time.

"The old sage weighed the jars in arms outstretched like balances. 'What you see before me are the distilled essences of the twin tides that govern our journey through life. Wisdom - and Ignorance. They ebb and flow through each of us; sometimes they fill us with the solace of truth, other times they erupt and their molten rivers weigh us down. This one, the Jar of Wisdom contains too much knowledge for one man comfortably to bear. And this, the Jar of Ignorance, swims with forces so dark and unpredictable it must never be unsealed. Would it could be destroyed. But ignorance isn't a force – it's a non-force. It subtracts. And that is its terrible threat.

"'As for me, well, I am old. I have see what I have seen. I have learned what I have learned. I have served my allotted time. Now I must pass on to unravel other, stranger mysteries. But before I go I ask you to take both these jars and guard them with your lives, lest they fall into the hands of ambitious men. Raise your hands and promise me that, and I will pass on my way in peace.'

"And so they raised their hands before him and they made their vows, and he laid the jars on the rock before him and closed his eyes - and died.

"After a period of mourning the jars were taken to a cave and laid to rest in the deepest darkest shadows. A pair of doors was erected outside, doors of ebony, bolted together with rivets of Purple Obsidian, and inside two sentries were appointed to guard the jars. They were the most trusted men in the village, and they carried with them swords so thin and sharp they were invisible until the light caught them – and there was no light within. A deep well was dug for and enough food was set aside to last twice their lifetimes. Outside, more sentries were posted. Three different sages held the keys to the doors – all three were necessary to turn the lock. No visitors were permitted – with one important exception.

"'When any of the pilgrims saw Death beckoning they were accompanied with great ceremony to the doors of the cave. The three keys were produced and they were permitted to peer into the Jar of Wisdom for a few seconds. This way all the pilgrims were assured of discovering the reason for their existence just before it flickered out. After that there could be nothing more to desire, and they would come out and go deep into the forest, never to be seen again. The final journey of the contented. The Jar of Wisdom would be sealed up again, and the cave doors locked.

"By and large the commune was a happy place. The village grew, children became adults who fathered their own, more houses were built, more children were born. But even amongst the happiest there will always be the discontented, the askers of the age-old question *is this all there is?* There were those who had heard their parents talk of the world left behind: a few became inquisitive and set off to see it for themselves. It must have been one of those who let the secret slip.

"A traveller arrived in the village. He was hungry and weary, and the sages put him to bed to recover. When he awoke, he heard two of his hosts talking outside his window. They were discussing the very Jars he had come to find. Wealth beyond the counting? Well, to a pilgrim seeking contentment, wisdom was indeed the most precious commodity of all. But this stranger thought that all wealth shone and glittered and clinked and clanked and fitted into pockets and sacks, and he wanted some.

"During his stay he did all he could to trace those precious jars. But wise pilgrims don't blab, and he was forced to concede defeat and return empty-handed. There his cronies gathered around him. *What was there?* they asked. *Wealth,* he said, *wealth beyond counting. But I couldn't find it.*

"Soon they arrived, hordes of them, greedier and more determined than him. Now that their secret was out the Council of Pilgrims locked the village gates and doubled the guard. The bounty-hunters amassed outside and the simple folk of World's End learned the hiss of the whispers of war.

"One night - when the moon was blocked by clouds - the plotters lit flaming torches, broke down the gates and swarmed in. In the battle many of the pilgrims died, robbed of their one chance to look into the Jar of Wisdom.

"At the Cave of the Jars the sentries were killed and the doors burned down. But the inner guards, hearing the commotion, had dug two deep holes and buried the jars. Just in time. The doors gave, the rampagers broke in, and found – nothing. The rumours had been lies. There were no jars. Enraged by the futility of their journey they stabbed the guardians with their own swords and burned down the village. But the Jars remained safe, deep below the surface in the cold dark soil.

"The disillusioned bounty-hunters left, cursing and fighting amongst themselves. All – all but one. In the dead of night he crept back to the Cave and began to dig. It didn't take long to uncover a jar – the sentries who had buried them were old, and weakened by their sparse diet. Victoriously he grabbed it, wrapped it in one of the pilgrim's cowls and ran off, deep into the surrounding forest, determined to keep his secret to himself. So puffed up with his success was he, though, he took the wrong turning and got thoroughly lost.

"Night fell. Alone in the dark, curiosity got the better of him. Power was a lid away – all he had to do was prise it open. He saw himself rising into the air, above the tangled branches of the forest, and flying home, *Rex Mundi*, King of the World. Unfolding the cowl and fumbling with the twine he uncapped the Jar - and peered in.

"A great wind rushed out, throwing him onto his back, uprooting the trees, chasing the moon behind the clouds - which had turned mauve and chocolate brown. As he lay there in the midst of the great storm, clinging on for dear life, he realised too late that he had unearthed the wrong Jar. He had run off with the Jar of Ignorance."

Nimrod's mouth hung wide open. Not even in his childhood days had he heard a story so rich in legend and mystery. When he managed to find his voice again, he asked:

"This man, what was his name? Is he still alive?"

Crepitus's face darkened. "His name was Virgil Podd – yes, I know it's an awful name, but he did, after all, come from *there* ... " Crepitus pointed in the general direction of Beyonder. "Wrapping himself in the pilgrim's cowl he pressed on into the Unknown. If he couldn't get his instant fix of power from out of a jar he'd grab it for himself. And there his story ends. We can only guess that he formed an alliance with the Creatures of the Night, and there they live to this day, planning vengeance from their castle high on a mountain-top. Trouble is, no traveller has ever returned with news."

"And the Jar of Wisdom? Was that ever found?"

Crepitus shook his head. "Men have given up searching for it. It still lies somewhere under the ground, never to be seen or touched again."

Nimrod tapped the floor with his foot. "You mean it could be under this very floor here, waiting for someone to find it? You mean I could be sitting over all that Wisdom right now?"

Crepitus's thin lips manoeuvred themselves into a smile. "It's possible, Nimrod. But unlikely. That jar could be anywhere, absolutely anywhere."

Nimrod wasn't giving up that easily. "Surely someone could go and find the cave and dig until he found it? Why don't they?"

Crepitus shook his head. "If it were as easy as that, boy, someone would have done it long ago. You see, when the jar of Ignorance was opened a whole chain of catastrophes was set in motion. Volcanoes erupted out of the mountains, laying waste to the forests and creating what is now the Plains of Ignorance: anyone bound for Nowhere has to travel through its barren wastes. The earth rumbled and shook; entire mountains collapsed, burying the Cave under rubble. Who can tell where it was – and even if you knew you'd need the assistance of another earthquake to uncover it. Shifting sands blew over the stones, and heavy overgrowth invaded the area. When Samuel Sagramort arrived, many years later and founded World's End there was no sign a city had ever stood here."

"Tell me more." insisted Nimrod. "If that Virgil Podd escaped alone with the jar to the Unknown, where did the rest of the Nowar ... the Creatures of the Night spring from?" He had almost spoken the unspeakable word again.

"Society always throws up its outcasts," said Crepitus. "The warts of humanity. Men rejected by civilised society and rejecting of it. When such outsiders heard of the existence of a place where normal rules no longer apply, they sought out Podd in his lonely domain. We still see them, those dark mysterious figures who stop over on their lonely journey, passing themselves off as travellers. You know the World's End philosophy as well as I do, Nimrod. No-one is ever refused food and comfort."

Thinking back, Nimrod did remember a dark figure that had once passed through the village. He had spoken to no one, and taken too lavish an advantage of the nectar freely offered to him. He had stayed only one night, but Nimrod had never forgotten him. There are some men that disturb your peace the moment you set eyes on them, and this had been such a man.

A shiver spiralled down Nimrod's back when he thought that such were the sort of men who peopled Nowhere.

Deep in the house something stirred.

Crepitus leaned forward.

"Quick! Drink up your tea! It must be icy cold by now, and you know what Mrs Crepitus said." He raised his own cup to his lips ... and spluttered. "Cold is the word. And it's all your fault, getting me to talk so much. It's all right for you; you could drink while I was talking. But I've never yet met a man who can drink and talk at the same time. The bubbles, you know."

He rose, cast a quick look in all directions and tiptoed across to a pot plant in the corner. Swiftly he poured the tea into the surrounding soil.

"Crepitus!"

The teacher spun round. Too late. Framed in the doorway, blocking out the light, stood Mrs Crepitus. And she did not look happy.

Crepitus tried to hide his cup behind his back. But his wife had already seen it. She strode into the room darkly. As she passed Nimrod, her shadow fell across him, and he suddenly felt as cold as Crepitus's tea.

"How dare you feed tea to my plants." she screeched, so loud the furniture shook. "I warned you, Crepitus. Now you're in for it."

She picked up a cuspidor from the floor and swung it a couple of times around her head. Nimrod had no doubt what she was intending to do with it, and by the look on Nimrod's face, nor had he.

Time for action.

Stepping between the two, Nimrod reached out and caught the cuspidor (which stung his fingers sharply), saying in a firm voice: "Enough! You're both acting like children! Now behave yourself or I'll pour your supper down the drain."

Mrs Crepitus stepped back, thunderstruck. Her face dropped, her mouth fell open. She made an incomprehensible snort (not dissimilar, come to think of it, of someone talking and drink tea simultaneously), which was presumably meant to imply that mere words were insufficient to express what words couldn't. Then she turned towards her husband who had already turned towards her.

"We don't like the sound of that, do we my dear..."

"Certainly not, snookums. No supper indeed!" She picked up Nimrod's almost full teacup, sniffed it, and smiled sheepishly. "Cold tea? Can't be having that. Let's brew up a fresh cup right now. Won't be long." And out of the room she shuffled on carpet slippers that had suddenly lost their menace. The sounds of clinking came rattling from the direction of the kitchen.

"You see?" said Nimrod triumphantly, "it only took a few kind words. Now. Back to another matter."

Crepitus looked startled.

"Another one? " He looked anxious.

"It's to do with, well, a sewing basket. Kabil said he lent one to you."

"Kabil? What's he been saying about me? What secrets did he tell you? Come on. Out with it."

"Oh, nothing. He just mentioned that he *may*, just *may* have loaned you his sewing basket."

"That's nonsense. What good is a sewing basket to me? I'm a teacher, not a seamstress. He's talking out of his hat."

In frustration Nimrod jammed his hands into his pockets and fiddled with the fluff in the corners. "I don't think Kabil was lying. Really. You can tell. It's in the eyes …"

The old Crepitus briefly resurfaced. "Are you arguing with me, boy? And take your hands out of your pockets! Where are your manners?"

Nimrod slid both hands free – and noticed the little snag of fluff still sticking to his fingernail. Looking furtively in the direction of the kitchen he said in a hushed voice: "He gave me this. The missing part of the spell. Magic fluff. To be applied to the tip of the needle, he said – otherwise it will work in reverse and she'll get worse. Kabil said you'd understand…"

Panic pounced on Crepitus's face.

"Give me that here, that fluffy … stuff." He plucked it away from Nimrod's finger, holding it like a precious object, studying it intently. "Kabil said that?"

"He said you'd understand. Frankly it makes no sense to me."

"Maybe I don't. Maybe I do. Hang on!" A look of dawning realisation passed over his face and clung there. "Oh, you mean that sewing basket! The basket with …. sewing in it! Dear me yes, now I understand."

Nimrod leaned forward.

"Where?" His voice came out like a hiss of steam from a train drawing to a rapid stop. "Where is it?"

"I sent it off to auction. What does a teacher need of a sewing basket?

The threads of knowledge, my boy, that's the only stitching I'm interested in. Needle and thread have no place in my curriculum…"

"Auction? Did you say auction?"

"You're repeating yourself again, Nimrod. Repeating yourself. Again. It's a habit you must get out of. If I were you I'd lay off the needless repetition and get myself down to the village hall. If you're so interested in that sewing basket you'd better step on it. Well, not on the basket. By my clock the sale begins in three minutes."

"Th-thanks…." Nimrod gasped as he got to the corridor … "very much" … as he reached the front door … "Mr Crepitus" … as the door slammed behind him.

*

At the ends of every corridor in the castle there hung a notice commanding in large letters of red ink that:

At 5am sharp every day
All residents of Dunroamin' Castle will
Lie face down on the stone floor
Until 5.50am sharp
Eyes kept shut
Brows pressed to the rock.
No exceptions.
By Order Of The Management..

5am sharp. That was the time of day Podd went for his jog. And he wanted no spectators.

Not that his fitness gave any cause for shame - winding his way through the cold tunnels at top speed every morning for countless years had trimmed him of every spare ounce of fat. But in a hierarchy constructed on fear, running shorts did little for his public image.

4.50am.

Up in his attic room Podd spat twice at the polished black shield that did double service as his mirror, buffed it up with a sleeve, grasped both edges of his hood and slowly peeled it back from his face.

Just as he remembered.

Hideous.

Short-cropped carroty hair. A snub of a nose, turned up slightly at the front. A peppering of freckles on each cheek. Wire-rimmed spectacles rusty at the bridge. And, worst of all, that flat unlined brow.

Dammit to hell, he looked all of fourteen years old.

Hastily he turned away from the reflection of his hideously youthful features.

His mother had kept a entire cupboard full of jars full of cream which she smeared on her face at various times of the day. To keep her youth, she said. What wouldn't he have given for a ageing cream to wipe that youthful smile from his face, replacing it with the sneer of cynical middle age.

It was a disease. *Rictus Sardonicus*, the doctor called it. A muscular condition. A face fixed into the grin of eternal youth. What a disgusting thought. And painful too – how often had his father accused him of smirking when he wasn't, how often had he doubled him over the desk and laid into him … all because of muscles he had no control over.

The trouble was, the more he seethed and fumed with bubbling hatred, the more the corners of his lips curled up in a mischievous smile. The more he glowered at it, the more he hated what he saw – and up went that lip again.

Muscles. Bloody cheek muscles.

Nobody in Nowhere had ever seen his face. Well, just that one time, that one inquisitive Nowart, but he had paid for his curiosity with his life. Now nobody dared so much as a brief darting glance in the general direction of the folds of his hood or guards would be summoned and the snoop would be dragged off for a spell in a damp cell, and that thing the guards liked to do with the sharp pole, the sour molasses, and the tiny but fierce hunger-crazed Blind Razor-Toothed Vole.

Serve them right too. If word spread that he looked no more fierce than a brattish kid his power would soon dilute.

He hated what he had once been. A boy. The very word made his skin crawl. All those stupid boyish hopes and boyish enthusiasm for boyish things... it made him want to vomit. And those short pants and that high pitched voice and the pimples with the black spots ... each a sign of weakness like a scar.

And the dreams ... those dreadful dreams...

There he stood, young and innocent, on the far side of a rocky chasm, beckoning ... beckoning himself back across the great chasm ... calling out in a high unbroken voice, it's not too late ... come back ... pick up where you left off... turn your back on your evil deeds...

But it was too late.

Far too late.

There was no going back now.

The things he had done, the actions he had taken to protect himself, there was no undoing those. Even if he wanted to. And he didn't.

Rage at the sickening innocence of someone who had once been him itched at his conscience and he struck his head hard on the stone wall to punish himself for that rare spasm of weakness.

Now more than ever he needed strength.

He remembered the warning clearly:

***When the Ninth Crystal Shatters and Breaks
Into Pieces
Brace Yourself, Thicken your Walls: use Stakes
Rest Ceases.***

***When the Eighth Crystal Trembles...
Drums Rumble -
An Army Assembles
Empires Tumble***

When the Seventh Crystal...

He shook the thought fiercely from his head.

The ninth crystal was a warning. No more than that. A clarion call to preparation.

He crouched down and scraped the plaster from around a stone in the lowest row in the wall below his war shield. Shuffling it backwards and forwards like a loose tooth he carefully extracted it from its place in the row … reached into the darkness within and withdrew a small rusty tin box.

As ever, the label read:

PLACE UNDER THE TONGUE AND SUCK

He held it up to his ear and shook it gently.

He knew the rattle of it like the midnight sigh of the wind through the portcullis. He clutched it to his chest, hunching over it, drawing strength from what lay within.

Then he slid it decisively back into the wall, replaced the stone, and rose.

Nothing like a good war to get the juices flowing.

Decisively he stripped off his cloak, pulled on his jogging shorts, struck the Great Gong in the corner so forcefully his whole body trembled, and set off to punish his body for its insolent youthfulness…

*

He skidded into the hall just as the sale was about to start. He hoped the sewing basket wasn't the first item to go on sale; after his helter-skelter dash he had no breath left to bid with.

Mr Vesperus, the auctioneer, was a huge, round man without a neck, and a head so precariously perched on his shoulders it seemed certain to roll off if the supporting trunk made a sudden movement. He took great pride in his work, and liked the villagers to know who was in charge.

"Right we are then folks," his rumbly voice boomed out, "where shall we start? How about this here luverly copper kettle. Isn't she a beauty? Wouldn't every one of you like to possess it for yourself? Folks, this kettle doesn't just whistle when it's ready, it tells you jokes over your tea." Mr Vesperus was prone to exaggeration. "How much am I bid for this luverly copper kettle?"

"Six janicles." came a voice from the back. The janicle, of course, is the World's End unit of money.

"Four janicles!" shouted a little old lady in the front row.

This is perhaps a good time to explain how a World's End auction works. Unlike most auctions, where the article goes to the highest bidder, in a World's End auction the article goes to the worthiest. The good citizens of World's End believe it's unfair that someone should get the benefit of a needed object just because he or she has more money to splash out. Often, the person who needs it most is the person who has least. So the auctioneer studies the bidders, and decides for himself who can put best use to it.

In this case the kettle went to Mrs Proud because, as she explained, her old kettle had sprung a leak and now she had to go without tea. Groans of sympathy all round. Proudly she took delivery of the kettle, and immediately plugged it in to make tea for everyone in the hall.

Mr Vesperus was holding up a bright red jacket. "Now here's a bargain for someone. Have you ever seen such a fine example of the jacketeer's art? Why, I've got one just like it myself. What am I bid for this stupendous, this incredible, this *magnificent* jacket?"

The bids ranged from one janicle to seventeen. Eventually it was awarded to the girl from the cake shop who had recently given birth to twins, so she could keep both her children warm with it at the same time. (It was an absolutely *massive* jacket.)

Suddenly Mr Vesperus' face dropped. It had just dawned on him that the jacket he'd just sold was his own, which had been hanging over his chair. But, by the rules of a World's End auction, once an article was sold, that was it. Sold is sold. This wasn't a case of see you later, jacket; it was goodbye jacket. It had been such a nice one, too. Immensely snug. His favourite, in fact. He wore it every day. His mother had hand-stitched it for him – four long years it had taken her, morning, noon and night ... stitching till her arthritic old fingers bled ...

A sniff, a dab of the eye and he was back to his cheery self. "Next, dear friends and relations, we have a once-in-a-lifetime offer," he announced, pointing to a tombstone. "Ideal for anyone with a sick friend called Simon. Any offers?"

Very few bids were forthcoming for this item. Nimrod took the time to size up his competition. The hall was jam-packed. Auction day was a public holiday, and most of the villagers came to pass a pleasant morning amongst congenial company. All the articles on offer were displayed on a platform, and Mr Vesperus selected them as the mood took him. The older people from the village sat on stools up front; everybody else stood. Mrs Proud had finished making the tea, now she was busy splashing it into cups and handing them out to all and sundry. She patted her new kettle fondly, forgetting it had just boiled. Her yelp was taken as a bid, and the tombstone ceremoniously handed over to her on account of her advanced years. She accepted without a word. Perhaps, suggested the auctioneer, she could change her name to Simon.

Next on the list was a bicycle without a wheel. Considerable interest was shown in this item, as there were very few bicycles in the town. Bids came from all over the hall. Mr Vesperus added his own words of encouragement.

"Come on, now, how about a few more bids? Here's your chance to own a bicycle of your very own. Why worry if the wheel is missing? Fifty per cent less chance of a puncture can't be bad. Any more bids? Do I hear sixteen janicles?"

Mr Vesperus did indeed hear sixteen janicles ... from none other than The Oastman, who explained how he could bake a wheel for the bicycle and, as everyone knows, tarts don't puncture. He collected his bicycle and carried it off proudly to his bakery to whip up a new wheel.

Still no sewing basket.

Instead, Mr Vesperus was holding up a picture of Lord Sagramort, the founder of World's End. A florid man, Sagramort, with cheeks like road-lamps and a flamboyant moustache he combed two hundred times a night to keep it silky. The story goes that he had come in search of the Jar of Wisdom but, feet aching after the many miles he had trudged, refused to go further than a mustard bath. His dog, Leopold, had wandered off, yearning for bones and sick of boiled cabbage, on the prowl for something it could sink its teeth into. Sagramort found the crumpled little animal digging for roots at a spot where the World's End town hall now stood. Too footsore to undertake the long journey home he built a home for the pair of them and they settled down to enjoy the quiet life. Word spread that the water was sweet and the land free, friends and relations arrived, then friends and relations of the friends and relations, and before long World's End was a thriving community.

Hence the interest in his portrait.

After patchy bidding it went to the man everybody knew would get it in the first place, Mayor Coolper, a descendant of Lord Sagramort. He announced proudly that the portrait would be hung in the Town Hall, and that the money for the bid would be taken from village funds. There was a ripple of applause from the civic-minded citizens.

But he was not going anywhere without a speech, not this Mayor. He balanced himself on the rounded end of Mrs Proud's newly acquired tombstone and cleared his throat.

"Fellow citizens of World's End," he said in a voice that rolled like a barrel of pebbles, "today is a crossroads in our journey forward. I think I can say that without any contradiction. Furthermore, as I have the pleasure to be the mayor of this town, I do say it, and expect no murmur of contradiction. Where was I? Oh yes. The Crossroads of Life. We've all been there. I know I have. And, like all crossroads, there are choices to be made. Go here? Go there? Turn round perhaps? Where now? Search me. We all have our own personal crossroads to bear. I know I have mine." He held up his new acquisition grandly. "Great picture, by the way. I particularly like the *impasto* of the palette brush on the moustache ends. Into the future, that's what I say. Onwards and upwards. And a rousing cheer for Lord Sagramort. Hip … hip…."

He sat down to loud hurrahs. He always like ending his speeches with a couple of hips … then he could persuade himself that the hurrahs that followed were value judgments on his mayorship. The fact that nobody had understood a word hardly mattered. He was the Mayor of World's End, and as such he was entitled to civic attention, no matter what. He staggered off with the painting, his legs emerging under Lord Sagramort's trench-coat giving the impression that the slender Lord Sagramort had sprouted tubby legs and was moving on to pastures fresh.

By now spirits were high. Mrs Proud's tea proved a triumph and people were already queuing up for seconds. Mr Vesperus – no longer the centre of attraction – announced that he would accept bids from anyone who wanted a second cuppa. The queue crumbled fast.

Nimrod peered over the head of the man in front to see what was up next. Surely it had to be the sewing basket now? But no, the object Mr Vesperus was holding up for sale was – Nimrod. Himself. A portrait painted when he was at his most flabbergasted.

"And now, folks, something for every home. This bee-yoo-ti-full incredible reflecting machine. If you've ever wanted to see yourself as others see you, here's the very implement. Just peer into the frame, ladies and gentlefolk, and what do you perceive? The best likeness of yourself you'll ever clap eyes on. Some folks pay many janicles to portrait painters for likenesses, yet here, my dear friends, is an ever changing portrait, one that changes as you do, grows older with you, loses its hair when you do, smiles back at you when you're happy, growls sympathetically back at you when you're down in the dumps . Don't miss this once-in-a-lifetime chance, good friends. Next week? Too late. Tomorrow? Still far too late. An hour's time? Too late by half. The time to bid is right now, so what do I hear?"

He heard absolutely nothing.

He dug a finger into each ear as if to clear the wax, creating a slippery squeak like the skid of a bicycle tyre on wet concrete. "What? No bids? I must be going deaf, my friends. Don't be shy, now. Do I hear five janicles for this beautiful reflecting machine?"

Unfortunately not.

"What about ten janicles?"

Apparently not.

"Twenty janicles? There you are. A bargain if ever I saw one, and I've seen many in my time.

Obviously no-one wanted something that reminded them how old they were. Now a mirror that fibbed … that would have been a different story.

Mr Vesperus tried another ploy. "I see. Well, let's try another sort of bid. Folks, the next person to make a noise of any kind, or move one twitch of a whisker will be the proud possessor of this bee-yoo-ti-full instrument for the fixed sum of nine janicles. Starting … now!"

The hall froze. Stillness. Silence. Nobody moved. Nobody wanted the mirror. Mr Vesperus pulled a pin out of its collar and dropped it. Everyone heard it.

Mrs Proud froze halfway through the act of pouring tea - even the tea co-operated by freezing mid-air.

A man near the back congealed halfway through bending over to tie his shoelace, with one foot on a stool and the other in mid-air he looked like a stork with arthritis.

The girl from the cake shop with Mr Vesperus's jacket heard the announcement with her finger a hair's breadth from the tip of her nose where a furious itch demanded her attention. There was nothing she could do, not if she wanted to avoid buying the mirror. The agony she was undergoing made her squint.

Then, finally, the silence was shattered.

It started at the back of his throat and worked its way up to his nose. A tickle. A twitchy, itchy tickle. The kind of tickle that, nine times out of ten, turns into a sneeze.

This wasn't to be the one in ten outside shot.

He fought back with everything he had. The tickle, which had started life about the size of a grain of rice, had passed through the gooseberry stage, expanded into a puffcake, and was now at that stage just before a balloon's skin can take no more.

Ah...choooo...OOOOOO!

It was, according to a normally reliable source, quite the loudest sneeze that had ever been sneezed within a two mile radius of World's End, even including the 1798 Great Flu Epidemic. This was the grandmother of all sneezes.

The guilty party had gone a bright red, even more scarlet than the auctioneer's ex-jacket. Everyone turned to look his way. He shuffled to his feet and looked sheepishly at the floor.

"I snoze," apologised Nimrod.

"Congratulations, young man," announced Mr Vesperus, "I accept your bid. The beautiful reflecting instrument is yours. You owe me nine janicles."

Nimrod trudged up to accept his fate.

"I, er, I don't really want it, you know."

"Nonsense. Of course you want it. You bid, didn't you? Well then. Now hand me my money, and let's get on with the sale. Some of us have homes to go to."

Nimrod dipped into his purse with resignation, counted out his last

nine janicles, and handed them over to Mr Vesperus. That left an
empty purse – empty but for a button and a secret stash of magic fluff.
What now? How was he going to bid for the sewing basket? He didn't
have another janicle to his name. It seemed as if he was fated not to get
those precious lenses.

"Off you go now, Nimrod. Enjoy your mirror. A big hand for Nimrod's
mirror, ladies and gentlemen…"

Clutching his unwanted mirror to his chest Nimrod staggered
dejectedly across the hall, parting the crowd like wheat in a field. Total
strangers clapped him warmly on the back and congratulated him,
but he was in no mood for their good wishes. He'd lost. He'd sneezed
himself out of the game.

Outside he let the tears flood out, adjusting his position to avoid
catching sight of his own reflection in the mirror. He had tried so hard.
Now - failure. What point was there in staying on for the rest of the sale.
The terms were strict. If you wanted to bid, you had to have money.
No matter how little, you still needed hard cash.

He flung himself down on the pavement, still clutching his mirror.
How could he make the journey to Nowhere without the lenses? He
was so busy commiserating over his fate he never noticed the shadow
that had fallen over him.

"Young man."

Nimrod looked up. Him! The Man Who Walked Alone! He was
dressed from top to toe in grey and had a complexion to match; shaggy
grey eyebrows shaded steel grey eyes. He rarely spoke to anyone, he
was a man of edges and borders who avoided the thick of things, a
perimeter man who watched and thought and kept his distance.

"Why are you so distressed?" Few had heard him speak, so Nimrod
was surprised by the gentleness in his voice. Weren't outcasts meant to
be grim and forbidding?

He pointed to the mirror. "It's because of this hateful thing, Sir, that's
why."

Then the stranger sat down on the pavement next to Nimrod and
looked deep into his eyes, so deep it was if he was penetrating his skin
and reading what was written between the folds of his brain.

"I think you ought to tell me all about it."

And Nimrod told him. Everything. As he listened, the grey stranger nodded wisely. But it wasn't just a everyday sort of wise nod, the kind you mechanically offer to disappointed friends, this wasn't that sort, it was as if he really, truly, deeply understood.

"So you're thinking of visiting Nowhere, are you? That's brave of you."

"I have to see what it looks like, sir. I don't know why, I just feel that I have to. I suppose that sounds daft to you."

"Not a bit, Nimrod." Nimrod wondered where the stranger had unearthed his name. "I think it's a noble plan. I wish you well on your difficult journey."

"Th ... thank you, sir. It's v-v-very good of you, sir."

"It's not good of me, Nimrod," replied the tall man, "it's you that it's good of. The credit belongs nowhere else." He stood up. Then, as an afterthought, added: "I don't suppose I can get you to part with that magnificent mirror, can I?"

"Part with it? Of course. Take it. It was an accident. I hate it. It's yours. Here. Don't care if I never see it again."

"No, Nimrod, I wouldn't think of accepting it for nothing. Here are five janicles. It's worth at least that."

"But ... but I only paid one," protested Nimrod.

"It's not what you pay for an article that gives it its worth," said the stranger, "it's the value put on it by those who need it. Take the money. As far as I'm concerned it would be a bargain at twice the price."

Nimrod watched as the grey man counted five janicles into a small pouch and pulled the draw-string, then solemnly handed it over, saying: "Look after yourself, young man. It's a hard and dangerous journey ahead of you. Once you've started, never give up. You'll be back safely, that I promise you. And I'll be looking out for you." Then he took the mirror and left.

If Nimrod had followed him round the corner he would have seen the stranger lift the lid from the first dustbin he came across and deposit the mirror carefully into it, doubling the rubbish, before continuing on his lonely way.

But Nimrod was already running madly back into the hall, his fingers gripped tightly around the little bag carrying the five precious janicles.

He was just in time to hear Mr Vesperus say: "Sold to Phineas Groper for one janicle."

And the article he was holding up was a sewing basket.

His mouth dropped open in horror. Lost again.

Phineas Groper shuffled up to Mr Vesperus to claim his booty. He was old, bent almost double under the weight of his years, dressed in rags. He never wore anything else. Obviously the auctioneer had decided that no-one needed a needle and thread more than this walking jumble sale.

The man of rags snatched it and clutched it tightly to his tattered waistcoat as he tottered out of the hall. Nimrod followed closely behind. He wasn't going to let his lenses escape so easily.

"Excuse me, Mr Groper," he called out, "can I have a word with you please..."

"Eh? Wharrayou want?"

"You've, er, just bought a sewing basket. The one you've got in your hand."

"So what of it?"

"Could I please see inside it?"

Groper brushed Nimrod's searching fingers away with a sweep of his hand, his arm-pit crying out for cologne. "Certainly not. It's my sewing basket, I bought it with my own good money. Now leave me alone."

"I just want to see something inside. I won't take up much of your time. Please."

This time he didn't even bother to respond. He turned his back and scuffled away, muttering things.

Nimrod watched him go. What rotten luck. Groper may need the needle and thread, but he didn't need the lenses. Surely something could be worked out...?

He knew that Groper lived in a tumbledown shack on the outskirts of World's End. Though he felt sorry for the ragged old man he also felt that, well, good manners cost nothing. Besides, he was quite willing to offer him five janicles for the lenses, five times more than he'd paid for them, a five hundred per cent profit in five minutes, and he still got to keep the basket into the bargain.

Keeping out of sight and using corners judiciously, he followed Groper back to his cabin.

When the ragman reached his front door he checked to make sure he was alone, dug into the depths of his rags and withdrew a small box, reached a finger down into his left shoe slid out a tiny key, and unlocked the box. Out of the box came another little box, out of his right shoe another key. More and more boxes emerged, each smaller than before, and keys popped out from all over his garments. Finally he unloosed from a string around his neck a wrinkled leather bag from which the matching half of the last key was extracted. Joining it to its other half he slid it into the keyhole, opened the door and let himself in.

What complicated precautions for the house of such a poor wretch. Who would rob a man who had nothing?

Once the door shut behind him Nimrod crept up. Peeping through the window he saw the ragman lay the sewing basket down on a tomato box which served as his grocery cupboard, and move through into the bathroom to wash his hands in an upturned scooped-out sun-dried half-pumpkin (his wash hand-basin.)

Pressing himself into the shadows he waited till he heard the water gush then darted forward and let himself in while the old man's attention was otherwise engaged. Inside, the house was a tip. The carpet was so threadbare it looked as if eight pieces of thin string had been laid haphazardly across the floorboards. What passed for chairs were old soap-boxes stuffed with torn paper. The table – more of those soapboxes but without the paper upholstery. Again Nimrod found himself overcome by pity. But two janicles is two janicles (the price had dropped during the journey) and that was still double what Groper had paid for the entire sewing basket. Truth be told he wasn't stealing, he was *giving*. The very opposite.

He reached out for the basket, a pair of janicles clutched in his sticky palm, poised to make the swap and get out fast; gingerly he raised the lid and leaned forward to look inside. There, on a pile of cotton reels and tucked neatly between two bodkins, they lay. The two lenses. Success at last. His fingers curled around them.

"Stop! Thief!."

He felt a horny hand on his shoulder and turned into the mean eyes of the ragman. He wriggled to escape the grip, but Phineas Groper was stronger than he looked.

"You know what we do with thieves, don't you? We punish them, that's what we do. You're going to pay for your crime, you felon, you thief, you light-fingered lawbreaker, you. You'll be wishing you never came to Groper's house to steal, you will."

Nimrod extended his left hand and rattled the two janicles. "Look – they're yours. I was never going to steal those lenses, honest. I had these coins ready to leave in their place ... and they're twice what you paid at the auction sale."

"Trying to blind me with mathematics, are you?" Groper's furtive eyes aimed at the coins and his hand swooshed in to sweep them up. "You smart kids, all the same, shoving your lessons down the throats of us what never had your privileges. Well you won't baffle me with your sums. I'm too smart for you, schooling or no schooling. Anyway. I don't need your money. Not yours ... not nobody's."

One after the other he bit the two coins to test their authenticity. Apparently satisfied he beckoned Nimrod over. "And shall I show you why? Follow me." He shuffled over to an ancient metal bed with legs as bowed and as weary as his and slid a rusty metal trunk from under it. Crouching to hide its combination lock from view he twirled in a secret code, raised the lid, and pointed inside. Even if the mean dimness of the single 4-watt lamp the coins managed a flicker of sparkle. Groper dropped the two new coins in to join their ancestors, raked his fingers through them and lifted up a great handful which he let rain down through his fingers, his lips jabbering away as he counted each jingle. There were more janicles in that trunk than Nimrod had ever seen. At least a thousand.

Groper seemed to read his thoughts and looked up. "One thousand and seventy nine, actually," he corrected Nimrod's mental estimate, "and that's including the two newcomers. They'll like it in there, they will - my janicles lead a peaceful life. None of the stresses of modern life for them. I won't disturb their rest, not me ... won't expose them to harsh sunlight or bounce them around inside purses. My janicles are slumbering janicles. That's why we get on so well together." He leaned forward, and Nimrod smelt his breakfast cabbage on his breath. "Know something? Inside this trunk is every janicle I've ever earned. First to last. See how they glitter in the light." Again he sifted his yellow fingers through the coins and let them dribble back into the box.

Nimrod could hardly believe his eyes.

"But why? Surely there are things you want? Treasures and treats? And what about food and drink?"

Groper snorted. "Money - that's all the treasures and treats I need. And as for food – well, what are gardens for?" he drew even closer. "See me smile? Know why? I'll tell you. Because now I can save even more. Shall I tell you why, little thieflet? Because from this moment on you remain here with me. I'm claiming you. You steal from me, I steal you. Only fair." Again he cackled triumphantly "Now I needn't get that grasping old woman up from the village once a year to darn and dust. You will do it free ... and every day."

"If you think that," said Nimrod, "you've quite another think coming. You may be older than me. You may even be wiser than me. But I'm bigger than you, and twice as strong."

"You'll do what I tell you," said Groper, reaching behind his back. "Bigger and stronger you may be. But you don't have one of these." He produced a gnarled branch, lumps everywhere and brandished it in the air. "You don't have a Beating Stick. And that's the big difference between you and me." He whooshed it in the air. "Did you hear what it said? It said - *on your knees*! " He whooshed it again. "Get to it, boy. I want every scrap of paper in my armchair replaced. It's losing its bounce."

Nimrod ducked the whistling sweep of the stick and did as he was told ... for now. He had an enormous respect for heavy sticks, particularly those with lumps on. Reaching into the soap-box he yanked out handfuls of ancient yellow newspaper which crumbled to dust in his hands. Groper moved in closer to supervise, stick at the ready.

"Now. Make new ones. Fat ones. Soft ones. Springy ones."

Nimrod tried. Groper stamped his foot, swung his stick, shrieked and had a tantrum, all at once.

"No! Too small! Bigger! Softer! Springier!"

Nimrod rocked gently backwards and forwards on the balls of his toes as he crumpled another sheet of paper into a ball, awaiting his moment. Suddenly he pointed over the ragman's shoulder.

"Mr Groper! Never suspected you had a wife! Or is that your mother?"

As Groper spun round Nimrod leapt up and kicked the Beating Stick into the air. Grabbing the soap-box he upturned it, paper and all, over Groper's head and without waiting to see what happened legged it, seizing the lenses as he passed.

He ran until he reached the village square. The crowds spilling out of the auction hall stopped and stared as Nimrod hurtled over the cobbles, waving his hands in the air.

"I got away." he shouted at the top of his voice. "I got away, I got away from the old money-grabber."

Soon a considerable crowd had collected around him. Mr Vesperus stepped forward.

"I think you owe us an explanation, young Nimrod," he said in his most official voice. "What's all this shouting in aid of? Count yourself lucky you left it till late, or I might have taken it as a late bid for the elasticated pyjamas. Now calm down and share it with us."

In ten seconds flat a panting Nimrod explained everything that had happened to him. The crowd pressed in on him, murmuring and muttering and wittering and whispering.

"I don't understand," said the auctioneer, "what on earth did you want with those lenses? Your eyes seem perfectly sharp to me."

"Kabil promised them to me," he said defiantly.

The crowd took a step back. From safely behind Tubby Tubmore, the Oastman's food taster, the Mayor's voice emerged.

"This is very irresponsible of you, Nimrod. Nobody ever goes near Kabil. He's a one-man No Go Area. But you haven't explained yet. Why do you need those lenses?"

"So I can go to Nowhere." Nimrod explained. "You see, I..."

But what Nimrod wanted was doomed to eternal secrecy. At the mention of Nowhere the crowd broke up and scattered like a herd of buffaloes, disappearing into the dust they kicked up, leaving Nimrod stranded in the middle of the square, one small lone figure amidst an acre of emptiness.

When it was clear nobody intended returning to hear more, he pointed himself towards his home and trudged off, kicking at stones along the way. The day-village curled up and dozed off as the evening village yawned and stretched and woke. Lights flickered on behind curtains, the smell of evening roasts in the oven mingled with the scent of lavender on the trees, and the fragrance of bath-soap and wet chubby children floated down the paths of houses as he passed them by.

Home. The red roses lining the pathway. The thin spiral of smoke streaming out of the chimney. The bright yellow door with the silver door-knocker, the chequered curtains fluttering in the evening breeze, beckoning him in. There lay the doormat that said WELCOME and meant it. He knew it all so well. And now he was going away.

"Hello, house," he said sadly.

Then he walked inside.

And got the fright of his life.

On his couch sat a gnarled figure leering at him through gnarled eyes; in his hands he held a gnarled stick.

Phineas Groper. Again.

"Come in, Nimrod. I've been waiting for you."

Some strange mesmeric quality in Groper's eyes forced Nimrod to draw closer when his every instinct advised him to retreat. He moved slowly forward until the miserable ragman was close enough to reach out and grab him by the collar.

"You're coming home with me, you are. And this time you won't escape. What do you say to that?"

Nimrod leant forward to whisper in the ragman's ear, where little furry insects scurried around and swung through the hairs like children in a playground.

"If you let me go," he said, "I can pay you. I have many janicles hidden away here in my house. Nice shiny janicles to add to your collection."

Groper's pushed him to one side and scanned the room, surprisingly strong for a man with so ancient a set of bones. His eyes shone and his hands twitched as if already counting the money coin by coin.

"Where are they, those lovely janicles? Give them to me. I'll look after them for you. They'll be safe with me. "

Nimrod shook his head. "Oh no, Phineas Groper, I don't trust you. Anyway, first we need to negotiate."

Groper raised his stick and shook it. "Negotiate? *Negotiate?* You're in no position to negotiate, you sticky-fingered thief. Now dig out the money and fetch it over here."

"No, Groper, first you must promise. No funny business. Then and only then I'll think about it." Seeing Groper's eyes darting around the room in search of hidden treasure, he added: "And don't think you can nose it out for yourself. Unlike you, I keep my coins well hidden."

Groper advanced on Nimrod, his stick waving nineteen to the dozen. "Lots of lovely janicles for Groper's collection. Nice gold janicles. Give Groper his janicles, Nimrod. Give them to Groper and he'll go away."

His eyes pleaded with Nimrod, who didn't trust him even a tiny fraction of an even tinier bit. He had two good reasons for not handing it over the money: in the first place he knew Groper would never keep his promise, and, in the second place, Nimrod had no more money in the first place.

Time for Plan B – or was that C?

"Look behind you, Groper!" he called out suddenly.

Groper cackled. "Don't think you can catch me with the same trick twice. It won't work twice in a row. At least be original. There's no-one there. It's just the last desperate ploy of a sneak-thief who knows he's cornered. Well you can just think again as you feel my stick across your..."

What part of his body had been reserved for Groper's stick Nimrod never heard for at that moment a vase splintered over Groper's head and he fell to the ground, stunned, revealing in all its magnificent glory the figure of Mrs Cassiopeia Small.

Sadly she studied the last shard of the vase still held in her hand. "What a waste of perfectly good porcelain," she said. "Anyway. All in a good cause. Dear me, it's lucky I came over just when I did. I had no idea Groper was such a wicked old beggar."

Cassiopeia Small was Nimrod's neighbour. Plump and eternally good-natured, she was the village's uncrowned Queen of Sandwich Makers. Many was the time that Nimrod, having heard the musical crack of knife through bread-crust, would count a slow five hundred before dropping in on the pretext of borrowing a cup of sugar. Were there ever more magical words than: "Nibble this and tell me what you think ..."

Nimrod stammered out his thanks.

"Think nothing of it, my lad," she said, holding out a ribboned parcel she had brought over for him, a parcel that smelt of warm bread and melted butter and … was that squashed purple-berries whipped up with goat's cream? Mrs Small's Sandwiches! What a way to go! "A little something for the inner traveller. Don't eat them all at once, now. As for Phineas Groper, I suppose one of us had better have a word with the Mayor. We don't need his sort in World's End."

She pointed to where Groper had been lying but now the spot was vacant. Groper had taken the opportunity to crawl off while Nimrod was concentrating on the sandwiches.

"Well," she said, "all's for the best. If he's wise he'll leave the village and never show his face again. And on that subject – leaving the village - I came to wish you good-bye, Nimrod. Can't say I think it's a good idea, but a neighbour's got to do what a neighbour's got to do…." She handed the parcel over. Nimrod thought, well, it may not be a good idea, this stupid journey, but if I stayed home I'd never have got these sandwiches…one of which, if I'm not mistaken, smells like cheese steeped in honey and goldenberry juice, my absolute favourite…

After she left Nimrod devoted himself to fitting the lenses into their frames. Under the flickering glow of the candles the slightly clammy purple material from which they had been made seemed to gently throb, like the neck of a lizard in the sun. He held them up to inspect the shapes scratched into the rims – held at a certain angle they seemed to represent tall, thin, grey men moving in procession. They seemed oddly familiar … they … yes, that's it, they resembled the Man Who Walked Alone! He shook them, holding them up to his ear, expecting a rattle … nothing; no, there was nothing solid in the little lozenges clamped to the arms, they seemed more like little parcels of tightly wrapped parchment. He picked at the sealing wax but the bonds refused to give.

Enough was enough. Too fatigued, that was his problem. It had been a busy day too stressful … too long. Now it was bed time. No more tinkering … rather give the body a good rest in preparation for the journey ahead.

Tucked up in his knitted woollen blanket like a larva in a cocoon he asked himself: "…" But he never heard the question. In a flash he was fast asleep.

Next morning, on the seventh chime of eight, he woke, rubbed at his eyes, and swung himself out of bed. After a good wash he devoured a breakfast of buttered flapjacks and tea followed by fried ham, eggs and hash browns. It wouldn't pay to eat too large a breakfast before walking. One wouldn't want to weigh oneself down with all those miles to cover.

He dug out his old satchel and set about packing. First in went the spectacles, carefully wrapped in cotton wool. Then the little compass, given him by Kabil, and on top, where they could readily be reached in case of an emergency, Mrs Small's sandwiches. In the front compartment went Kabil's wafers and the flask of nectar.

Time to be on his way.

He set off down the path, swinging his satchel jauntily as if he hadn't a care in the world. Through the waking village, past the orchards, feeling the dabble of pink morning light through the apple trees on his cheeks. Climbing the last gentle rise before the descent into the valley he wanted so much to stop and smile at his favourite sight in all the world - World's End – but he didn't. When he stepped through the wicket gate at the end of the path he would be crossing an important barrier. Behind, security and comfort and the pull of the familiar. Ahead – he just didn't know.

If he'd looked he'd have seen the village shrink behind him until it was just a dot in the distance. But he kept his eyes fixed on the horizon. By the time the sun had risen over the mountains, Nimrod was well on his way. Out of World's End. On his way to Nowhere.

*

For the first time in his life Nimrod was wrapped in emptiness. Soon after leaving World's End the trees shrunk into shrubs, then even these threw up their branches and surrendered the struggle. Little knots of gorse, curled by the sun, buried their heads in the dust; now all that remained were bleached stones and ribs of rock heaved out of the depths of the earth long, long ago.

Ahead - the yawn of nothingness. Behind – and he daren't look, for fear of losing his courage - the twinkling lights of home.

It dawned on him that being on his own (which he loved) was a different matter to being isolated (which he rapidly discovered he didn't). Before his parents died he'd often sought solace in his bedroom, where his dreams lived; afterwards, when the emptiness of the house was forced on him, it lost its appeal. To shake off the loneliness he tried humming a cheerful tune. Trouble was, he didn't know any. Like history, or maths, or long distance running, music wasn't his strong point. So he made one up. But it was so boring it only made him lonelier. So he cast around to find something else to distract his anxiety.

Halting by an anthill crawling with scurrying insects he thought and thought – and had a brilliant idea. Of course. He could have an early lunch. Dipping into his satchel he pulled out Mrs Small's parcel of sandwiches, untied the bright red ribbon and breathed in the puff of aromas rising from the thick hunks of fresh-baked barley-bread. Then paused. Might it not be better to wait until he was really hungry? He argued with himself for the time it took an ant with an injured leg to drag itself up from the bottom of the anthill, along his arm and onto the rim of the greaseproof paper, grinding its mandibles. Of course, that would be the sensible thing. Save them for later, when he really needed them. But would they keep? No, he decided, catching sight of sliced raspberries smeared in goat's cheese and poppy-pollen jutting out from between two crisp lettuce leaves, rather eat fresh bread now than boot-leather later. Besides, he'd only have one. Possibly two. Or, at a push, three.

Seven sandwiches later Nimrod began to wish he'd saved some. Only one left. One fat one. Carefully he parted the bread which had been glued together with fresh honey from bees reared on the pollen from the Ginger Tree. Bliss! It was still so fresh he could almost hear the bees buzzing in his ear. That was the thing about truly great sandwiches: they looked good, they tasted good, they smelt good, and they sounded so authentic you could almost believe…

The bee flew straight into his ear and buzzed madly around. Nimrod dropped the last sandwich and galloped up the winding path. If you can picture an acorn with wings, and a bodkin for a sting - that's the size of the bee that was sizing his ear up for the site of a new beehive. Even the crippled ant found the energy to run and dive into the folds of his jerkin.

With his last sandwich gone – scattered in the path behind him with the bee and an army of ants fighting for possession - he trudged miserably on. His feet were swollen and blistered, the sun had brought him out in a sweat, he had no one to talk to, and there was nothing left to eat. Why had he started on this stupid journey in the first place?

He looked around. World's End had vanished over the horizon; now he was truly alone. Silence pressed down on him. Even the bee would have been something to listen to.

He thought he'd try his made-up song again, but he'd already forgotten it, so he submitted himself to a silence broken only by the crunch of boots on gravel. His throat was parched and dry and needed a good sluicing out. There was always that bottle of nectar, of course ... but no, he wouldn't repeat the sandwich mistake. He'd save it for later - when he really needed it. But what else was there to drink? Where could one find water in such a barren place?

What was that?

Was his imagination playing tricks on him, or was that really water he heard? He turned his listening ear this way and that. It certainly sounded like soft, cool, clear, trickling water. But where did it come from?

Then he saw it. Just off the path a spring of crystal water gurgled invitingly out of a huddle of rocks. Butterflies swooped and dived, their vibrant colours reflected in the playful water. At last he could drink without dipping into his precious nectar. He stepped off the edge of the road, his dry tongue already lapping up the cool water...

... and ground to a halt.

Hadn't Kabil warned him not to desert the path? Ah, but surely he meant later, *beyond* the plains. He wasn't actually *in* Nowhere yet.

The beckoning bubbles proved too much for him. Just a sip.

Off the path the silence became fiercer. His boots bit into the dust without a sound, the insects clammed up and the wind vanished. It was as if he'd suddenly gone deaf. He called his own name out loud but his voice was swallowed up in the wide treeless air and seemed to be a plaintive cry from far away. Only the water sounded real.

Not far now. He went faster.

So far so good. Nothing had jumped at him from behind a rock yet … no unimaginably monstrous creatures waited there to scare him out of his wits. Thirstily he anticipated the flick of the cool water striking his throat. He clambered down the rocks to the grassy slopes. How comforting to be among grass and flower once again. He stripped off his shoes and socks, stretched out his legs and wriggled his feet as the stream-cooled breezes tickled them. He felt the long green grass slither up between his toes as he approached the water then bent and lowered his mouth.

Nectar never tasted this good. He let it lap around in his mouth and trickle down his throat. It had the scent of fields of waving poppies under a late autumn sun, the warmth of a favourite shirt, the playful zest of tiny kittens chasing leaves around a tree. The dappled waters cast lazy reflections on his face as he lapped up the most marvellous water ever wrung from cotton-wool clouds.

His thirst quenched, Nimrod lay back on the grass. A soft drowsiness washed over him, the sort that anchors you to your morning bed just before you let go and open your eyes. The bubbling waters seemed to be whispering: *stay a little longer, Nimrod, don't go. Lie back and we'll sing you to sleep. Rest your head on the long green grass and forget all your cares for ever and ever. Give yourself over to us .. let go … let go …*

All thoughts of Nowhere leaked from his mind. Who wanted to slog along a dusty road when you could lie on green velvet forever? When you could dip your body in the limpid water and feel this delicious drowsiness for always …

Somewhere between a dong and a clang, an alarm bell tolled in the cathedral of his skull, asking: couldn't this be as much a trap as a pack of Nowarts lying in ambush? This peaceful glade could keep the most determined traveller away from the beckon of Nowhere. Nimrod pictured himself lying forever among the waving grass, fingers trailing through the bubbling stream, until he grew old and grey, as surely trapped as if he was locked away in a dungeon.

He tugged himself up and shook the drowsiness from his sleepy feet. Quick! He had to get away from this deceitful glade. With the slap of the cool water calling him back he forced himself to scramble back up onto the rocky plain. At least –he assumed he was on the plain. A heavy mist had settled, covering everything in a thick veil. He couldn't see further than the tip of his nose.

Which way was the road?

Where was the path that lead him back to it?

Despair sapped his resolve. Every step might take him further away. The mist was so dense Nimrod felt as if he was drowning inside a milk bottle. What chance had he of finding the road again? Suddenly he remembered the crunch of his boots on the soft sand between the rocks. If he could just locate the outline of those footprints...

He knelt down and fanned his hands out, feeling. Nothing. He moved them to the left ... the right ... ahead ... behind. Maybe the sand had been too hard to take an impression? But no, his fingers travelled over the pattern of his palm: if the sand could remember that it would surely have kept the imprint of his boot pressed in by the full weight of his body. Slowly, now ... not so much of a hurry ... they're there somewhere...

Just as he was contemplating returning to the glade and waiting for the mist to clear his pinky finger fell into a dent. Found it. The print of his heel.

Slowly, desperately slowly, he patted and stroked his way back along the path. Once or twice he missed a step and crawled off in the wrong direction but never too far to retrace his mistakes. At long last he felt the welcoming ridge of the edge of the path - and collapsed gratefully on the road.

Then an odd thing happened. The moment he stood up the mist cleared, whoosh, just like that, as if it had given up trying to trap him when it saw it had lost.

He breathed a long loud sigh of relief, the sigh of a wind before a storm. Deep down he was proud he hadn't used up any of his three chances to call on Kabil when he really needed help. He may have overdosed on sandwiches, but at least he'd been prudent with the magic.

Off he went again, down the narrow path, filled with fresh energy. His little victory had given him heart. If he stuck to the path nothing could touch him. He'd reach his destination, take a quick look around, turn on his heels, and head back home. Why, if he was quick about it he could be back here in three, maybe four days.

To give himself something to do he counted his footsteps. When he got to a hundred he silently congratulated himself on his fortitude. When he got to five hundred he began to wonder what Mrs Small was rustling up for supper. When he got to three thousand the only think on his mind was bed.

He checked the position of the sun. Give it another half hour. He'd rest for the night when it had sunk behind the horizon, then wake up refreshed enough to tackle the most difficult part of his journey to Nowhere.

What … what was that?

He stopped and turned. Was it his imagination − or were those footsteps he had heard behind him?

Nonsense, Nimrod, you're tired. You're hearing things.

On he went - and there they were again, slow, stealthy footsteps. He tried to convince himself his imagination was still working overtime, but they sounded too real for that. He was being followed. By someone … or something … who didn't want to be seen.

He counted out another five hundred steps without turning, going faster and faster until he was running at a trot.

The pace of the footsteps behind him picked up too.

Then, without any warning, he spun round.

Nothing.

Nobody.

The path was quite empty.

The little rocks on the plain had grown into boulders, quite large enough for a grown man to hide behind. Which hid his predator?

Then he remembered the spectacles Kabil had given him. If that was a Nowart following him, here was a chance to get his first glimpse of one.

He plunged his arm into his satchel. But wait, was this a good idea? This was a journey that had to be made. There was no turning back. And if he were to see a Nowart at this stage of the trip he might very well catch fright and return without ever completing it. So he slung his satchel over his shoulder and told himself: two thousand footsteps more and that's it, bed time, wherever the sun might be, however loud the footsteps, imaginary or not.

The sky dampened and darkened and purple fingers reached out to suffocate the horizon. Behind him there was only greyness. His beloved village was far gone. Dark oily clouds gathered over him, unfriendly clouds, nothing like the cotton-wool clouds of home. He missed the crickets, too … and the barking dogs. And the reassuring evening bustle of friends And the aroma of all the village suppers mixed into one. There was so much he had taken for granted. When he got back he'd spend one long night awake just watching World's End drop off to sleep, listening to it snore, smelling its cosy warmth.

Which brought him back to the sandwiches. Why had he been so greedy? Now he had nothing to eat, nothing but the little biscuits Kabil had given him - and these he needed to save for later.

He wondered if silly old Kabil was watching him now, through his crystal ball. He wondered if, sitting before the glowing embers of the cake-oven in his cottage in the woods, the wizard could guess just how cold and miserable he was. He pulled his jerkin around his body to keep out the little chilly tongues that licked at his spine. It didn't help. Oh for the chatter of a friendly cricket or the reassuring glow of a lamp behind patterned curtains.

Four thousand nine hundred and ninety eight.

Four thousand nine hundred and ninety nine.

Five thousand steps exactly.

He stopped and raised his eyes,

Standing just ahead a vast tree blocked his path like a giant with a bowed head. The sap had long left its veins; it was black and leafless, as if it had been engulfed by flames which had gobbled up everything green. Its branches reached out wildly as if to ward off another fire. A pair of grey bats circled above. Very slowly. As if keeping watch for strangers.

He didn't like the look of it, but it would have to do. Tonight he would lie beneath its branches, close his eyes and let all his nervous doubts gently slip away; he would let sleep close out this strange unfriendly environment where footsteps had no feet and fountains were not to be trusted. He missed his four-poster bed with its knitted blankets, he missed *desperately* the little fridge next to it, at hand for emergency hunger attacks. He missed most of all his fireplace, missed sitting crouched before it, watching the flames acting out their stories for him, each one different, each with a surprise ending. And he missed the cup of warm cocoa that would be warming his hands just about now. He pictured it, that fat mug with the corkscrew handle, a spoon dug deep into the middle of the warm thick chocolate, steam floating up and forming two distinct tributaries, each scrambling up a nostril to meet again at the back of his throat.

But there would be no cocoa tonight. No warm bed, no knitted blankets, no midnight snacks. Just the chilly night air, a bare tree to lean against, and two grey bats to keep him company.

Come now, Nimrod, pull yourself together. You're going to have to get used to this darkness, young man, because Nowhere is shrouded in continual night. You're going to have to get used to the cold as well. And if you think you're enduring hardship now, how will you take the hardship that awaits you round the corner?

He told himself this with conviction, but try as he might he couldn't comfort himself. When you're cold, you're cold, and talking to yourself is no substitute for a flaming log.

He drew closer to the tree. A wind rose up from the darkening ground and it waved a branch at him: *back, go back, you don't belong here.*

Further in the distance a patch of darkness broke the horizon and stretched across the plains. By screwing his eyes up he was able to penetrate the gloom and make out the ragged edges of the bare forest on the borders of Nowhere. He quickened his pace to get to the tree before night hid it.

One step … two steps … three steps … four.
Fifty steps … sixty steps … seventy steps … more.
Six hundred and six, six hundred and seven six hundred and … thump.

The tree. His first milestone. One day down, one day closer to journey's end. But if he hadn't arrived "there" yet, where was he now? This wild and wasted stretch of nothing with its bare trees and its air of utter hopelessness, was this really still Somewhere? Or was it a kind of Snowhere between Nowhere and Somewhere?

Weighed down by adverbs he gathered together a heap of shed branches and ignited them with his tinderbox.

When the fire was blazing brightly Nimrod raided his satchel for the wafer biscuits and extracted three, determined not to polish them off as he had the sandwiches. No chance of that. Though they looked decidedly unappetising, after just one Nimrod felt as if he'd eaten a five-course meal. He washed his one-biscuit banquet down with a sip of Nectar and, tossing another crackle of dead branches onto the fire, rolled himself up into a ball and settled back against the tree.

Sleep eluded him. As the night thickened the tangled branches came alive with eerie creaks and scrapes, and the night wind rustled the twigs against each other so that they hissed out: *Stay away, Nimrod. Sssstay away.......*

When at last he fell asleep the glowing embers from the fire lit up his small hunched shape against the black lump of tree. A little later the embers themselves surrendered to the night and Nimrod became just another gnarled root. Which was lucky, for soon after that a stooped figure emerged through the night and scanned the plains with eyes that could see only in the dark. Seemingly satisfied he urinated into the soil and then scurried back to the security of the timberline.

Nimrod slept on, long, deep, and noisily.

He woke just as the sun rose, and sat up, confused. What had happened to his four-poster bed – had someone stolen it from under his sleeping body? Where was his bedside lamp, and why was there nothing cold and shiny where his trusty fridge always waited with a handy wake-up snack? Slowly, as he rubbed his eyes awake, he remembered where he was, and wished he wasn't.

It was a cold dawn. Nimrod rose and dusted himself off; after another nibble of wafer and a swig of nectar he packed his belongings into his satchel and took one last, lingering look at the path that led back to World's End before turning towards Nowhere.

Far in the distance a dark arch punched a hole in the waiting forest. Although it appeared a short walk away, three hours later he seemed to have got no closer. The nearer he got the more it seemed to retreat until Nimrod, angry at the tricks his eyes were playing, shut them tight and stumbled blindly forward. It worked. In what seemed like minutes he bumped his head on the first of the trees.

In he went, eyes wide open now.

The forest wound a dark arm around him. Its canopy of branches kept out all light but a few pale rays that cast gloomy shadows before him like crossed swords of mist.

He kept his eyes pinned to the ground ahead of him, watching his boots flatten the leaves and fallen branches. Luckily he didn't turn round, or he'd have come face to face with a hooded figure trailing him at a safe distance.

The Guardian of the Forest.

Deep in his underground lair he had been plucking the feathers from a fledgling raven who had fallen from its nests (three ravens, a chopped cabbage, a dozen small peppercorns and a drizzle of root-oil – his favourite supper) when he heard the trample of brush. Waiting until the vibrations subsided he climbed out to investigate. There was no mistaking the back. A man-stranger! Podd would pay him well for the tip-off. In all his years of duty only one other man–stranger had dared cross his territory. He'd been well-rewarded for reporting that one … a boiled pig's head and a pair of warm hog-skin trousers. A jacket to go with the trousers would be nice … the nights were drawing in. And, what with inflation and the cost of living, the going rate must be at least three pig's heads by now. He rubbed his hands together gleefully. Pay-pay time. And another man-stranger would bite the dust. Ever since his own dismissal from the man-tribe he'd come to detest these pinklings. Off through the trees he scuttled, to do what he had to do.

Oblivious of his pursuer Nimrod had just clambered over a huge fallen tree blocking the path when the ground began to shake. He stopped and listened. Someone – or something - was forcing its way through the undergrowth, and it seemed to be heading straight for him.

He grabbed hold of a branch from the fallen tree and tugged with all his might, a fat nobbly branch, just the thing for whacking unfriendly creatures over the head with. Unfortunately it was also a stubborn branch. Desperately he levered it this way and that.

The rustling and crashing grew louder.

More tugging.

More levering.

Just as he was about to give up and run for it the branch snapped and over he tumbled, head over heels, backwards.

This probably saved his life. As he rolled over, the creature sprang… and landed with a thud on the very spot Nimrod had just vacated, expelling from its mouth a hot green puff of half-digested forest matter.

It was a horrible thing. A giant caterpillar, matted hair dribbling like Spanish moss all over its fat squelchy body. When it realised it had been thwarted its upper lip rose in a snarl to reveal gnarled yellow teeth, remnants of previous meals still clinging to the roots. Clawing at the undergrowth with its banks of feet it concertinaed round to face its prey. By now Nimrod was back on his feet again. Threateningly he wielded his stick like a sword, curling it in front of the creature's eyes. It followed every tiny movement as it looked for another opportunity to pounce.

For a while they watched each other. Nimrod swayed from left to right, like a goal-keeper awaiting a penalty kick; the caterpillar chose to sway backwards and forwards as it judged its spring ...

Licked its lips..

And leapt.

But Nimrod had sensed what was coming. On the p of pounce he stepped to one side. The brute's hot breath hit him like air expelled from an oven, searing his eyebrows. With a gasp it flopped next to him with a thump, its legs clawing at the forest floor, shaking the ground all round.

Nimrod brought his stick down on its head. Take that. And that. Not fast enough. With one snap of its jaws the creature lunged at the stick and bit it clean in two.

A rhyme danced into Nimrod's memory.

He who fights and runs away
Lives to fight another day.

Sound advice. Summoning up all his reserves of strength Nimrod shot off through the trees. The creature scrambled to its multitudinous legs and set of in hot pursuit. Nimrod could hear it panting and snarling and licking its chops, that and the pounding of hundreds of pairs of feet, as if a huge hostile army was pursuing him.

The forest thickened. The swish of the whipping branches amplified Nimrod's panic. A plan. That's what he needed. Just one would do. But where did you get those in the middle of a forest, far away from the High Street?

It arrived in his head uninvited. He leaped up suddenly, grabbing a branch just above his head, tucking his legs under him as the creature whizzed on below, unable to activate its two hundred brake pads at a moment's notice. As it passed under him Nimrod dropped on to its back and clung on for dear life. Gobbets of matted hair came off in his hand, unearthing a squadron of writhing bugs that lived in the darkness of the creature's own hairy jungle.

He reached out and snatched at a passing branch. Thanks to the furious momentum of the creature it snapped off in one. Where he sat, right on the middle of its back, the creature couldn't quite unpick him with its snapping teeth, try as it might. It snarled and squeaked in wild frenzy. Nimrod beat it over the head with his branch, creating hollow, echoing booms. The caterpillar bucked and thrashed, desperate to unseat him, to topple him and finish him off, but Nimrod tightened his knees around the creature's centre, gripping it like pliers of flesh.

The beast slowed down, deafened by the thumping so close to its ear-holes. Nimrod took this as a sign of weakness and bashed at it with added vigour.

He felt the back muscles start to slacken. Encouraged, he went for the mother of all slams. Drawing on all the energy left in his body's reserve tank he whacked the branch down hard on the top of its head then spun it round and poked the sharp end into its ear-hole. Something inside punctured and popped. With a howl it stumbled and rolled to its side, flinging Nimrod off to crash against a thorn-bush.

Scrambling to his feet and plucking the thorns out of his jerkin he cautiously approached it. Its eyes stared with a glazed expression up towards the forest canopy, its underbelly heaved in and out, and great wrenching snores echoed in its nostrils like the whistle of a train in a tunnel.

Before it could regain consciousness Nimrod struck out along the path as fast as his fear could carry him – in other words faster than he had ever travelled in his life.

Part of him glowed with pride at his victory. But only a small part; the great majority of him suspected that worse things awaited him around the next corner.

Worse? Worse than a giant caterpillar with teeth? Worse than that?

The further he penetrated, the more sinister the forest got. Snide creaks sneered at him from the darkness. Unseen forest life laid odds on his making it (16-1)... or failing (evens). Warm breezes fanned the branches and hissed at him. Even the slap of his own footsteps on the damp forest floor echoed as if something wet and slimy was close on his heels.

On and on.

Deeper and deeper into the forest.

Further and further from home.

Closer and closer to Nowhere.

Suddenly, one by one, the noises switched off.

First the hiss of the wind - gone.

Then the muttering from either side – no more.

Even the slap of his feet on the wet leaves faded into a dull and deathly hush.

It was as if the forest was preparing itself for an attack, silently pausing before it inflicted its *coup de grace* on the trespasser.

If you've ever been locked away in an almost totally dark sound-proofed room then you may be able to share Nimrod's anxiety. If you haven't, please engage your imagination.

What kept him going was the thought that Kabil was watching every step in his milky crystal ball. Despite the bluster there was something deeply reassuring about the old wizard whose spells didn't work properly. Or – and Nimrod didn't like to face this alternative – was it just that one old fool was better than nobody?

Nobody else knew where he was right now.

Nobody else trusted him.

Nobody cared.

Then, from out of the silence just ahead came the sound of breaking wood. A little later, through the dim murk, he made out a shape. A crumpled, bent figure trudging through the forest and dragging two heavy bags behind him. There was something familiar about it ... something about its grunting and groaning and general-purpose moaning...

Phineas Groper.

Scrambling along with his moneybags.

Nimrod felt a sudden surge of pity for him. His obsession with money had unhinged his judgment. He was doing a foolish thing. He was greedy ... not evil. He had to stop him.

"Mr Groper? Wait. It's only me. Nimrod."

The ragman spun round. When he recognised Nimrod, he gave a growl and scuttled off into the trees.

"Wait!" called Nimrod. "I'm not after your money ... honest!"

But the only response was a cry of anguish and the crunch of dead branches which softened and dimmed and retreated into the silence.

Silence. That awful silence again.

When it eventually broke it did so in such a surprising way it took Nimrod's breath away.

The whispering of the leaves, the hissing of the wind and the wet slither of the branches under his feet, they were history.

Instead, he heard the most beautiful music in the world.

Though the melody had little effect on him its strange harmonies drew out of him memories he never knew he had. There he sat, on the floor of his nursery surrounded by broken toys ... there in the garden the first kitten he ever called his own stumbled over its own shadow. Suddenly he was five years old ... sweet girls with bows in their hair held up party plates piled high with pink cake and sweet marzipan ... he heard nectar ice-bocks cracking against glass. It hardly mattered to him that he'd never seen a nursery, nor had he ever owned a cat. Pink cake brought him out in spots and marzipan, even the sweet variety, was less agreeable to him than boiled cabbage.

Such music, though ... so haunting ... weaving the echo of a reed pipe with the voice of a young girl, surely the most beautiful ever born. He pictured long flaxen hair hanging down to a narrow waist, gentle eyes with long curved lashes, cheeks blushing pink... what was she doing here, of all places, deep in the heart of this unpleasant forest where no leaves grew?

"Nim-rod ... Nim-rod ... over here...."

"Where are you?"

"Nim-rod ... Nim-rod ... put your feet up and rest your aching bones. Come sit before my fire and melt the chill ..."

Still fresh in his mind was the false promises of the grotto in the plains. But this was different. Surely nothing evil could weave so sweet a song? And she was right, his feet *were* tired, his heart *was* weary, his bones were as cold as a debt-collector's heart. Wouldn't it be wonderful if he could lie down and rest his head on the soft lap of a beautiful young girl as she calmed his forehead with cool boneless hands and hummed him to sleep with her plaintive lullaby ...

"Come, Nimrod, come to me and lay your head upon my apron ... "

With a cry of delight, he called out: "Wait for me! Don't go away! I'm on my way!"

Of course, as you and I know, Nimrod should have been suspicious of music that seemed to know his name without being introduced. But give him his due: he was far from home, eager for company, and enchanted by the wistful voice.

So, unheedful of Kabil's warning, he broke away from the path and went off in search of the nymph of the trees.

Silly boy.

Come, Nimrod, we're waiting for you!

The music seemed to be drifting out from everywhere at once. Blindly choosing a direction … any direction … he ran into the thick of the forest. The music floated away. He turned. Another direction. Softer. Further away.

Again and again he tried, again and again the music soared away to hide behind the trees.

"Wait!" he called. "Don't go away… I'm coming… won't be long now …"

Taunting him with its sad melody the music approached him.

In desperation Nimrod dipped into the satchel. He remembered the spectacles. Perhaps they would light up the way for him. He hadn't yet called on any of his three cries of help… but spectacles, well, they were a different kettle of fish. This is what they were designed for … to become his beacon in this dark, unfamiliar no-man's-land. And there they were, glinting in the pale light that had fought its way through the canopy of the branches. Lifting them out he breathed on them, buffed them up against his shirt, and rested them on the bridge of his nose. They fitted perfectly.

Where was he?

What was this place?

He saw things he had never noticed before. Amidst the trees, all bunched together like groups of mean old men, he glimpsed hundreds of footprints, leading everywhere. And they looked fresh. As if the feet responsible for the tracks were still sticky with their mud.

He panicked. What was he doing here? What had made him leave the path he knew to venture into the tangle of a forest he didn't?

The music drifted closer.

He ran towards it. Got it this time.

It stopped. And started up right behind him.

His ears were playing tricks on him. This was impossible. Music couldn't be at two places at once. (Stereo hadn't yet reached World's End.)

Gripping his satchel tightly, he turned and headed for the source of the song. This time he wouldn't be side-tracked. This time he would run straight into the arms of the lovely girl with the long, flaxen hair and lie back as her fingers caressed his weary body.

The forest closed in on him. But Nimrod pressed through the narrowing gaps.

Then, for the umpteenth time, the music stopped again.

He looked around. He was lost. Completely lost. The path could be anywhere ... or nowhere. It could take him forever finding it again. And no use trying his trick of following his footprints back, for there were footprints everywhere.

So it had been a trap after all. The forest creatures had been slyer than he estimated. They had lured him off the path with little chance of finding his way back. He might as well lie down and die, right now.

There had to be a way. There always is.

The dust flittering down from the branches had formed a film on the lenses of the spectacles, blinding him. He took them off, spat on them, washing off the frothy brown spume with the corner of his shirt. Again he raised them and slid into them, curling their tips around his ears.

It was if somebody had turned the lights on. The purple haze glowed, the shadows retreated and the clouds revealed their silver linings.

He turned slowly round, searching for landmarks.

Halfway through the revolution he felt something on his shoulder.

A horny hand.

With a shriek he spun round ... and cast his eyes on his first Nowart.

*

The creature whose hand rested on Nimrod's back was a slap in Nature's face. Not much shorter than Nimrod, into its small frame were packed so many revolting features it was bent under the burden of them. (As you know, a smile raises your head up high – but the weight of a frown sinks your head on your shoulders.)

Its head was hammer-shaped, like a praying mantis. From the crown down it dripped matted hair, like a turnip, which hung off its body in knotted tussocks, with frequent bald patches revealing the nasty pinky-green rash a Nowart was prone to due to the high level of ammonia in its system. Its powerful arms hung loosely by its side, the muscular sinews rubbing and chafing against the sides which caused more unsightly rashes. Three tentacles on each hand, that's all, but, being a creature of manual habits, more would only have been a nuisance. The feet (just three toes) were horny and corny – indeed each sole was a single huge corn which acted as a damp-course against swamps. Their leg muscles were coiled springs, able to inflict severe damage with just a gentle kick. (How could anyone know? When a Nowart kicked, it never kicked gently.)

The face – well, put it this way, mirrors were banned in Nowhere and puddle-stirrers were employed to agitate the surface of still water when Nowarts approached, to prevent them seeing just how repulsive they looked. An (unconfirmed) account reports a face speckled with lizardy scales and coal-black eyes with the capacity to glow like embers when angry; smoke was sometimes spotted. Its mouth was a morass, soggy from the constant attention of a lolloping tongue which darted out from full lips. A Nowart needed no teeth, its gums being harder than rock.

When they saw the satchel hanging off his shoulder they pounced, clawing at each other to get to it first. One of them managed to snatch it away and run off with it – he was just gnawing with his hard gums at the press-stud (which his dim brain was unable to get to grips with) when the leader of the group bounded over and with a single swipe struck him to the ground.

"Give that back!" he snarled. "The creature belongs to Podd – and so does all he carries with him. Steal from him and you steal from our Lord and Master."

The Nowart on the ground whimpered and sniffed and made generally disagreeable sounds. He tried to roll away but the Nowart-in-chief planted a foot on his chest.

"Now say sorry."

The pinioned Nowart made a stifled sound which could have been any word in the Nowart dictionary. His superior trampled on his nose.

"Say it again."

The Nowart said it again, the same odd word but this time with a flat-nosed intonation..

"Now go and give it back. Hang it over the prisoner's shoulder where you found it and I may not ... the word was *may* not ... report you to Podd. Off you go."

The creature scrambled to its feet and scurried along close to the ground, the satchel in its teeth. Gently he hung it back over Nimrod's shoulder, so gently and courteously it became a studied insult, all the more so when it patted and stroked his shoulder with an exaggerated affection. Its eyes, however, blazed at him with fury. It was saving up its revenge.

Nimrod tugged himself away and two more Nowarts rushed forward to pinion his arms behind his back. Though he put up a bit of a fight it was an uneven match, and before long he was trussed up with heavy twine.

The Chief Among the Nowarts stepped up and looked him over.

"So you thought you'd invade our forest, did you?" His voice was a nail drawn across a blackboard. "We'll teach you different. We've a couple of surprises in store for you, and none of them very pleasant."

"I only wanted to visit Nowhere," explained Nimrod in as brave a voice as he could muster which, sorry to have to report, came out more like a squeak.

"See Nowhere? You'll see Nowhere, all right," snorted the Chief Among the Nowarts. "We'll give you your own personal conducted tour. No holds barred."

The cruel rasp of his laugh reverberated round the forest. The other Nowarts joined in, until the forest was ringing with their cruel sniggers.

Chief Among the Nowarts held up his hand.

The laughter stopped.

"Come. Time to go. Nowhere's a long way off yet."

He signalled the other Nowarts to grasp his arms. In the muttering that ensued, Nimrod heard the word *Xero* crop up frequently. A Nowart? Or a kind of punishment? Nimrod decided that it was the name of the

Chief Among the Nowarts.

"Get a move on, Outsider," said Xero in the voice of a 90-a-day smoker.

"I can't," said Nimrod. "My feet are too sore."

"I told you - *move!*" grunted the Nowart. "You won't even half-know what sore feet are when we've started with you. Now *move!*" Nimrod heard him whisper to a nearby Nowart: *Look - he's got toenails! Fantastic! We can use them as gum-picks once we've eaten him!*

The Nowarts nipped him with their tentacles, trundling him along between them. Xero walked a few paces to one side, as if superior to the Nowart rabble, of whom Nimrod counted seven. There was Xero, the two who had him by the arms, two behind, and two up front. Had his father fallen into the same hands? Had he even reached this far? Nimrod longed to interrogate his captors ... but didn't dare. Their expressions didn't invite conversation.

Such a sad, silent journey. The Nowarts were wrapped up in their malevolent thoughts, and Nimrod was too busy feeling sorry for himself to speak.

The ground raced under their feet. Clouds gathered and darkened in the sky; nervous trees raised their branches like frightened hands warding off threats. The air was sour, flecked with tiny sparks of bitter pollen like ash from a fire; it made Nimrod cough.

"Hear that?" one of the Nowarts sniggered. "You know what he needs? He needs a lozenge!"

Lozenge ... lozenge ... the word spread, accompanied by peals of mirth. Very soon they were all at it until Xero picked out the perpetrator of the joke, raised his hand, and gouged three long streaks down a cheek. End of laughter.

"Enough of that. Go get us branches. Time to recharge."

Soon a blazing fire was burning in the middle of a clearing. The Nowarts huddled round it, pushing and shoving to get to the warmest spot. Nimrod was bundled to one side, the ropes digging painfully into his wrists. Foul-looking food was produced, but not a scrap came his way. From a leather bag one of the creatures fished out a private stash of some hard strips of old meat, tearing off strips off with his bony gums. Two others pounced on him, kicking him to the ground, snatching the fetid meat from his fingers and plucking undigested strings of it from his mouth. Nimrod turned his head in disgust.

After the meal Xero produced a leathery cask. Removing the stopper he raised it up and took long noisy slurps then, without wiping the neck clean, flung it over to the Nowart sitting nearest him. One by one they had all had a noisy suck of it. Something in the liquid loosened the Nowart's tongues - they started laughing raucously and slapping each other on the back.

"What a find," boasted Xero. "The Lost Knight. Podd will reward us handsomely."

"I know what kind of reward I'd like," announced another. "I'd like to be Torturer-In-Chief for a day!"

"Only one day?" a particularly ugly Nowart chimed in with a sadistic cackle. "Someone's easy to please!"

"Bags I get to use the Poking Stick," said another. "I have a feeling I'd be good at it."

"Nonsense," piped in another. "You're too slimy. It would slip out of your ugly mitt."

"Enough! You're behaving like children! Back on your feet, the lot of you."

Xero struck out with a short length of chain he carried with him to underline his authority and the Nowarts sprung out of its way, cursing and hissing.

Nimrod shot forward, propelled by a kick in the small of his back.

"Get a move on, ugly pink thing. From now on you'll have my kicking foot to answer to."

Two Nowarts stamped out the fire with their bare soles and the party set off again, grumbling.

They crossed a wide plain, saturated with puddles. After a while the trees thinned out and dwindled away completely, unable to survive in the encroaching swamp. The path broke up into stepping stones over a bubbling black marsh smelling of stagnant water, oozing blackness and belching up gassy bubbles; the Nowarts hopped confident across them but Nimrod more than once nearly lost his balance and toppled in.

Then something awful happened. Treading on a slippery patch the foremost guard lurched and lost his footing. He swayed around, trying to right himself, but the rock was too slimy; with a shriek he tumbled headlong into the bog, his hands beating the air like the blades of a windmill. Down, down, down he sank, until the swamp closed around him. The surface settled. Then, a froth of tiny bubbles appeared and the Nowart's head broke the surface, even uglier now with its coating of green slime and the ridiculous almost comical addition of a frog gulping pop-eyed atop his head. "A hand! Give me a hand!" bubbled the unfortunate Nowart. "I'm sinking fast!" Desperately he reached out an arm for his cronies to grab hold of and draw him to safety.

But the Nowarts only laughed raucously at his plight.

"Don't drink it all at once!" shouted Xero, and the others hooted with laughter, as if this was the joke to end all jokes.

Nimrod struggled to his feet. "Grab him!" he cried. "He's your friend, and he's going down. Quick! Someone do something!"

But nobody made a move.

The struggling Nowart became desperate.

"Help! Help your old buddy before it's too late. Funny joke, but joke over. Someone give me a hand ... I'm sinking fast!"

The head sank again below the surface. There were more bubbles, then fewer bubbles, then no bubbles at all. Just mud, oozing black mud where recently the Nowart's head had been.

Then, as they watched, a gurgle came oozing out from below the surface. Nimrod thought he heard the word *please*. If it was, it was a hopeless plea. After a polite pause, the marsh burped up one more big bubble, as if it had just enjoyed a hearty meal, then settled back for an after-dinner snooze.

"Another tasty snack for the Hungry Bog," announced Xero without emotion, and signalled the party on.

Nimrod swallowed back the sourness that had risen up from his stomach. These creatures - did they feel no pity at all, not even for their travelling companions? If this was how they acted towards their own kind, how would they treat intruders? Like him? It didn't bear thinking about.

After this he became obsessive about the stepping stones. Every time one of them so much as quivered underfoot he would leap across to a flatter one, just in case, his head filled with visions of a slow sinking death in the black depths of the slimy mud. But he was in safe hands; his guards kept a tight grip on his arms. They wanted nothing to happen to him until he had been safely delivered – and the bounty for bringing him in had changed hands. Perhaps after that the rules would change.

Weariness rinsed his body of hope. Just when he was wondering how much further his feet could possibly struggle Xero pointed into the distance.

"Behold the gates of Nowhere."

Straining his eyes, Nimrod could just make out a hazy tower pressing its shape through the clouds. It had an air of brooding of peril, of vague unsettling shapes in restless dreams. Tiny figures moved about on its surface like ants on patrol, appearing and vanishing in the shifting haze. There were quick glints and flashes when the pale sun caught … what? Their spears? It all seemed fanciful and unreal.

They pressed on along the winding path. The bogs dried up, ponds became puddles and then bleached out into broad salt-pans. A little further and everything was rock, great flat sheets of it. They were on the foothills of a mountain.

He felt a prod in the small of his back from the large of a foot.

"Faster, pinky. Slow down and you'll have me to answer to."

A guard leaned forward to prod him viciously between the vertebrae and Nimrod felt hot sticky breath on the back of his neck.

Onwards. Upwards. Shift those ugly pink pins.

They crossed over a hump-backed bridge and started their ascent of the mountain. The clouds lay low, like waves in an ocean; when they drifted briefly apart Nimrod saw below them a chasm that fell away into inky blackness. On a track halfway down an enormous bald Nowart with a whip chivvied up a band of slaves from the mines deep in the belly of the ravine, followed by two weary yaks who snorted steam as they dragged up a cart laden with sacks of ore. Higher up on the jagged mountain peaks a goat with a corkscrew horn clattered up one of the nearer peaks and stood surveying their slow progress with a contemptuous sneer.

The path narrowed as it steepened, and the calf muscles in Nimrod's leg glowed from exertion. No wonder Nowarts had such sinewy legs.

They turned another bend and there in the distance stood the Middle

Tower of the Great Wall of Nowhere, briefly free of its scarf of clouds. It appeared and vanished, appeared and vanished as the clouds gathered and parted, managing to look more forbidding each time.

They skirted a bend and came to a narrow bridge balanced on boulders and guarded by a pair of bored Nowarts. Any threat of trouble and the bridge could quickly be levered off and rolled down the mountain to splash into the raging torrent below, along with whoever happened to standing on it at the time. They crossed in silence. Below, ravens swooped and croaked, turning in their flight to peer up at them as they passed over.

From a distance came the tolling of a bell. Their party had been spotted. Xero raised his chain in the air and swung it round a number of times in some sort of secret signal. A little later the sound of a ram's horn floated back.

The last mile took forever. The rocks here were sharper and denser and seemed to draw energy out of Nimrod like a magnet. The prodding in his back became faster and more furious, the guard's breath hotter and stickier.

And then, finally, they were there.

The Great Tower of Nowhere.

On its elevated battlements guards patrolled in a relentless circle. Others passed back and forth behind the windows, armed with copper spears and steely eyes. At the base of the tower stood a massive door, sliced out of a single sheet of red-veined granite. Xero stepped up and with his horny knuckles rapped out a special code – one long, two shorts, three longs. After a short pause the great door slid open and a Nowart in full battledress came out to meet them. He looked Xero up and down, inspected Nim with a pitying expression that suggested he had read the torturer's afternoon agenda, and motioned them in. Behind them the gate slid shut again - and Nimrod took his first step into Nowhere proper.

His first reaction was: what a cold city. The worst kind of cold, moist and clammy cold, not like a World's End winter which could be kept at bay by investing in suitable knitwear, this was a penetrating sort of cold equipped with icy barbs that pierced the surface of the skin.

"Move along there." The guard with the hot sticky breath again. The prod in the small of the back. The horny kick against the back of the knee.

"Leave off. I'm doing my best."

A cobbled road rose up the hill, past mounds of soil heaped up around ladders lowered into deep black holes. The homes of the Googlions.

As they passed these warrens suspicious heads popped out of the holes: tortoise-skinned old women with mistrustful eyes, miniature Googlions with mauve faces, men sucking at blackwood pipes and puffing spirals of what smelt like burning rubber into the sky. There was no confusing them with Nowarts, who were sinewy and spare: these Googlions were squatter and more thickset, their arms long enough to reach the ground and propel them along as they ran. heads less mantis-like and rather more human, though human only in a freaky sort of way with their close-strung eyes, flattened noses and – where the Googlions only had cavities – small curly ears like dried apricots.

"Here! You! No peeking!"

A sharp stone struck him on the forehead, drawing blood, which dribbled into an eye and briefly blinded him. He raised his hand protectively and stumbled over a rock, shooting forward like a missile, causing a row of Googlion children to shriek with laughter and clap their hands together with leathery slaps.

Turning into the main street of Nowhere they passed a massive pile of discarded rubbish visible only partially through the flapping wings of flocks of diving scavenger birds. On either side stood a double line of apartment blocks seven and eight stories high, reeking of boiled roots and rotten meat, and thrusting out ugly paunches where the mud-bricks bulged. Rats crawled out of nests burrowed into the dried bog-turf, weakening them – one hard shove, Nimrod thought, and they'd all come tumbling down; even the wooden struts that held them up leaned like drunken giants, unsteady, rotten and worm-eaten. The architect – if there had been one - seemed to have taken pleasure in displeasing the eye; such flamboyant ugliness could never have been unintentional.

Another bend and the Main Square sprawled out before them. Nowarts lolled out everywhere, scattered like discarded garbage, their eyes empty and deficient in hope. Some dragged themselves to the other side in slow motion, dropped down, and stared hopelessly back at where they had come from. From one of the buildings came an agonised shriek; a woman ran out sobbing and collapsed on the side of the road in tears. Nobody took any notice of her.

In the centre stood a granite statue of a man so ugly a black sack had been placed over his face to hide its terrible features. In big, bold letters on the plinth were engraved the words: OUR MAYOR. His horny tentacles hands were so realistically carved they seemed ready to grab whoever walked within grasping distance. Nimrod noticed that all the Nowarts gave it a wide berth.

Every Nowart went by foot; there were no vehicles of any kind, not even for the old. Nimrod missed the bustle of cobbled footsteps, or the lazy clatter of bicycles. Come to that, he missed any kind of noise. Nowhere was swaddled in silence.

A swirl of chocolate clouds hung over the city and the air was smoggy and damp. A dreadful storm seemed minutes away.

A maze of narrow paths wound away from the square. Here the wealthier Nowarts had their houses, just as ramshackle as the hovels of the dispossessed but with smaller windows so they had less of this hideous town to look out on. And they could afford bars on their windows. Again, there was no attempt at pleasing architecture here … they were just places into which the lazy Nowarts could crawl when they wearied of cheating and plotting.

Beyond a rickety perimeter fence waited the quicksands. To keep outsiders out and insiders in. Here, on the edges, lived more of the squat, hunched creatures the Nowarts kept as slaves. Everything about them – their faces, their posture, the way they moved – was furtive, for they had to scheme and plot for every scrap of stale root. Theft was rife amongst these wretched creatures, who communicated in bleats and whines. No Nowart ever went near the swamps, not unless he was tired of life (many were). With great relish Xero shared with Nimrod an anecdote of one Nowart who had ventured too close after a heavy evening of cabbage beer; the Googlions had captured him and trapped him in a wicker cage suspended over the Quicksands, where they threw him scraps and exhibited him to their children, lowering him an inch a day until he disappeared under the swamp-water.

On the far side of the square Nimrod identified the food store, a wicker shed where the Pantryman-in-Chief dried the thin strips of root which kept the lesser Nowarts' stomachs full and stoked their energies just enough to do Podd's bidding. Years in the damp soil gave these roots a musty, sour flavour which appealed to the coarse Nowarts. They were unearthed by Googlions (their mouths stitched shut so they couldn't snack on them), and soaked for a year in vinegar. Under a low roof the crook-backed Pantryman wandered up and down the rows to select the roots as they became mouldy enough for consumption. Two guards, appointed personally by Podd, kept permanent watch against thieving Nowarts and Googlion. To earn a hunk of root you had to devise a wicked plan which met with the approval of officials who reported directly to Podd. As even Nowarts had to eat, the city was steeped in wickedness.

Next to the food store lay the Crypt, a long stone hall devoted to the worship of Podd. Every morning the Nowarts would gather together to pay homage to a discarded cloak stuffed to resemble their leader. Guards passed up and down inspecting the faces of the worshippers, and any supplicant who did not look enthusiastic enough was removed and thrown into the Penance Pit. Civic allegiance flourished.

Next came the gambling den, the most popular building in the city. Here Nowarts gathered to cheat and swindle each other and contribute their meagre earnings to the War Fund in the hopes of increasing their possessions. It was as raucous as a slaughter-house. There were stabbings most days, and muggings in plain view. The law of the jungle prevailed, but that didn't stop parents sending children in to duck and dive through the crowds and pick the pockets of the winners.

In the centre of the square a trap in the ground led to a flight of stone steps which emptied into the Pit. Beneath his feet Nimrod could hear the hollow moans and cries of the better-behaved Nowarts who had been rounded up and crammed into a long narrow cell carved out of the rock by the Googlions. (In Nowhere, prison worked the other way round: should a Nowart inadvertently commit an act of kindness he was immediately bundled into the Penance Pit for periods up to a year until he repented of his good deed.)

Next to the prison stood a low squat building. The Guardhouse. Here Podd's personal guards lived. Their task was to patrol the city, eyes skinned for generous deeds, ear-cavities cocked for rebellious talk. Anyone who so much as whispered the name of Podd was immediately collared and sent up to Dunroamin' Castle for trial. Needless to say, no Nowart had ever been found *not guilty*. The civic guards wore tortoise-shell armour and stone helmets, and carried pointed spears for prodding purposes. They were selected from the most loyal of Podd's subjects, which meant that next to Podd they were the most disgusting men in Nowhere.

Outside the Guardhouse, on a structure resembling a hangman's scaffold, sat Podd's favourite pets, a pair of huge grey vultures who took it in turns to circle the city, listening and watching. Every evening they flew back to their Master and passed on their reports. (Podd never set foot in the city himself, for fear of being mobbed by fans.)

A crowd of Nowarts had gathered to inspect the prisoner. They kept their distance as Nimrod was marched through the square, pointing at him and whispering to each other, aghast that such a creature trod the same earth and breathed the same air as they did.

A few paces from the Guard House Xero stopped. He turned to face his fellow Nowarts, gesturing with contempt at his prize.

"See what I have brought you!" he proclaimed. "A Beyonderling. Pink and soft. Gaze at him, Nowarts, and be grateful you were born the right side of the track."

A loud cheer went up from the Nowarts. Xero smiled smugly at the response to his words.

One or two of the younger creatures ventured closer, sniffing.

"Wait." Up went Xero's horny hand. "No-one is to touch the Outsider. He is to be delivered personally to Podd. And he must arrive in one piece. You know how Podd dislikes soiled goods."

At the mention of Podd, the muttering stopped. A handful of guards drew closer, and the vultures left their perch to hover around Xero's head, their cold eyes raking the crowd.

"You may file past and study the Beyonderling," barked Xero. "But keep your distance, and remember – absolutely no touching."

The Nowarts rapidly formed themselves into a queue ... of sorts, jostling for position, fists flying all over the place. One by one they filed past, their malevolent eyes glinting without blinking as they looked him up and down before the queue pressed forward and the next in line shuffled up to ogle him. At the tail-end three Googlions cloaked in sacking had snuck in for a look until a guard spotted their pathetic disguise and kicked them away.

Xero grabbed Nimrod's shoulder. "This way, pinkling," he said gruffly "You spend tonight in the Pit. Tomorrow you meet Podd."

He shoved Nimrod across to the trapdoor. A waiting sentry produced a massive key, spat on it to oil it, rotated it in its keyhole, hoisted up the trap, and booted Nimrod in.

The door slammed, and all light vanished.

It was like being lowered into a bottle of ink. He was blinded by darkness. He held his hand inches away from his eyes. Still nothing. Not even a shadow.

He waited for his eyes to acclimatize to the darkness. Far below in the belly of the dungeon he heard the scrape of talon on rock and smelt stale air, unwashed bodies and rotting carrion.

As the minutes passed the blackness slowly separated into industrial grey and he made out a descending flight of steps hacked roughly out of the rock. He cautiously extended a foot and moved down one. Then another. And another. Eventually, after what seemed like a hundred steps, he stood on level ground. He ventured forward. He was in a narrow passage. Slime dripped in gobbets from the roof. A bit further forward. He rounded a bend and found himself in a massive underground dungeon with a roof so low he had to stoop. Terrified Nowarts scuttled off to hide in the corners, whimpering, pressing themselves against the walls. One particularly skinny Nowart, braver than the others, stood his ground and pointed a horny finger at him, smacking its lips. "Look!" it said. "Lunch!"

"No!" growled another, creeping out of a dark corner, "he's a spy. Podd sent him here to trick us so we'll say the wrong thing. Then he'll hand us over to the Torturer. Grab him. He must be destroyed."

A murmur of blood-lust ran through the prisoners. They unpicked themselves from their dark corners and advanced on him.

Nimrod struggled frantically with his bonds. Xero hadn't told them he wasn't to be harmed. Now they were going to tear him to pieces. He tugged a hand through a loop of twine, feeling the blood rush to the wrists and leaving his fingers numb. It was the numbness that did it. Without any feeling he was able to torture a hand through a tiny loop and slither it free, just as the Nowarts came into grabbing reach. With a quick, desperate movement he lifted his throbbing hand up to his face and snatched off the spectacles.

Darkness fell like a kidnapper's blanket. And, as the light disappeared, so did the Nowarts, so did their glinting eyes, their outstretched arms, their clutching tentacles. Just in time, too; he could still feel their breath on his cheeks and hear the swish of their waving tentacles.

He stepped back, out of reach, and waited, heart in throat.

The first reaction was a chorus of frightened gasps and cries. They weren't just baffled – they were terrified out of their wits. Even in Nowhere people didn't just vanish into thin air, not unless accompanied by the clatter of the guards' boot-studs. An encouraging start.

Then he heard them dart back into their safe corners, bumping into one another in the darkness, cursing, grunting, whimpering, and Nimrod knew that for the time being at least he was safe.

Clutching his spectacles, fearful of losing them in the dark, he reversed through the darkness, feeling with his hands, until he found a length of wall free of hairy forms. Lowering himself back and down he settled down to pass the night.

The Nowarts never stopped fidgeting and fiddling in the dark. All night they were at it, grunting, huffing, puffing, snorting. Did they never need a good night's sleep? But what was night to them? They were permanently enclosed in darkness, so how could they ever knew when it was night, when day? So they simply laid down and took their rest as they pleased, day, night, whenever, grabbing their moment and, probably, their neighbours and their few possessions.

Exhausted as he was, Nimrod could get no sleep. Every scratch became a threat, every snort a new plan to grab him.

Hour upon hour passed.

On and on went the muttering.

On and on went the shuffling.

On and on went the grunting.

On and on went the snorting.

Until Nimrod's frustration boiled over into anger. He *had* to sleep.

He needed all his energy for tomorrow, all his wits about him, all his reserves of resistance. Cupping his hands around his mouth to create a hollow echo he said, in the deepest voice he could muster:

"The next person to move will feel the vengeance of Podd on you. You have been warned."

Silence. Immediate, absolute silence (not counting heavy, nervous breathing – and not that far away, either.)

Again he laid his head back against the wall and waited to hear if … if … if…

It seemed like minutes but was probably more like hours when a voice penetrated his sleepy haze and stirred him back into consciousness.

"Outsider!"

Where was he? And what was that dreadful *smell?*

"You! Beyonderling! Wake up!"

He shook his head. His eyes were still crusty. How long had he slept? He fumbled for his precious spectacles.

Gone.

Stolen.

He sat up, suddenly very wide awake indeed.

"Outsider. Step up here immediately."

It was Xero, calling from the top of the stairs.

Again Nimrod fumbled for his spectacles. Again his fingers closed around stale air.

No question about it.

His precious spectacles were missing.

While he slept one of the thieving Nowarts must have crept up and stolen them from the very shadow of his heaving body.

Frantically he scrabbled around. His fingers closed around his satchel. He fumbled about inside. Nothing. With rising panic he broadened his field of search, patting the floor of the dungeon around where he had slept, in an ever-increasing circle. They had to be there somewhere … just *had* to. Without them he would never escape, he was fated to spend the rest of his life in Nowhere, blind as a bat, lower than the lowest of the Googlions.

"Did you hear me, pinkling?" Xero wasn't in a good mood. "I told you to step up here, chop-chop. If you're not at my feet by the time I've counted five you'll wish you'd never been born. One … two…"

Still he fumbled. Still the spectacles were nowhere to be found. They had to be there somewhere … surely no Nowart would have had the courage to creep up on a snore without a body. (The very thought of a growling, purring huddle of nothing!) No, sometime while he slept he must have kicked them into the darkness. If only he could get just *half* his vision back then he could run up the stairs, slip past Xero, and run all the way back to World's End.

"Three … four…"

Just as he was despairing of his future he remembered slipping them into the top pocket of his jerkin to keep them safe from the same thieving hands h now suspected. With a loud sigh of relief he fished them out and hooked them back over his ears.

"Five! Right - now you suffer!"

"Wait! I'm here! I'm coming!"

The reaction of the Nowarts was, well … can you imagine looking over this page into the corner of the room and seeing a strange figure suddenly materialise out of nowhere? So when Nimrod suddenly fluttered into view … literally out of Nowhere … they reached for each other and huddled together, whimpering like frightened dogs.

He hoisted up his satchel and ran up the stairs to where Xero blocked the grey morning light. Angry tentacles grabbed him and shook him.

"So. Our Beyonderling wisely decided to be obedient. One second more and I'd have made mincemeat out of you. I tasted it once, you know. Meat. Mr Podd had some left over, after a banquet. Nasty stuff. All gristle and no juice. Not like a nice piece of boiled cabbage." He looked him up and down as if to say: what wouldn't you give for a spoon of cabbage now, eh?

A crowd had collected in the square. Wherever he looked there were Nowarts, pointing Nowarts, gibbering Nowarts, Nowarts climbing on their children's shoulders for a better view.

"Shut up!" screeched Xero. "Shut your ugly traps, the lot of you." He returned his attention to Nimrod.

"Today," he said, "you have an appointment with our Lord and Master. But before you meet him you must be made ready. Cleansed of Beyonder. He hates everything about it, you know. Every tiny speck.

But it's not just your personal hygiene he'll attend to. Oh no, my horrid little pinkling, there's more than civic sanitation to what Balik has up his sleeve. He's the most powerful wizard anywhere, that Balik; he will cast such a spell on you that will never again even *think* of escaping, the word will *vanish* from your personal dictionary." He leaned in closer, until Nimrod saw his scared face reflected in Xero's purple eyes. "Do you read me? If anyone so much as whispers *escape* to you an hour from now you'll say, escape? *Escape?* What can such a thing be? Is it a bird? Can it fly? Is it food? Can I eat it? *Escape?* Pray tell me, what breed of fowl is an *escape?*"

He made a sweeping gesture to encompass the throng of Nowarts, adding in a whisper: "Do you really think they stay here voluntarily? Here, where the air is cold, the food rotten and the most sought after reward is freedom from punishment? Don't make me laugh. That's Balik's doing, that is; they don't escape because they don't know how. They don't escape because they don't have the faintest idea what such a thing is. They've lost their will!" He nudged Nimrod in the ribs and guffawed. "Good one, what? And within the hour you'll be as escape-proof as every one of them. What do you say to that, little pinkling?"

Trouble was – he had nothing to say. If just *half* of what Xero threatened was true, he'd had it. He might as well leap into the swamp now and have done with it. He was finished.

"Grab him."

Xerox snapped two tentacles together and two of the guards came running over.

"If he gets away again you both die. Painfully. Get me? Now … tie him up again and this time make it tight. Next stop … the cave of Balik!"

*

Forming a set of brackets around him they marched Nim down one of the side streets leading off the square. It was early morning but already the town teemed with Nowarts. A queue had formed outside the Root

Drying shed; mothers held up their squalling children to increase their chances of hand-outs.

At first some of the townsfolk wandered over to watch the prisoner's progress and jeer at his plight, but when the party turned off towards the Cave of Balik, none of them followed.

"They don't dare," said Xero, guessing what Nimrod was thinking. "There are two kinds of fear – jabbering fear and trembling fear. Our great Lord Podd inspires the first variety; Balik arouses the second."

They passed an open field where Googlions were digging for roots; Nimrod could see the great red threads passing through their lips to discouraging snacking. A pair of Nowart guards stalked up and down, on the lookout for slackers.

"I suppose," continued Xero, becoming philosophical, "that's what becomes of isolation. Lock yourself away from society and questions will be asked. When there are no answers to those questions we enter the realm of speculation – and speculation invariably assumes the worst." A woman carrying a scrawny baby on her back passed them by on the way up to the square. She shrank into the shadows as they passed.

"Take her now. She's never seen our Lord and Master, but she knows what to expect of him. And for why? Because us honoured few …" he puffed out his chest with pride… "…because we who inhabit the privileged Inner Circle, we are able to pass on to rubbish like her what we have seen and heard. But Balik, well, he's a different story. That wretched woman, she lives just up the road from his cave but he might as well be the other side of the swamps. None of us have clapped eyes on him; we know him only by his voice and through his deeds." He cast a sidelong glance at his prisoner. "Deeds. You'll soon be one of them, pinkling. They say he can turn a grown man inside out."

Nimrod thought about that, but only briefly. Certain thoughts were not for thinking.

Seeing the effect of words Xero sniggered - and his entire throat shook, shaking gobbets of breakfast off the matted hair on his dewlap.

"You'll enter his lair a Beyonderling … and come out - well, who can tell. A Nowart? A Googlion? Or worse?"

The worse thing was, he didn't even laugh. This was business.

The end of the road was blocked by a rock so dense the pick-axes of the Googlions hadn't been able to break it up when the road was built. There was, however, a narrow cleft between its two lobes and it was down this that Xero tugged Nimrod. As they drew closer the Nowart guards swallowed back their fear, their dry saliva falling with little wet plops into their gastric juices, with unfortunate after-effects. Even Xero seemed uneasy. Nimrod noticed his fingers clenching and unclenching as he approached a pair of enormous iron gates. Outside hung a bell pull. Xero grabbed hold of it and tugged hard, twice. A bell tolled solemnly, deep within the cave, its sounder dampened by slime.

There was silence, broken only by the clicks and pops of the guards' saliva. Then a deep, throaty voice emerged from within.

"Who is it? Identify yourselves at once."

"It is I, Xero. I come on a mission from our Lord and Master. I have an outsider needing the Treatment. Podd wishes you to attend to him before he sees him this day. He said I should command you to do "the usual." He said ... he said to say you'd know what he meant. Let us in, Balik."

"O Balik, please. That's the way I like to be addressed. Bit of respect. Now let's hear it again, this time properly."

"O Balik," said Xero, the O six times louder than the Balik. "You mean like that?"

"O Balik what? You're addressing a wizard. What's the magic word?"

"O Balik *please* let us in."

There was a pause as the wizard considered, then:

"Wait!" commanded the voice. Moments later, without any apparent aid, the gates creaked slowly open to reveal a dim passageway.

"One at a time. You know the rules. I hate crowds. I'm claustrophobic."

The guards shoved Nimrod forward. It was obvious they weren't a bit keen on this.

Up they went. Soft pink light bathed the tunnel and strange music floated through from the inner depths. Weird pictures adorned the walls: pictures depicting various body parts reacting to the application of pain. The only light came from small candles set high in the rocky walls, pink candles which flickered and guttered and sizzled in the damp.

Nimrod heard Xero muttering behind him: "Hope he's quick about it. I've an urgent appointment at half past ten." If Xero was ill at ease, what kind of terrifying demon lived here?

He would soon learn.

The tunnel opened out into a rocky ante-chamber, its walls draped with purple cloth embroidered with spiders. Throaty organ music filled the air, and the nervous breath of the guards sent the candlelight flickering. Xero motioned Nimrod towards a stone bench studded with shackles.

"Leave the Beyonderling with me," ordered the disembodied voice. "No need to chain him up … I've just made a fresh batch of knockout gas. You can wait outside. I want no-one to witness my spells. Leave him with me until I summon you back."

Xero was clearly not keen to leave his charge unattended, but Balik had spoken. Unwillingly he turned and strode down the passage followed closely by the swallowing, hiccupping guards, their horny hooves clattering and clumping until even their echoes had been swallowed up. There was a hollow clang as they gates slammed shut.

Nimrod waited.

And waited.

And waited.

Then the far end of the cave rippled and Nimrod made out the curtains, identical in colour and pattern to the cave wall. The lights flickered, the organ swelled, the breathing grew heavier, and the curtains parted enough for a tall figure to step through. It was clad in a plum-coloured mantilla embroidered with death-watch beetles. His face? You could hardly call it that. Nimrod had only once seen such a face before … on a skeleton. It was a bleached skull.

He was so terrified he fell over backwards.

"Arise, Beyonderling!" came the voice of Balik. "Step forward into the light so I can get a good look at your face."

Nimrod did no such thing.

Instead he said:

"Get lost, you wet lump of slime. Why, you're so useless you don't even have any skin, like a normal person!"

Where had that come from? Nimrod couldn't believe he had said it.

He stepped back.

"I mean… That is to say …"

Balik advanced towards him … and stopped. He raised his skeletal hands up to his skeletal face, twisted - and lifted. Off it came. Skull, eye-sockets, teeth and all. What sort of wicked magic was this? But there was more. The same skeletal hands grabbed hold of the mantilla and flipped it back to reveal another figure beneath. Even in the dim light there was something familiar about the shape. And then it clicked, and he nearly screamed for joy.

"Kabil!" he shouted, and reached out to hug the old wizard.

"Sssh!" cautioned Kabil, "Not so loud. You don't want the guards to hear you. Words carry for miles inside a cave … even whispers, so you'll have to talk softer than that. "

"What are you doing here?" asked Nimrod in less than a whisper.

In reply Kabil put an arm around Nimrod's shoulder and walked him towards the curtains parting them and leading him into another rocky chamber, larger than the first. It was equipped as a laboratory.

The wizard sat Nimrod down on a stool and paced up and down in front of him as he explained.

"You're the first person to discover my secret, Nimrod," he announced gravely. "I've been coming here for years. You see, I have certain … ah … *means* of getting here without plunging through forests and braving empty plains. Many years ago, when I first learned the trick, I transported myself to Nowhere and disposed of Balik, the original wizard of Nowhere. Not a nice man. He won't be missed. I took over his cave, and pretended to the Nowarts that I was him. Not a very difficult task, I must admit, for no-one had ever seen him. Too scared. Just as no-one ever sees me. For some time now I've been plotting the fall of this land of Nowhere. And am I glad to have a little assistance!"

His words were drowned by a low rumble of thunder; very slight thunder, admittedly, but thunder none the less. And, all the more surprising, this was *indoor* thunder.

Nimrod followed Kabil's eyes across to the corner. In the darkness of he could just make out an arrangement of tubes and pipes and glass bottles breathing steam. Above them hovered a small, immensely black cloud.

"My secret weapon," announced Kabil proudly. "Nearly there. Give me another couple of decades and I'll have the bugger. Just a tweak here and there, a few twists of a screwdriver, the half-turn of a shifting spanner..."

"But ... but ... but...... Nimrod stopped, took a deep breath, and started again. "But why didn't you tell me all this before? I've had a terrible time!"

Kabil paused before looking back at Nimrod.

"That's a difficult question, Nimrod. I'm not sure I can really answer it. But I'll try. When you visited me and announced your intentions of travelling to Nowhere I nearly clapped you on the back, shook hands with you and did a jig, all at once. At last I had found someone brave enough to address the Nowhere problem. But first I had to make sure you were up to it. I watched you most of the way, young Nimrod, and I have to admit I thought you were a goner when you answered the call of the Mesmeric Glade. Convinced you were going to succumb, I was. Must say you coped very well. And as for the fight with the Caterkillar ... well, nice one. You really excelled yourself there. You had me on the edge of my seat."

The miniature black cloud gave another tiny little rumble, like a hungry stomach, which the wizard ignored.

"But do you know what impressed me most? You never once called on me for help. You had three chances and you used none of them. How proud am I of that? No, I don't think I could have found a better assistant to help me wipe out Nowhere. Not anywhere."

Nimrod swelled with pleasure. Particularly as the compliment had come from Kabil Mark Two. Not the doddery old wizard he had first visited, but this proud, wise man.

"Thank you, sir," was all he could say, and meant it.

Kabil pulled back a sleeve to reveal a small sundial strapped to his wrist. He removed a tiny torch from his pocket, and shone it at the sundial. "Goodness me." he declared, "time does fly. Enough of explanations and on to action. If I don't hurry, those guards of yours will be back. "

"What do you want me to do?" asked Nimrod, suddenly feeling less brave. "Am I going back to World's End with you?"

"Goodness, no!" exclaimed Kabil, "that would never do. You're a useful ally in the camp of the enemy. I'm not going to lose that chance in a hurry. You must do as the guards tell you and get behind the walls of Dunroamin' Castle at all costs. There's still a chance that your brave father is alive, although not a very strong one, I'm afraid. They may lock you up and torture you a little, but fear not, I'm working on an escape plan right now, and I'm sure I'll have it up and ready before they move on to the sharper instruments. Leave that side of things to me."

"If .. if you come up with a plan," stuttered Nimrod, "how will you convey it to me?"

Kabil waved a hand at him. "Don't go confusing me with the finer points," he said, "that's one of the little details I must still work out. Never forget, though, I'm a wizard. I may not be a great wizard, but I still have the power of magic at my beck and call. I know there are only two of us against the forces of the Nowarts, but I still think we stand a pretty good chance."

"If I mange to escape from Dunroamin' Castle," continued Nimrod, fingering his spectacles, "how can I get back to this cave?"

"Use your compass. I hope you haven't lost it. And then call out your name. The gates will open for you. But mind you scurry in, for they close fast."

"With a pack of Nowarts on my tail, I'm sure to hurry." said Nimrod with feeling. "They really are the nastiest creatures I've ever clapped eyes on. I'd hate to live here for ever."

Kabil arched his eyebrows darkly.

"You've yet to meet Podd, my friend. Make sure you take a deep breath before looking at him. He's a Bad Man. If his hood slips, turn your head. Never look him straight in the eyes. They a have a strangely hypnotic power, one not even a brave lad like you will be able to resist."

He glanced once again at his sundial. "But we've spoken enough. At least you know now that you've a friend close by. When the guards return I want you to walk as if a spell has been laid upon you. Cast your eyes to the ground, keep your voice low and obey whatever orders the guards give you. Is that clear? "

Nimrod nodded.

"Right then." Kabil drew his clock around his body once again and replaced the skull mask. The result looked so frightening Nimrod could

114

hardly believe a friend lived within.

"Come along with me - and remember all I told you. Look after yourself, now." He led Nimrod back into the chamber, stopping only to turn over the gramophone record of organ music and blow the dust off the stylus.

When Nimrod was seated again on the beach, Kabil raised his head and called out in a booming voice: "Return, O Guard of Podd, and collect your prisoner."

A few moments later footsteps echoed up the corridor and Xero marched in with the two Nowart Guards. When they saw Kabil, they lowered their eyes.

"Remove him from my presence. The spell has been cast. From the stroke of midnight tonight he will do what he is told. Come dawn you will have no more trouble from this one."

Obediently, the guards grabbed Nimrod and turned him to face the exit. Remembering what Kabil had said he looked down at the ground and shambled down the corridor like a donkey on a rope.

As they reached the gates Kabil's voice boomed out after them: "One more thing: I don't want that Beyonderling harmed in any way. One tiny scratch and a thousand curses will hail down upon you and make you wish you were dead. He must be delivered to Podd unhurt."

Then the great gates slowly parted to let them through.

Xero led the way, the guards half marching half carrying Nim. Back up the road, back into the square, past the Guard House, Nimrod kept up his spellbound act, walking as if asleep. His mind was going over what Kabil had told him. So he planned the downfall of Nowhere. All on his own? Just like that? How could one man defeat all these awful Nowarts, creatures versed in scheming and plotting and fighting amongst themselves? One man – and a wise, gentle, kindly one at that. And yet ... and yet he had seen a new side to old Kabil this time, something in his eyes, a trick of the light perhaps but there had been a definite glint ... a spark of steel ... an edge ...

They stopped at the very edge of the village. A narrow path wound its way up, but no castle was yet visible.

Xero turned to face Nimrod.

"Right. Now listen you here, Beyonderling, and listen well. From this point you are to hold your tongue. Podd dislikes noise of any kind, and that includes superfluous talking. Never speak unless you're spoken to, and when you do, keep it short. The more you complain, the worse off you will be. Is that clear?"

"Clear enough," answered Nimrod in a low, flat voice. He had to keep up the pretence that he was completely under their power, which was, really, not that far from the truth. No suspicion must be thrown on Balik at all costs.

Xero motioned to the guards. "Hold him tight. As you know, no stranger is allowed near the domain of Podd unaccompanied. There are watchers everywhere, the rocks have ears, the sky has eyes. Every move we make, every word we utter is being passed on to the Master. Don't give them any opportunity to report ill of us."

The guards made gruff noises.

Xero stepped forward decisively.

"I will lead the way. Stay close to the prisoner; the All-Powerful Lord of Nowhere will reward us well for delivering into his hands this useless twig so that he can snap it at his leisure. By the left…"

From the great watch-tower behind them a bell began to toll.

Dong … dong … dong.

A wave of fear swept through Nim. Suddenly he no longer trusted Kabil. The old man was a dreamer. Why had he listened to him? He should have run when he could, when he had a chance…

Dong … dong … dong.

Oh dear, now he was in real trouble. He would never descend this hill. He struggled to suppress the panic: panic would only make everything worse; what he needed now, more than anything, was presence of mind.

Wrong.

What he needed was the very opposite. Absence of body.

With a sudden jerk he pulled himself away from the tentacles of the guards, took a deep breath – and snatched the spectacles from the bridge of his nose.

*

116

His ears buzzed. His eyes swam. It was as if some rushing force had plucked him up and plunged him into muddy water. The skyline of Nowhere had turned into a hazy smudge that rippled and swelled, rippled and swelled, and his captors – whose foul breath he could still smell – into vague smears that stretched out for him like waving strands of seaweed. And the bell ... the solemnly tolling bell from the guard tower ... its toll went from clang to dull heavy thump, muffled like a bass drum.

The whole world had become invisible ... sort of. He took a step back and it was like walking underwater with lead boots on. He reached out to steady himself, flummoxed, unable to put two and two together, before sense slowly filtered back. So this was what *invisible* meant. Shapes became smudges ... noises turned into their echoes. Nothing quite vanished.

One sound, though, was unmuffled ... his own voice calling out to him from inside his head, *escape*, it said, *escape and run, do it now*, and that's just what he did.

He dodged the waving tentacles and aimed for a gap between the blurs. He half-remembered a narrow alley between the guard-house and the root-drying hall. Sidestepping the smudges he sprinted towards it.

A shape crossed his path. He bumped into it and it was like colliding with chocolate pudding. He wondered: had it felt him too? The answer came in the form of a low echoing howl as if from the end of a long tunnel.

No time to think about that. The gap loomed before him and he darted down it, flinging himself back against the wall ... more chocolate pudding. He slid the spectacles over the bridge of his nose and curled the tips over his ears. The wall grew solid and cold behind his back and vision swam back, but everything was still blurred ... had the collision perhaps dislodged something behind his eyes? Of course. He had been clutching them in his sticky hands while he ran, now the lenses were coated in his sweat.

He unhooked the tail of his shirt from his trousers and gave them a quick polish. Light flooded through again, and he saw that he had fetched up in one of the residential streets radiating off the square.

Vision brought sharpness back to his hearing. A klaxon was honking out its alarm message in the square; he could imagine Xero striding backwards and forwards and barking out orders. *Sound the alarm. Snare him. Truss him. Bring him to me.*

On the other side of the lane an upper window opened and a wizened old-lady Nowart's head emerged, squinting up towards the source of the alarm. He shrank back into the shadows. Below her a door crashed open and a soldier hurtled out, still buttoning on his breastplate. He disappeared in the direction of the klaxon, nearly tripping over Nimrod's feet. The old woman shouted something after him and he called back what sounded to Nimrod like yeah, yeah, yeah.

Huddled in the shadows Nimrod hugged his knees to his chest and wondered what to do next.

Call it out, Nimrod. "Kabil, Kabil, Kabil - by the powers of light and goodness I direct you to send aid."

Surely the time had come. One call, just one; that would leave two if the first failed, and if it didn't, well, he wouldn't be alone any more, alone and cold and frightened…

"Get a move on or I'll clip you round the ears!"

He parted his knees and peered through the gap. Bustling towards him a she-Nowart was chivvying her two children down towards the dark end of the lane. The hair on her head had been plaited into spikes, the latest thing, Nimrod imagined, in Nowart chic. She was plug ugly, but clearly thought she was the bees knees.

Her children had surly eyes, crabby at being hustled away from the action. The girl, her hair styled to resemble her mother's, was pulling faces and mouthing her mother's words … *stop dawdling … shift those lazy feet … stop pulling those faces … don't think I can't see you …*

The boy, younger than his sister, wore an expression of dumb insolence, his eyes flashing with rage at being removed from all the action. Yes, thought Nimrod, there's a future Xero festering slowly away in there somewhere.

He watched them let themselves into a house at the far end. The door swung shut, struck the latch and bounced open again. The mother's voice carried up the road: *straight up into your rooms and lock the doors behind you, do what I tell you or I'll give you what for your nasty little worthless articles* …

What if…

The plan arrived fully formed in his head. He rose to his feet and scuttled down the lane keeping his back in contact with the wall where the shadows clung, towards the open door. In he darted, pulling the door shut behind him.

Done. Safely behind closed doors. Even if they were somebody else's.

It was dim in there but the embers from a flickering fire at the far end showed a long, rather narrow room dominated by a cauldron steaming over coals. Whatever was stewing in there it smelt foul, acidic enough to bring tears to his eyes. His stomach churned. Hunger - or disgust? The rest of the room was taken up by a stone slab that served as a low table just a foot or so off the ground, and cushions filled with straw.

Stairs led up to the next level, and an internal door to the next room. To the right of the fireplace a low door opened out onto a courtyard. As Nimrod accustomed his eyes to the smoky light a squat figure in a shapeless sacking dress came in, mopping at its brow. A moment later she was followed in by another Googlion servant, in loose britches; he gave her a rough push - which sent her sprawling - and slithered over to the cauldron to dip its finger into whatever bubbled away in there. It withdrew something limp and flabby and sucked it into its mouth … *hmmm* is *hmmm* in any language.

The she-creature picked up a fork from the table and jabbed it into the side of her companion, who just chortled and finished off the lump in its mouth with a loud slurp, the fork sticking out like a hog's tail.

Nimrod darted through the door into the adjoining room - the sitting room. Here three easy chairs nailed together out of rough-hewn wood and two tree-stump stools were ranged around a pond in which swamp-lobsters tethered by chains tugged and yanked to get within attacking distance of each other; their claws snapped, churning the water up into a lather.

A portion of the far wall had been painted black, and a length of chalk on a string had scratched out what looked like a score-card. At the far end of this room stone steps led down into the cellar. There were no windows.

Next door the servants were still bickering and scrapping; he heard a splosh as stew was flung. Then footsteps. Then a shrill yell of rage. Then slaps. Then grunts and yelps. Then more yelling. Nimrod recognized the voice of the spike-haired woman.

"Steal food from my children's mouth, will you? Well I'll learn you, you stinking blobs of carrion. Just you wait till your father gets home. Until then, *this* will have to suffice … and *this* … and *this* …"

Each *this* was accompanied by a howl, some of them bordering on a dangerous-sounding snarl. There was revolt seething in there, just below the surface.

His suspicions were confirmed a few moments later. After sighing and generally bemoaning the standard of servants these days the mistress of the house stomped upstairs. The Googlion servants started up again. But gone was the animosity of the fork-stabbing incident, now they were fellow conspirators, united in their hatred of the Dreaded Enemy.

"*Stinking blobs of carrion!* Who does she think she is, she whose neck smells of vinegar-water, dabbed on to snare that swamp-lobster of a husband of hers. Disgusting. Nauseating. Vomit-making."

"Learn us? She'll be learning her own lessons when the time comes, and it's not far away."

"Hard lessons."

"Sore lessons."

"Long lessons."

They collapsed into hysterical giggling. Nimrod heard the thumps as they clapped each other on the backs and shared their fantasies of revolt. No chance of that. The Googlions were too obsequious to rise up against their oppressors, the Nowarts far too sly and cunning.

"Send us down the swamps for roots, will they? Well we'll see who ends up wallowing in those swamps, we'll see who ends up with the slimy mud caking the backs of their throats, we'll watch their ugly heads rise from the mud and spit out the frog-spawn before they beg for our tender mercies."

"And will we be merciful? Will we, Gluçilla?"

"Will we hell, Glydnyg. We'll show them the same mercy they've always shown us. A kick up the dirty end, if they're lucky."

"And if they're not?"

Again they collapsed into peals of laughter, cut short only by the slamming of the front door and the return of what Nimrod assumed was the Man-Nowart of the house.

He retreated hastily into the stair-well over the dank cellar.

The smell was foul down there. Human waste, festering roots, stagnant water. He clung to the wall, testing each step before he set a foot down in case he stepped into something revolting.

Then he froze.

He was not alone down here. Something was clicking and splashing in the darkness, something small, something that breathed.

It seemed to hear him too, for it stopped whatever it was doing and waited ... waited and listened and thought.

For minutes on ends they both remained still, each waiting for the other to make a move. On the ceiling, condensation fattened into drops and slid off to plop and echo in the cold, eerie stillness.

Then the creature took a step forwards.

Towards him.

It stepped out of the water and onto the cellar floor. Water careened off its back. It stopped. Clicked. Took another step forward ... then another.

Click.

Clack.

Claws.

Nimrod gulped and froze. Nowarts he could just about cope with ... but this ... this thing that breathed and clicked and had the sense to bide its time, this invisible creature at home in the wet and the dark ... this creature that was now slowly approaching ... without shape or form to get a fix on ... it terrified him a hundred times more.

Wait.

He remembered the tinder-box in his satchel. Perhaps if he could identify the thing that clicked ...perhaps then disgust would replace fear. He fumbled for it. The creature listened, trying to work out what he was up to. Shuffling through the crumpled sandwich papers ... the flask of nectar (no, not now) ... the change of socks ... Nimrod's fingers closed round it and slowly drew it out.

The creature took another couple of steps forward. Perhaps it had an apparatus to smell his fear ...?

121

He drew the flint across the touch stone. The scrape seemed to draw the creature on ... or was that a step backwards ... a retreat...?

He tried again.

The creature stood its ground, clicking.

The trusty little tinder-box seemed to take a deep breath and then, whoosh, out it spat a tongue of flame which curled round the wick and sent a circle of pink light sputtering into the darkness.

As the light erupted he saw rocky walls dripping with slime ... green icicles clinging to the ceiling like snot ... a pond spread with heaving moss ... drips and slimy claw-prints leading across to ... to the bottom of his steps ... and there it stood, looking up at him, tapping its claws on the floor.

He recognized it immediately. It was a giant version of the swamp-lobsters in the pool. Oh yes, thought Nimrod, now I know what you are, you're the factory, the thing that breeds those gladiator lobsters upstairs that maim and kill each other to entertain the Nowarts through the long boring nights.

Slowly, so as not to startle it, he reached in and grasped Mrs Small's grease-proof sandwiche paper ... easy does it ... wait ...

Then, as the creature clambered up onto the first step ... up towards him ... he held the tip of the paper into the fire until it blazed – and flung it down the stairs.

It floated down in a blaze of angry flame.

The creature drew back its feelers and made a horrible screeching sound (which could have been the friction of shell against shell) as it turned and scuttled back towards its pond. Nimrod saw that the surface of the water was agitated now, as if a school of tiny fish had swum to the surface for feeding, then he saw hundreds of tiny snapping claws and thought, she's only being a mother, she's only protecting her babies. He felt a stab of pity for their useless lives.

Back up the stairs he trotted, two at a time, sending a blast of air to snuff out the burning paper ... then tiptoed across to the connecting door. Outlined against the courtyard door a Nowart dressed, like Xero, in the uniform of the Captain of the Guard was shaking its tentacles in the air. It was in a dreadful mood.

"This kitchen's a disgrace. A shame. Just look at it. Just because you lot have crawled out of the swamps doesn't mean we want to share your messy habits. Think about your superiors for a change. Now get on with my dinner. I've had a terrible day, absolutely bloody terrible, and I need my victuals. Later, when we're all tucked up in our beds getting our beauty sleep, I want you, Gluçilla, to come down and tidy this mess up. You hear me? Every last scrap. No, not you, what's-your-name, not you, I've got other tasks for you tomorrow, and a weary Googlion won't be any use to me. Do you understand me? Have my words penetrated your thick ugly skulls?"

There was a grunt ... or was it a sneer? To Nimrod it sounded insolent but the Nowart didn't ... or didn't care to ... notice.

"Now crack open some of that root wine. I've got a sick head on my shoulders tonight."

Nimrod darted back to the head of the cellar stairs in case the Nowart came through to take his bad mood out on the swamp-lobsters. Instead he went clumping up the stairs, calling out to his children to tell him exactly what it was they'd learned at Nowart-school that day, and woe betide them if they didn't show signs of being smarter than they'd been this time the evening before ...

In the kitchen the muttering had started up again.

"I'll wait behind the door, Gluçilla. Then, when he next comes in, *whop,* I'll pounce on him and *thwick,* stab him with this here knife. A nice slow slide between the ribs: that should do for him. I know just where to aim for ... I've practised many times on myself ... with a blunt stick, of course ... until I learned just the spot. He'll fall like a tree with wormy roots."

"Oh don't be ridiculous, Glydnyg, just grow up. You know our ribs don't match theirs. Us with our two bellies and them with only one, poor things. They don't need as many as us. Less to protect. How I *weep* for their plight. How I *pity* their emptiness." Her sarcasm rippled like fingernails on silk.

"Tell me to grow up, will you? And who has to creep back at midnight to mop up the floor? Who'll be scrubbing out the boiling pot when the other's stretched out fast asleep, snoring like swamp-bubbles? Just you tell me that, two-bellies!"

Nim left them at it. He had spotted a chest in the corner, large enough to curl up in, and he had much catching up to do in the sleep department. The eating department too, but ... those roots! Forget it!

He'd rather starve.

He eased open the lid and peered in. The chest was half full of dry root-husks. He tested the makeshift mattress with a suspicious foot. Nothing yelped … or raised its head through the straw to peer at him with venomous eyes.

He climbed in and let the lid gently down until he was sandwiched between softness and darkness.

"Kill him!"

Was it a second – or was it a month he'd been asleep?

Judging by the exchange muffled by the lid of the trunk the family had eaten; now each of them was urging its adopted swamp-lobster to annihilate its opponents. He'd slept an hour at the most. Far too short.

"Tear his claws off!" came the keyed-up cry of the little girl.

"Blind him!" screeched the most junior of the Nowarts.

"Kill! Kill!" Mother Nowart was beside herself with ecstasy. "Trap them in the corner and use those claws! Go on – you're bigger than both of them!"

"Wait!"

The voice of Daddy Nowart cut through the din. Nimrod heard him distributing slaps and cracks across the head. "I told you: we're not playing *To The Death* tonight. Loss of Limbs? Why not … they grow again soon enough, but no killing. The new brood downstairs aren't big enough yet … waste this lot and what'll we do for next week? Eh?"

"Look, ma – my one snapped your one's eye off! Brilliant! This is a wicked game, this is!"

Nimrod felt an army of pins of needles march along his feet … round his ankles … and up his legs. Little by little he shifted position …. slowly … gently … silently …

Then … one of the straws stuck straight up one of his nostrils and began to tickle a sneeze out of his nose.

He remembered his last big sneeze, the auction sneeze; that had almost cost him his spectacles - and won him a mirror he didn't want. The price of this one could be a lot steeper. If he let it loose they'd yank the lid open and … well, he didn't fancy his chances against the swamp-lobsters.

He felt the sneeze-tickle travel up one nostril, chicane round the bend, and hover there, trembling.

Now that death was no longer an option the Nowart family had lost interest in the lobsters. The room had gone still; even a trivial sneeze would explode the silence, and there was nothing trivial about the sneeze building up there at the back of his nose.

Think about something else.

Mrs Small's sandwiches … focus on them, on those fat, juicy fillings spilling out of the hot bread – no, on second thoughts, think of something else again … those are tummy-gurgles building up down there, as dangerously explosive as the sneeze.

The library. Concentrate now, Nimrod, how many titles can you remember? Row A-B, starting at the top … *Aardvarks and Other Curious Beasts … Abernethy Biscuits and How to Bake Them … Acrostics For Beginners … Articles Up the Nose: Their Part in History* … no, that wouldn't do either.

The sneeze was reaching the point of no return … a few seconds more and the touch-paper would catch. Then – wham-bang-ouch!

Amidst the husks his hand curled round a spike of bark. Just as the sneeze reached the top of the hill and prepared to release its brakes he plunged the pointed end into his nearest body surface - which happened to be the meatiest part of his thigh - and the pain took over. He swallowed back a yelp– and clenched his eyes tightly shut. The pain ebbed. The sneeze spotted the gap and headed for it. He gave the husk another shove and the pain returned - with a vengeance. He clamped his teeth shut like a castle portcullis, holding everything back. But for how long?

Then …

"Don't know about you lazy lot but I'm off to bed. What a day I've had. I'm bushed. Somebody tie up the lobsters."

There came the scrape of wood on stone, mutters, grumbles, yawns … and in a minute flat the room was empty. Good thing too. A few seconds later all his suppressed explosions joined forces and detonated: a yelp of pain, a gigantic sneeze and the earthquake rumble of a hungry tummy, all at once.

More silence.

A little later another sound rolled into his consciousness. A low, grating rumble … like wind stirring gravel. He blinked, struggling to place it.

Of course. Snoring. His own. As heard from the inside. He shook his head and surfaced from his sleep.

No, it wasn't his own snoring that had woken him. A slow, steady scrape had done that, the scrape of straw against stone.

He reached up to ease open the lid and let in a finger of pale light. And listened hard.

From the next room came a clatter, then a thud – and the scraping suddenly stopped.

What ...?

In the next door room Gluçilla had been cleaning up as instructed, that was clear enough from her martyred grunts as she dusted and washed and swept. But that thump?

He slid out of the chest, wriggling his legs to chase away the pins and needles, and dusted himself off. The detached husks floated down into the pond and the lobsters woke, straining and snapping to be the first to get to whatever it was that had disturbed the surface.

Then ... a hoarse whisper.

"Alone at last. Together. C'mere, you lovely foul thing, you ..."

He pressed himself back into the shadows. The Master of the House had spoken. But what was he talking about?

There was a scuffle, and a petulant whimper.

"Gerroff of me! Gerrout of it! Leave off!"

He worked his way round to the door, leaning forward until he could get a better view into the kitchen.

In the fireplace the embers were still glowing. Gluçilla was pressed up against the mantle, her straw broom discarded on the floor, her face turned away from the Nowart who was, well, there was no mistaking what he was doing, he was forcing her face back to face his, he was squeezing her cheeks, he was ... he was trying to kiss her.

Nimrod felt nauseous. That he could do this while upstairs his wife and children slept! He tried to imagine catching his own father with Mrs Small next door, say ... or the girl who sometimes came to tidy up when his mother was poorly ... and couldn't. Unthinkable. Inconceivable. Hideous.

He looked again. Perhaps he'd misread the situation..?

No. It was as bad as he thought. Worse. Because the Googlion was so much smaller than him the Nowart had to crouch down in a contorted position to reach her. She was snuffling and whimpering and picking at the hair on his back with her fingers. But he was too strong, she didn't stand a chance.

And then ... the clumsiness of his posture gave Nimrod an idea.

Leaning against the wall was a net and pole for clearing scum off the surface of the pond. Urged on by Gluçilla's muffled grunts he grabbed it by its business end, ran through, and brought it smartly down over the Nowart's head, netting it amidst the strands of green slime.

There was a mighty loud roar and the Nowart spun round, its tentacles clutching at the air. Nimrod leaped back and the rod swung like a pendulum as the Nowart floundered about, temporarily blinded. The servant girl lay on the floor, against the wall, clutching her cheap labourer's frock to her chin, sobbing and watching through tearful eyes.

The Nowart opened its eyes. Realising how he had been caught he gave a growl of fury and grabbed at the rod with both tentacles, yanking hard. Still the net remained in place, trapping and contorting its face.

Again it tried ... again it failed,

Raising its upper lip with a snarl it unrolled its purple tongue and hooked the netting back into its mouth so it could bite through the cords one by one, *snap ... snap ... snap.* Then it turned and plucked the last strings of slime out of its eye sockets, breathing heavily and blinking stupidly, unable to believe anyone would dare do such a thing to him ... and in his own house too.

"What the ....!"

Nimrod caught a sudden whiff of vinegar-water. Standing at the bottom of the stairs, tentacles clapped to cheeks smeared with dark pink cream, stood the Nowart's wife, her spikes of hair rolled up in miniature versions of the net that had trapped her husband's face. He only managed a quick glance but it was enough to glimpse something in her eyes, a look, a weariness, a coded message that said: *this isn't the first time.*

Then the Nowart opened its mouth and roared.

"Pinkling!"

Nimrod took a couple of steps back and collided with the wall.

"Xero!"

The creature's horny foot kicked out and everything went dark.

*

Waking, he felt a stream of air fanning his cheek. He tried raising an arm to flick it away ... still too dopey to remember that breezes can't be idly dusted away like that ... and found he couldn't move a muscle.

He tugged open an eyelid – at least that worked - and black specks swam into view. He opened the other eye, just a fraction, and the specks became ravens wheeling and swooping against a sky thickening with rain.

He looked down and saw that he had been tethered to a wooden frame. His mouth felt rough and dry and powdery.

"Water. For pity's sake give me a drink of water." He hardly recognized his voice; it was more a croak than a sentence.

"The pinkling wakes. Shall I knock him back into oblivion for you, Captain?"

"Leave him be. He's not going anywhere in that state."

He recognised the voice of Xero. He clamped his eyes shut again, not ready yet to face up to the reality of his plight. Where were they taking him? And why?

He pieced together his last conscious moments. The servant girl crawling away into the shadows. The blazing eyes of the Nowart. The sudden pain. The nothingness.

As consciousness ebbed back he became aware of the scrapes gouged out of his chin by Xero's talon. At least the spectacles still rested on the bridge of his nose ... though only just. He mentally examined the rest of his body ... any other damage? Nothing he could put a finger on, which was hardly surprising as his finger was securely attached to a hand attached to an arm attached to a stretcher with rough twine.

He became aware that he was moving uphill in bumps and jolts. The Nowarts at either end of the stretcher grunted as the path grew steeper.

"Too heavy for you, is he?" came the mocking voice of Xero. "If you're not up to it, grunt one more time and I'll relieve you of your duties. Send you somewhere cushier. How does swamp-draining sound to you? No steep hills down at the swamps. I'm sure the Googlions could do with a little help down there."

The guards drew in their breath. Xero inspected his prisoner.

"As for you, pinkling, I find myself in a quandary. Balik's treatment should have purged you of resistance. Yet last night … that business with the net …" His eyes caught Nimrod's and for just a moment a shadow of complicity, a secret shared, passed between them. Was that just a hint of blush beneath his matted facial hair? Then he looked away.

"My instincts tell me to send you back for more of the same. Just to make sure. But Podd is eager to inspect you, and there's no time for that. I shall have to report Balik's failure … it seems his powers may be deserting him."

What had he done? By protecting the servant girl he'd gone and blown Kabil's carefully laid plans.

His mind raced.

"Yes," he said in a hushed, subservient voice aimed at Xero's retreating back. "You do that. The Lord and Master must know everything. Nothing must be omitted. I too will tell the Great Lord all. Everything. *Everything.*"

Xero halted briefly in his tracks and Nimrod knew he was weighing up the odds. If Podd were to learn of his weakness…

"That may not be necessary. We'll see about that." He spun round and his eyes were blazing. "But remember this, outcast: you take your orders from me. Do you understand? Only from me!"

"I will do as I'm told. Speak as instructed. Answer as commanded."

Xero studied him. After a moment he unhooked the flask from his belt and splashed his face with a dollop of the contents; though it was bitter and sour he managed to catch enough of it in his mouth to wet his parched throat … enough to murmur a subservient thank-you before the Captain of the Guard turned and continued his climb. Nimrod gritted his teeth. Had he planted a seed of doubt in a nature festering with suspicion? Time would tell.

Onwards. Upwards. Towards … what?

Up in the castle Podd stood at a window, his eyes glued to a giant telescope, watching the procession wind its way up towards him.

Did you really think you could creep up on me without me knowing? This is my territory. You don't belong here. You think you're brave … well you're not. Stupid is the word. Stupid like all the other man-creatures I left behind all those years ago.

My castle is impregnable. Even if there were a thousand of you I'd still defeat you. There's not a brick to tumble … not a joist to split and fall. We carved it out of the mountain rock … me and my obedient servants. To keep out meddlers like you. What a fool you are, what a blind fool.

He turned away from the window and cast a glance at where the little tin was squirreled away in its hidey-hole. In it, amidst his other treasures, lay the picture he had slavishly copied the castle from, dog-eared but safely hidden. He had carried it about with him since he first thrust it into his pocket. It was only a copy, a small copy torn from a book, but the original was burned into his memory. The castle in the clouds … the winding path … the pilgrims struggling up like the little party who even now bore the stranger up to him. He saw it all as if it were yesterday … every detail fixed there as he waited for the stick to fall … rise … fall again. The river swirling in the valley … the jagged rocks … the squiggle of the artist's signature … the title trapped in its frame.

Pilgrim's Rest.

Not a week went by when he wasn't hauled before his father and doubled over the desk for some trivial offence. The picture hung on the wall facing him as his father laid into him with his birch, his Nemesis - but also his salvation. It became his castle, his haven, waiting for him at the end of the winding path, pressing its shape through the mist as the cane bit into him. With the pilgrims he climbed the hill, braved the rocks, reached for the door they would never reach.

In those days it had stood for Power and Authority and Don't Argue With Me Boy. Later it became his symbol of escape. Now … now it was his, all his, now he had the power, he wielded the big stick …

In time the castle and his home had merged into one. He had even given it the same name spelt out by the brass letters hammered into the wooden plaque over the letterbox of the red-brick bungalow at the end of Delphinium Terrace. Dunroamin'. In that moment victory was his.

One of the Nowarts stumbled and cursed, jolting Nimrod, and a pair of massive gates swung into view, blocking their way.

Xero stepped forward, presenting himself with a low bow to the waiting gatekeeper.

Name ... place of birth ... reason for visit ... planned length of stay.

Nimrod saw how nervous Xero was. And not without reason. Hit the wrong note and the gatekeeper would hit a lever. Then ... bang, whoosh, splash ... the rock would crash open and down you went, bound for oblivion.

The gatekeeper walked over to where Nimrod lay tethered on his stretcher and thrust his face forward. His breath smelt of rotten carrion-meat, fed to him three times a day by the vultures. His eyes lit up with malicious glee.

"Ah. Our Visitor from the Outside World. We've Heard All About you, Outsider. They've Been Preparing for you for Days." He spoke in capital letters. "You're In For Quite a Time, Let Me Warn You." His laugh creaked like an old rusty lock.

The rock beneath them trembled unsteadily. From deep below came the dull rumble of rushing water.

The gatekeeper studied Nimrod's tethers and seemed satisfied. Producing from within the folds of his jacket a ring of keys he unlocked the great gate, taking his time over it, casting slow, meaningful glances over his shoulder. Then, with a groan like a cry of pain, it swung open and they passed through.

"On your feet, pinkling."

Horny tentacles fumbled with his knots, dug into his shoulders, hoisted him roughly to his feet. His hands still tied behind his back Nimrod swayed unsteadily as the blood rushed back into his feet.

"That's enough molly-coddling, you lazy pink monstrosity. You can walk the rest of the way on your own two feet, like the rest of is."

A horny kick in the small of his back indicated that it was time to move. Now. And fast.

They set off again up the path following a steep zigzag route. Nimrod's legs ached. He longed to beg permission to rest. But he had been "treated". And the "treated" never begged.

The Nowart behind him, guessing his thoughts, grunted – and prodded him with unnecessary force.

The higher they rose the rarer the air became. Nimrod gasped for breath. Even the Nowarts seemed to have trouble breathing. The winds howled and the sky darkened. Then they rounded a turn ... and there it was, Dunroamin' Castle. It was the coldest building Nimrod had ever seen. He felt a shiver run up and down his spine like the red and white stripes of the pole outside the World's End barber shop. Red for cold, white for freezing.

Suddenly a dreadful scream echoed out from somewhere deep within, hovered in the air and then died as suddenly as it had formed. All was silent again. The Nowarts took no notice; it seemed as natural a phenomenon to them as a sudden breeze or a cloudburst. Not a good omen.

They drew up to the great castle door and Xero taped out a secret code. (There was no knocker; the hands of a Nowart are so horny knockers are redundant.) It opened almost immediately and out marched four identical Nowarts armed with lances. Recognizing Xero they gestured them in.

The air inside was stale and dingy and cold. Corridors burrowed out in all directions, lit by blazing torches high on the walls. *Forward … left … forward again.* Podd had incorporated into his castle's impregnable stone walls the bewilderment of a labyrinth to bamboozle all but his inner circle. *Left … right … right again.* He noticed how even Xero's self-confidence drained as the castle wrapped round them. The set of his jaw softened and his eyes blinked nineteen to the dozen. Seeing such a hard man visibly weaken sent his own courage into a tail-spin.

Left, left, right, left, straight, right again… or had that been right before left …? Nimrod sank into despair; the map he was trying to draw in his head had become a tangle of spaghetti.

Another scream – and this time even Xero blinked. Somewhere close by a fellow Nowart was being tortured. The howl of a Nowart is not a pleasant sound (nor, come to that, is its giggle), and though Nimrod detested the creatures with every fibre of his being he still couldn't help finding a tweak of pity for its owner.

They drew up at a high door at the far end of the darkest of the corridors and Xero tiptoed reverently up to it, nodding at the armed guards at either side. They ignored him. He rapped sharply on it with his horny tentacle, once – twice – three times.

Nimrod had no doubt who waited beyond.

Like a wayward boy standing before the door of the head teacher's study Xero adjusted his belt and patted down his matted hair. A strange choking noise emanated from his throat, and a little ball of phlegm struck the door as he cleared his throat.

Then he found part of his voice.

"Master?" he called out, "it is I, Xero, your abject and servile servant, who grovels beyond. Do you grant me leave to enter?"

Silence.

"I have what you asked for. He is with me now, as I speak."

A longer silence.

"It is the Beyonderling. As commanded he has not been damaged."

The silence was broken by a hushed, nasal voice, as if the speaker had a bad case of laryngitis. "I commend you, Xero. Remain outside and send him in."

Xero turned. His Adam's Apple stuck out as if he'd swallowed a leg of mutton. Pressing his mouth hard up against Nimrod's ear he whispered loud and hard: "Remember what I told you ... not a word ... keep it brief ... and nothing ... *nothing* about that incident...." Then the door swung open to drown the rest of his words, and a guard shoved Nimrod into the room. The door slammed shut behind him like the lid of a coffin.

He looked around. He was standing himself in a deep hall with high vaulted ceilings. Its tall, narrow windows had been draped with damask curtains richly embroidered with scenes from the history of Nowhere. There was Podd, bravely clambering up a towering peak ... there he stood, weary but proud, aloft on his precipice, surveying his new land, ravens swooping around his shoulders. On another the Nowarts crawled on all fours from their caves to inspect the new arrival ... and there, on the largest tapestry of all, the kneeling masses kow-towed to the all-powerful being their traditions had long prophesied, he who would make them powerful and rich ... bloat them with luxury.

The drapes on the far wall were devoted to the building of Dunroamin' Castle. Nowarts – their eyes lifted to the skies and burning with visions of a new world - marshalled swarms of Googlions with whips. There were Googlions everywhere ... hewing the stone ... felling the forests ... exposing the ore ... forging and smelting the iron over glowing fires. Rocky outcrops became castle towers, saddles of rock battlements ... trees became planks became drawbridges. It was a celebration of the deep and painful roots of the city, a testament to cruelty. Power lay in the stick, not the carrot … kindness was just another word for weakness.

The floor was a slab of cold marble with red veins splintering out in all directions, and Nimrod saw his eyes reflected back at him, made bloodshot by the veins in the rock.

Deep within the shadows under a low canopy a shape crouched like a spider.

Nimrod coughed, to check whether he had any voice left.

"So." That throaty voice again. "So there are still creatures left on this earth that resemble me. Step forward. Let me study you from up close."

Nimrod ventured forward. His feet echoed on the cold marble, doubling and redoubling until he sounded like a vast army on the march. All part of Podd's grand plan, all designed so that if treachery should turn the loyalty of his guards they could never creep up on him unexpectedly.

"That's close enough. Wait there."

A cloaked figure disentangled itself from the shadows and emerged, walking all the way round Nimrod, studying every inch of him. When it spoke again all the hoarseness was gone; to Nimrod's horror the monster he had so long dreaded meeting had a voice like … like … well, a human being!

"Hell's Furnaces, Outsider, aren't you *hideous!*."

In response Nimrod said nothing at the top of his voice.

"I see you tremble," continued the voice from behind the hood. "Good. When you stand in the presence of Podd you tremble. No other behaviour will do. You're learning fast."

In the absence of a suitable response Nimrod cleared his throat again, not very confidently.

"Well, well," said Podd. "It's so long since last I last saw a face from Beyonder I'd almost forgotten how contemptible it can be. Look at you! All smooth and pink. Such weak blue eyes. And so little hair! Whatever must my Nowarts think, seeing such a creature?"

(*Translation: this is what they would see if my hood fell away. How would they react? Would their fear disappear? Would they … laugh? Would my power vanish overnight?*)

"Well I think it's quite a nice face," replied Nimrod stubbornly. "My friends all like it."

A humourless laugh emerged from the hood. "Friends. *Friends?* Forget that word, Outsider, for you will never set eyes on them again. Not when I have cancelled you."

"Cancelled me? By cancel could you possibly mean *kill* me?" Nimrod had never used the k-word before, and it tasted unpleasant.

"Kill you? Too easy. The swish of a sword and, phffft, you cease to be. Like snuffing out a flickering candle. What a waste. One day, Outsider, one day you may become superfluous to my needs and I may put you out of your misery. But first I need to inspect you, like a germ under glass. You are the wrong turning I might have taken … a weakling, a victim. You are me – as I once was!"

He leaned in closer to Nimrod, who snatched a glance into the hollow of the cowl. Was that a glint of … *spectacles* he saw in there?

"That's one reason why you will go into my menagerie. But there is another. If I were to let you go and you were to return to your home I would be sending back a signal. Podd is weak. Podd can't make his mind up. Podd has lost it. Then they would come for me. Bring their armies. Invade my castle. One feeble creature like you could bring it all toppling down. I said you were just a germ, Outsider. But one small germ can bring an elephant crashing to the ground. An elephant today … a kingdom tomorrow. My kingdom. That's why I need to … disinfect you."

He was breathing heavily. Flouting Kabil's advice Nimrod stared deep into the cowl and caught the flash of a white tooth with a gold filling.

Podd sensed his ill ease, and laughed. The filling flashed again.

"How did you like our village, creeping hairless thing?"

Nimrod made a gesture that didn't actually commit himself one way or the other. (You've been treated, remember, he kept reminding himself.)

"Not up your street? Well, you'll like our dungeons even less. They have absolutely nothing to recommend them. But in time you will grow to like your cell … for it will be your haven from what we have prepared for you during your stay."

Nimrod found his voice again. It had been hiding all the while at the back of his throat.

"Wh-what are you going to do with me?"

"Do you want the short answer or the long one? Let's start with the short one. We are going to Hurt you." Podd, pronounced the H in Hurt with a capital letter, a trick he had picked up from the Middle Gateman. "The long answer? Now is not the time. Surprise is pain's most loyal comrade. After your first session you'll lie in your cell and wonder – *what next?* If I told you now we'd lose the initiative. What do you think of that?"

Nimrod had three reactions.

The first went like this: What *was* this rubbish? Who wrote his dialogue? Had he fallen asleep over a chapter of a book from the World's End Library *Fantasy Fiction* section and dreamed himself into it?

The second was: this is a madman. A nutter. A total loony. You can't deal with people like this.

The third was the sudden return of that old weakness of his … temper. Treatment or no treatment Podd had it coming to him.

The blood rushed up to his head, his cheeks flushed and he blurted out: "You want to know what I think? Well I'll tell you. I think you're the *nastiest* man I've ever met. There. Said it."

"Do you now." Nimrod could hear the grin from within the cowl. "Well, flattery will get you nowhere. Don't think you can soften my heart with your compliments."

"I wasn't attempting to do anything of the sort," said Nimrod. "Where I come from, nasty is a measure of poor character. It's a negative word. Nasty people are hated people."

The cowl shook. "Thank you again. You say all the right things. But I still won't ease up on my plans."

It was the smugness more than the words that snapped Nimrod's temper. "I hate you!" he screamed. "Hate you hate you hate you…!"

"Good, good, good." Podd sounded yet more delighted. "It seems that Balik is even better at his treatment than I gave him credit for. We'll make a Nowart our of you yet."

Nimrod froze into silence. A Nowart? Him? Like Xero? Like those blank-faced unblinking guards in the passage?

"*Me?* A *What?* Did you say *Nowart?*"

Within the hood the shadows deepened as Podd scowled. "I seem to have let my plans slip out. But now you know, I may as well admit it.

Yes, Outsider, one day you, even you, with your pink hairless face and your baby-blue eyes, will be a Nowart. It may take years, it will certainly involve trial and error, but a Nowart you will eventually become. Like all my subjects. You'll look like a Nowart, think like a Nowart, behave like a Nowart. When I get it to work on you, halleluiah, the world becomes my recruiting yard. Think how I'll be able to magnify my army ... brigades of Nowarts converted from outsiders like you ... snatched from beyond the Plains ... and then beyond that. "

Nimrod thought of the matted hair and hunched figures of his captors - and shivered.

Podd seemed to read what was going on in his mind. He inserted two fingers into his cowl and emitted a shrill whistle. The door crashed open and a line of Nowart guards ran in, lances at the ready.

"Stand there. Don't move. Do you see them, Outsider? Study them closely. You're looking at yourself, years on. Like the hairstyle? You can throw away your comb. Appreciate the way the teeth and the gums have become one single hard entity? No brushing in the mornings, bet that appeals to you. It won't happen overnight. But we'll get there. One day you will resemble them. And how will we achieve it? I'll let you into a secret." He drew closer. "Stage one is to force you to perform acts of ... what was that word again ... nastiness. Morning, noon and night. Unrelenting nastiness day in day out, month in month out, year in year out, that'll break you down."

He leaned in, even closer, and whispered into Nimrod's ear. " Even the Nowarts were unwilling pupils in the early days, even they displayed foolish moments of kindness ... " Nimrod felt him quiver as he said the word *kindness* ... "but look at them now. Nasty as you like."

Nimrod pulled away. "You won't succeed, you know. I can be very stubborn. I'm famous for that."

"Then," explained Podd quite simply, "we will have to kill you. That's always a last resort. But don't go writing your will out, not quite yet. Because we *will* succeed. We always do. We'll find a way, never doubt it."

Nimrod weighed up Podd's words. What alternatives! Either turn into a Nowart ... or die. He decided that if it came to the push he probably preferred the second.

Podd strode back into the centre of the room.

"Remember, boy, we are trained persuaders; failure is not an option. If Xero doesn't succeed in turning you into one of us, he will suffer for his failure. The threat will make him work that much harder at it. One by one members of his family will be tossed over the precipice into nothingness. If still he doesn't succeed, over he goes too. There are always others. More ambitious. More cunning. More likely to succeed where others have failed. More terrified of the consequences."

To Nimrod the really frightening part about all this was … it made sense. Cruelty probably worked where kindness failed. Was this what had happened to his father? Was he now one of the Nowarts he had met along the way? Perhaps that was him, the guard standing by the door and picking his nose? Him with the squinty eyes and the broken nose and the cut above his lip … *daddy?*

"In that case," announced Nimrod, quite matter-of-factly, "I will escape."

Podd strode back over to Nimrod, and gripped his face with clammy fingers. His breath smelt (Nimrod guessed) like the fumes from a freshly opened mummy's sarcophagus.

" *What did you say?* "

"I said," repeated Nimrod, "that I will escape. Didn't you hear me the first time?"

Podd let his face go, clapped his hands - and laughed. If you can call it a laugh. It was more like the groan from an industrial engine running out of oil. It echoed hollowly on the marble floor, doubling up and then doubling again until the hall echoed with the insane laughter of a teenage boy who had taken too many wrong turns.

Podd turned to one of his lieutenants. "Did you hear that? He said *escape*. Tell him how many prisoners have escaped from Dunroamin' Castle. Go on. Tell him."

The laughter of the two lieutenant guards joined Podd's, crashing against Nimrod's ear-drums like stormy winds on a sail. One of them raised an arm and formed two tentacles into a misshapen zero.

"I will escape," repeated Nimrod. "Just wait and see, I'll be out of here before you realise it."

Podd's laughter switched off. Suddenly. Just like that.

"I really wish you hadn't said that. Because it introduces a note of failure into the proceedings. It seems as if our wizard is not doing his job properly. I will have to have words with him. He was told to cast a spell on you to stop you wanting to escape. He didn't. He'd better explain – or off the edge he goes. Guards! Collect Balik and bring him to me!"

Two of the Nowarts marched towards the door.

Nimrod went all cold. This would never do. If they got hold of Kabil, all hope was lost. He had to think fast.

"Good! " he said, "so you have your weakness after all. Thank you for letting me know."

Podd was cold with anger. How dare he use that word!

"Weakness? What are you talking about? I have no weakness."

"Ah but you do. You're impatient. Impatient – and rash. Always fatal flaws in a general. Do you mind I stay and watch? I always like it when people want things in too much of a hurry. More chance of things going wrong. If I were you I'd get him in here now, immediately, tell him you want the instant version. Please. I'd appreciate that."

Podd beckoned the guards to wait.

"The *instant* version?"

"That's what I said. He told me he was using his new super-strength spell. The industrial-quality version. Takes fifteen hours to work itself up. Apparently I won't just stop wanting to escape - I'll start growing Nowart hair while I sleep. But you go ahead, you get him up here now. Tell him to cancel the old one and replace it with the instant version. Oh, you're smart, you are. Now I see why they made you leader."

"They? Who's they? I made me leader, boy, never you forget that. They doesn't come into it." He sniffed. (He had a permanent cold, was that mentioned?) "I knew I could trust my wizard. So I must double the guard on your cell until midnight, must I? Thanks for warning me."

Nimrod's heart sank. Had he blown it? With a double guard Kabil didn't stand a hope of getting to him.

"No guards or cells will hold me." More mock-bravery while he played for more time.

"*My* guards and *my* cells can," snapped back Podd. "Now get him out of my sight."

He snapped his fingers deep within the folds of his cloak. Two lieutenants stepped forward and gripped him fiercely, bundling him roughly towards the double doors. Just as they got there Podd called out: "Wait."

The Nowarts loosened their hold slightly, just enough for Nimrod to turn and face him. Podd leaned forward - and the space within his hood had never looked blacker.

"Empty that satchel on the floor."

There was nothing to do but obey. Unhooking it from his shoulder he fumbled with the press-stud, still slimy from the Nowart's gums, and managed to snap it open. Podd's eyes never wavered.

My most treasured possessions I keep in my lozenge-tin, bricked up in my secret place, he thought. *What is it this man-creature holds so dear he carries it wherever he goes? It must be precious indeed.*

He stepped forward as Nimrod shook out the contents.

INVENTORY

1 (one) jar of nectar.

6 (six) dry wafers, one half nibbled.

2 (two) scraps of greaseproof paper - empty.

1 (one) compass, needle points south.

2 (two) socks, not a pair.

"That's it?"

"That's it." Nimrod looked up at him, unable to work out whether Podd was mocking him – or just inquisitive.

"Those there are your most treasured possessions? In all the world?"

"They're all I brought with me, if that's what you mean." Mocking. Definitely mocking.

Podd snatched the satchel off him and tore at the seams. With a ripping sound the threats parted and the satchel was reduced to its constituent parts.

Nimrod thought: I could do with a nice long swig of that Nectar now. And I could die for the rest of those wafers.

A hand emerged from the hood and pointed to the floor.

"Pick that up. Have it analysed. Likewise those funny looking biscuits. Take them away and report back to me. His secrets must be buried inside."

He shook his cowled head; he was missing something. This didn't add up. Nobody would travel to the ends of the earth carrying just ... *that* junk!

Nimrod took a step back.

"Grab him!"

His voice contained an unexpected quiver of panic which Nimrod thought it wiser not to acknowledge.

The Master of Nowhere pointed to the great double doors.

"Lock him up. But ponder this: if the Outsider escapes, I will personally see to it that both of you are hurled off the end of the world. Do you understand that?"

As they grabbed him Nimrod felt his captors stiffen. They growled obediently back then used his body to thump the doors open. As they swung apart Xero leaped back into the ante-chamber, the pattern of the keyhole imprinted onto his cheek.

Handing him over the guards grunted the warnings Podd had given them, but Xero just smiled. He didn't fail. Not him. Not Xero.

Down the corridor again, deeper, lower into the depths of the castle, the feet of the Nowarts rattling out a rocky tattoo like a drummer's roll accompanying a prisoner to his execution. Eventually they turned off into the pokiest corridor of all and stopped before a small rusty door dripping with condensation. Two of them untied the cords binding his hands.

"Here," said Xero gruffly. "Your cell. Get in."

And, with a little assistance from a stout kick in the small of his back, Nimrod did as he was bid.

*

The cell enclosed him like the arms of a beggar with walls rough and jagged, like a cave's; what little light there was drained through a small window high on the far wall opposite the door. It smelt of straw and animals though there was no sign of either, just emptiness and dark corners. The door clanged shut behind him, one of the guards said something coarse, the other one laughed, and their voices echoed up the corridor, followed by horny footsteps.

Then silence.

Nimrod raised his head towards the whisper of fresh air that leaked through the window and breathed in deeply. He was simultaneously cold and hot as wind from the mountains and the fever of fear fought for control of his body. No wonder Podd had sneered at his threat to escape. It was unthinkable. The window was too high and too small, the stone too hard to burrow through, the door too well guarded.

Scccrat.

What was that?

It clawed at the floor, the sound reverberating out of the darkness.

Scccrat. Scccrat.

Insistent scratches from tiny claws.

Scccrat. Scccrat. Scccrat.

Nimrod listened hard and revised his opinion – nothing tiny about those claws: they were big and dangerous, and whatever was making the sound was locked in with him.

Rats.

Or worse:

One enormous one.

The scratching grew louder, and by cocking his ear to one side he worked out where it was coming from. There. The dark corner to his left. He peered closer and detected a movement deep within the shadows. Whatever it was was big – and it was creeping towards him. If this was a rat, then it was the largest rat in the world ... or one that had crawled up out of the abyss. Nimrod stepped back and struck the wall. The creature kept coming ... forward... forward... forward ... bright eyes fixed on him.

Into the middle of the cell it crawled, into the wash of pale light from the window. Nimrod gasped, and clapped his hand to his mouth. This was no rat, this was no creature from beyond the world's borders. It was covered from head to toe in scraggly grey hair, but it wasn't a body-coat like a four-footed animal's; this was human hair, uncut for years and years, tumbling down from its head like a cataract, so that all he could see of the body which crawled forward on all fours was a heap of barber's clippings through which two nervous eyes peeped.

The eyes.

Those eyes.

"You!"

And forward he ran, flinging his arms around the stranger's approximate centre and hugging it so tightly its expelled breath blew up the corners of his jerkin.

"Dad!!"

The woolly thing shook its hair and two ears emerged. Another shake and there were the eyes, studying him suspiciously. From the overgrowth hands reached out and felt Nimrod's face like a blind man – nose, eyes, mouth, chin ... and recognition dawned, lifting the corners of its mouth into a smile and lighting up its cheeks with splashes of rosy pink. It rose off its haunches, hesitantly at first, squinting through the pale light, then stumbled forward arms outspread and embraced him weakly.

"Nimrod! Is it really you? You bad boy. Why did you risk your precious young life on a failure like me?"

He stepped back, and turned his head away.

"Got it badly wrong, didn't I? Leaving you and your mother for this cold cell ... whatever must you think of me?"

Nimrod reached out for him, feeling the resistance in the arms protruding from the dusty grey parcel.

"Nonsense. You're a national hero. They're thinking of putting up a statue of you in the town square. Brave Lemli. The first citizen to look further than his nose. And as for my youth – there's not much of that left, not now. Two days ago it was my Final Youngday. Next year I'll be an old fogey, like you."

The hairs at the front of the tangled face knitted together in a frown.

"A statue? Of me?"

"Yes," fibbed Nimrod, vowing that the first thing he'd do on his return (well, after a huge meal and a long sleep) would be to arrange the statue, even if he had to carve it himself. "Now come on over here. We've years of hugging to catch up on."

And that's what they did, for ages, just stood and hugged each other tight, and shook and swallowed and gulped just a little bit.

When they parted, there were tears in the old man's eyes.

"I never thought I'd ever see a World's-Ender again," he stammered, "let alone my very own flesh and blood. What are you doing here?"

"I've come to rescue you, of course" announced Nimrod. Not strictly true, but it seemed the right thing to say under the circumstances.

"Me?" Lemli looked puzzled. "I thought you'd all forgotten about me. How's Larana?"

At the mention of his mother's name Nimrod felt all his excitement gurgle away like water down a drain. Of course. His father was already gone when the accident happened. He didn't know. He stared into the hopeful eyes – and his stomach lurched with pain. He just couldn't bring himself to break the tragic news now.

"She's – no, father, let's not mention her name where those terrible creatures outside can hear it. I'll tell you all about her when we're safely back on the road home. Do I smell straw? Is there straw here? I need a rest. There's a lot to be done tomorrow, and I need to catch up on my energy."

A snack would be nice too, he thought, uselessly.

But the old man had years of questions saved up, and out they spilled. "How is everyone else? The Oastman ... is he still baking? And Mr Vesperus? How about what's-her-name, that fat woman who gossips? I don't suppose you brought any of Mrs Small's sandwiches...? It all seems so long ago, so far away."

They exchanged questions and memories about World's End until the grey sky behind the window blackened and the cell sank into darkness and the old man's voice grew hoarse from lack of practise. Under the window, on the cold rock floor, they huddled up for warmth. Nimrod found Lemli's grey beard even warmer than his knitted blanket back home.

"But how about you?" asked Nimrod." How have they been treating you? What have you been doing all these years?."

"Sitting, Nimrod. Sitting and moping, most of the time."

Nimrod was astonished "You mean they haven't made you work for then? They haven't tried to turn you into one of 'them' yet?".

"Oh, they've got all the time out of the world to do that. Time means nothing here. Well, once a week they take me on a conducted tour. They instruct me in the habits of Nowarts, the laws of Nowhere, all the sordid details of their sordid lives. I did the swamps yesterday. Dreadful place. And those lobsters... As for their treatment, well I could do without all that pricking and jabbing and poking just to show me who's boss around here. They must be very low in self-esteem."

"One thing puzzles me," said Nimrod. "Well, many things puzzle men, but as of now this puzzles me most. How do you see in Nowhere without special spectacles?" He wriggled his nose and the spectacles followed suit. "Without these everything's a blur."

Lemli lowered his eyes. "I couldn't, at first. I was blind for weeks. Of course, they couldn't see me either. How they caught me was, I ran into one of the nets they stretch out to catch escaping Googlions. I was just a smudge. But one of the Nowarts noticed this moving smear, this blur of movement, and trapped it in a barrel. That was me."

"And then…?"

"They rolled me off in my barrel to this wizard. Name of Balik. Nasty piece of work. Lives in a cave. Like me. Like you, now. He cast a spell on me. It only half worked on me, because I was thinking kind thoughts. That always works, you know. Even when you don't mean them. But it was enough to lift the scales from my eyes. It also brought me into focus. You should have seen how they shrank away from me when I solidified in front of their very eyes. Their first Outsider … they call us Beyonderlings, you know. From Beyonder." Under the fringe of hair the eyes looked inwards. "I still dream about it most nights. Oh for the blazing fire and those toasted marshmallows. Oh for the slippers I mocked. Oh for anywhere but here …"

"Give it time," said Nimrod, in his most reassuring voice, which wasn't firing on all its cylinders. "We'll escape from here yet. You and me."

Nimrod felt the hairy old head turn towards him. "I don't think so, my boy. I've tried hard enough without success."

"Two heads are better than one," explained Nimrod, who secretly believed quite the opposite: when it came to escaping, the more the heads the harder the hiding. "We'll be out of here in no time, just you wait and see. Now. All those tours you've been on. What can you tell me about the Googlions?"

"Don't go near them. They're a bad lot. If they weren't terrified of the Nowarts they'd be up and at them at the drop of a whip. The Nowarts use then as slaves. Treat them very poorly. If there's one thing worse than being a Nowart it's being a Googlion. They both lead hopeless lives – but the Googlions have to work harder."

Nimrod shivered. "I'd hate to meet one of theme in a dark street. They frighten me."

"Well the Nowarts feel the same way. That's why they stay far away from their valley."

"I don't blame them," muttered Nimrod. "I don't think..."

But what Nimrod didn't think was lost to history. At that moment the cell door rattled open and two Nowart guards marched in, followed by Xero.

"You two are coming with me," he announced. Then, seeing how the citizens of World's End were huddled together for warmth, he added: "Better take advantage of each another's company tonight. Because tomorrow we separate you. A cell down the passage has become unexpectedly vacant, and it's got your name on it, pinkling. Podd doesn't like shared cells. Sharing soon becomes plotting. Not that it would do you any good. Plot away, much as you like, while you can ... Nowarts of Tomorrow." He clapped his sides and guffawed, long and loud.

"Where are you taking us?" asked Nimrod.

Xero reached out and pinched him viciously on the cheek. "You'll learn not to ask questions, pink one. Do as you are told and don't argue. That way you get hurt less."

"Yes," said Nimrod, his cheek smarting, remembering that according to his story his treatment ought to be beginning to take effect about now. "Yes, sir."

"Guards!" ordered Xero. "Grab one each and follow me."

The guards obeyed gleefully – grabbing seemed to be what they enjoyed most. As they stumbled out into the corridor Nimrod shot a questioning look at Lemli, who just shrugged his hairy shoulders. No idea. Search me.

Along the corridor their footfalls echoed and multiplied. Xero had been the bearer of the worst possible news. Lemli's company was the only silver lining in a bank of coal-black clouds. Now they were going to rip it out The future looked grim.

Nimrod wondered which of the wizards had cast the spell on Lemli: the evil Balik - or kind Kabil? If it had been Kabil why hadn't he told him? Your father's still alive. You can save him. And if it had been Balik

… why hadn't he crushed his resistance?

They descended into the dingy depths of the castle. The air was particularly stale down here, stale and cold, and Nimrod envied Lemli's coat of hair. He blew into his hands as he walked and rubbed them over his face, but rather than warm his cheeks he only succeeded in chilling his palms.

They came to a broad arch and Xero pushed them through. Dominating the room sat the hugest Nowart Nimrod had yet seen.

He wasn't just huge – he was vast. His motionless body was parked behind a shiny stone table with a reflective surface which doubled the image, like a mountain in a lake. His head, perched atop rocky shoulders, was completely round – round and flat and wrinkled, with two deep gashes carved out into folds beginning each side of a pair of flared nostrils and enclosing a fat-lipped mouth constantly on the move, nibbling, chewing, munching.

His voice was like a little avalanche of rolling gravel.

"So these are they, are they? I see ... I see."

As he looked them up and down his eyes bulged out of their sockets and he rubbed his palms together with greasy slithers.

Then, sighing with the weariness of a much overworked man, he pressed both hands hard down on his desk and eased his bulk up, panting slightly from the effort. After getting his breath back he advanced on Nimrod and Lemli, and scrutinised them closer up. "Hmm. It's not going to be easy, not at all easy."

"What isn't?" asked Nimrod timidly.

The huge Nowart clipped him over the head. "Keep quiet, slug. When I want you to speak I'll ask you. Until then, keep your mouth shut."

Xero stepped forward.

"This is Dyle, cleverest man in all Nowhere. He has been entrusted by our Lord and Master with the task of turning you both into Nowarts." He paused, smiling at the reactions to his words from his prisoners, and continued: "He's been working at the theory for years. Now it's time to put all those charts and equations into practice. Isn't that right, Dyle? That you've come up with a foolproof system? How long will it take?"

Dyle yawned and stretched his meaty arms high above his head. All his slow, deliberate movements had a great force to them, like ancient rituals still practised. "Five, maybe six days. But after two, they won't remember where they came from. After three, they'll begin to sprout nice thick hair like ours; body, arms, legs, everywhere. And their fingers will fuse: five goes into three, for maximum manoeuvrability. After four, they'll begin thinking like us. The last two days, well that's to round off the finer points of what makes a Nowart a Nowart. Posture ... attitude ... the intensification of the Cunning Factor ..."

He dug a pair of huge hairy tentacles into a pocket and fished out a length of knotted twine. Sizing up Nimrod and Lemli from under rocky brows he unrolled it and took their measurements. Legs ... arms ... body ... head ...

"Hmm," he mused, "we'll have to do a little squashing here and there. A couple of heavy rocks should help. They're not short enough, and who wants tall Nowarts. Filthy thought. We'll start the squeezing process tomorrow, eight o'clock sharp. I'll want at least a dozen rocks. Two flat ones for the heads. And some cord."

Nimrod watched Lemli out of the corner of his eye. He was shaking like a leaf. He had been too long out of circulation. All his hope had drained away; all his determination had been kicked and prodded out of his system. Now he was a husk, a shell, a shadow of the father he had once worshipped.

Dyle prodded them in the ribs with merciless tentacles. "They're too fat, both of them. They'll have to be starved and squashed. No more food until I give the word. Perhaps when I come back from Pain School we can start them on a berry a day so they don't waste away."

Nimrod flinched. Had he heard right? No more food? This was the worst of punishments. The rocks he could take, at a push, even the empty cell. But no food? What kind of mind could have devised such a dreadful torture?

"I see our visitors are unhappy. Doesn't the thought appeal to you, pinkling? Well you'll just have to learn. Nowarts aren't big on eating. Just enough food to keep the blood flowing. Do I make myself clear?"

Nimrod nodded mournfully. Lemli copied him.

Dyle consulted a tablet of stone, and made scratches on it with a stylus. "You have curious measurements. Yer arms are too short, yer legs too long. Never fear. Bit of pulling, bit of pushing and they'll soon be nothing to be ashamed of. Muscles need building up. And as for those pink tongues – "he shook uncontrollably – "nauseating!"

He made a few quick calculations and returned to his chair. As he ponderously lowered himself back down his reflection in the table-top looked like a great ocean-going liner sinking into the sea. The ground shook.

"Seven inches off the top, five inches around the waist. Easy enough. Give them plenty of cigarettes to smoke. That'll keep 'em short."

Cigarettes? Nimrod had never heard of such strange things. Were they some terrible means of torture, known only to the Nowarts? He ventured to ask what they might be. Xero replied:

"Dried crumbled leaves wrapped up in tubes of paper, you ignorant fool. We set them alight and force the smoke into your mouth and down your throat. Keeps you from shooting up. Now do you understand?"

Nimrod most definitely did not. What a ghastly torture. How could anyone be expected to eat mouthfuls of stale smoke? These Nowarts were indeed vicious creatures, thinking up such punishments. Old dried leaves indeed.

"Quiet!" ordered Dyle. "Don't go passing our secrets on to such ignorant fools. I've a good mind to blindfold them when the process begins." He turned his bulk on Xero. "And to gag blabbermouths!"

Xero touched his head in apology, and moved out of the way.

Dyle continued: "As for the introduction of iron into their flabby systems, well, let's make no bones about it, that's my greatest challenge. I think we'll begin by making them torture a Googlion or two. Bring some up the day after tomorrow. Torture Chamber Number B19. The one with the red basket of paraphernalia and the chains on the wall. Five am sharp. Nice early start. Then they can fight each other. They'll be pretty hungry by that stage, and the winner will get a boiled pea. Give 'em something to fight for, I always say."

"I'll never hurt Nimrod!" declared Lemli fiercely. "Not a hair on his head."

Dyle reached out and grabbed Lemli and drew him across the table until their faces were level. "You'll do as you told! If I say fight, then you fight. See?"

"No," replied Lemli stubbornly. "I just won't!"

Dyle gave him such a shove he went skidding across the surface of the stone table and slid off the end, collapsing in a heap on the floor. Nimrod knew that if he let his temper go now that would be the end of everything. Fiercely he dug his heels into the ground to hold himself back and shut his eyes tightly, but he couldn't block his ears, couldn't help hearing Dyle say: "Extra tortures for that old fool. He should never have said that."

Lemli picked himself up and dusted himself off. Nimrod opened his eyes again. Dyle stared into his face and said:.

"And what do you have to say about all this, you irritating brat? Eh? Do you also refuse to fight?"

"No." answered Nimrod. "I'll fight all right!"

Lemli turned, startled, unable to believe what he had just heard.

Nimrod continued: "Oh, yes, I'll fight. But not that fine man over there. I'll fight you, you pop-eyed lump of rock. "

He braced himself for Dyle's fist, but it never came. The fat Nowart just laughed out loud into his face. His clammy breath smelt of frogs. "Wait and see. Podd has promised me great rewards if I turn you into Nowarts, and I aim to earn them one and all. Dyle doesn't fail."

He fixed Nimrod, then Lemli, with his bulging eyes. He was trying to picture them as Nowarts. He could see their hairy bodies, their short, squat frames, their horny hands and feet, their twisted features. He'd make sure they were the ugliest Nowarts of all.

"Take them away!" he suddenly commanded. "I don't like Outsiders cluttering up my place of work. Tomorrow we'll start work on them. Make sure you get in a good supply of flat rocks. Put two guards outside their cell door tonight – no, make that three."

Xero's lip curled. "Don't worry, Dyle. They won't escape. No-one escapes from Dunroamin' Castle!"

Dyle looked unconvinced. "Let's hope not. Now get rid of them. I need my beauty sleep. I'll see you all at eight tomorrow for the squashing. "

Back along the corridor they marched, Xero first, followed by Nimrod, them Lemli, then the two guards. Back in their cell Xero stood over them, eyes twinkling with anticipation.

"Enjoy yourselves. Your last night together. Your last night as Beyonderlings. Tomorrow you start to become Nowarts. Like us. Be proud!" With a chuckle he turned on his corns and left, slamming the door behind him.

"What are we going to do, Nimrod?" asked Lemli. "I didn't like the look of that big man with the poppy-out eyes."

"Oh, he wasn't as bad as he looked. Nobody is, you know. We can handle the likes of him."

"Do you really think so, Nimrod?"

"No," admitted Nimrod, "not really."

There was a long silence.

Then: "I'm still not going to fight you, Nimrod. You can fight me with all your might if you want to, but I won't fight you back."

Nimrod patted him on the back. "Of course I won't. We were always the closest family in all of World's End, and they'll never force us to dishonour that heritage When they tell us to fight we'll just sit down. They can't do anything to us."

"Do you really think so?" pleaded Lemli again.

"No," said Nimrod, "Not really."

"I don't think I'd make a very good Nowart," said Lemli. "For one thing, I couldn't harm a flea."

"I could," said Nimrod. "If it bit me."

Another long pause.

"What are you thinking about?" asked Lemli of Nimrod.

"I was wondering what you were thinking about," admitted Nimrod.

"I see," said Lemli. "That's very interesting."

Nimrod occupied himself by making shapes with his fingers, while Lemli began to count the hairs on his beard. They kept on like this for a good ten seconds, then looked over at each other.

"I'm unhappy." said Lemli.

The cell was growing colder and darker by the second; all Nimrod could see of his unhappy friend was a grey hairy shape huddled up in the corner.

"You know what I'm thinking?" asked Nimrod.

"No," said Lemli, "What?"

"It's not a very original thought, I must admit," apologised Nimrod.

"I'd still like to hear it," said Lemli.

"I've mentioned it before," Nimrod went on, "and nothing much came of it. "But now I think I must mention it again."

Lemli moved closer to Nimrod.

"I'd very much like to know what you're thinking, Nimrod. Would you please tell me?"

Nimrod took a deep breath. "I was thinking, Lemli, that the only way for us to get out of this place ... is to escape."

Lemli held him at arm's length and studied his face. Then he smiled, proudly.

"That's my boy!"

*

Under his billowing cloak Podd's legs measured out long strides like a pair of compasses as he plunged down the corridor to its lower depths. Something was wrong. The Outsider was locked away in his cell with that other hairy buffoon ... neither of them was smart enough to cause him a moment's anxiety ... yet something was very wrong. He felt in the marrow of his bones.

"You had no trouble with him, Xero? He came like a lamb?"

He turned to fix the darkness of his cowl on the face of the wiry Nowart who trotted along beside him, two paces to every one of his master's.

Xero averted his face. Had Podd heard something? Had word filtered back through the telegraph system of rumour and gossip? Had his wife dared open her mouth to someone? What about the Googlion or her brother? Impossible; too much to lose. Anyway she knew her terms of employment: he asked for it, she obeyed. Whatever "it" was – a plate of dinner or a cuddle in the corner. Couldn't have been the birds, either. The vulture-frightener on his roof had been in good working order when he left with the pinkling ... first thing he had checked. No, he had nothing to fear. Podd was just being cautious.

He turned and looked straight into the darkness of the cowl.

"He tugged and wriggled a bit. There was some grumpiness. But that's only to be expected. A few well-placed kicks in his tender bits soon reminded him what's what. No, Master, you'll have no trouble with him. He's soft, softer than swamp-mud, and as pink and wet as a sore eye."

A growl emerged from the darkness.

"Of course I'll have no trouble with him. He's from Beyonder. They're all weaklings there. No grit. No spunk. Too much appeasement, that's their problem ... not enough combat. Anyway, it's you that needs to keep his nose clean. One whimper of protest from your prisoner and you'll find yourself sobbing twice as loud. You know the rules, Xero. Trouble from a prisoner earns twice the trouble for his guards. He goofs - double the punishment for you. I hope you've been frank with me ... hope you've told me everything ... everything that matters. You have always been my most trusted lieutenant. But hold something back ... anything ... well, you've seen the shape my disappointment can take."

Trust. The word meant nothing to Podd. He used it like a prod ... a threatening weapon. He pronounced it with the same scornful curl of the lip as when he spoke of duplicity ... or betrayal.

He remembered them, those three obsequious Googlions crawling out of their cave that day he first set foot on the mountain all those years ago. Well, four, at first. But a well-aimed shot from the pistol under his cloak taught them a lesson they'd never forget. They'd never seen a gun before ... couldn't understand how a bang here could result in a death there ... they chattered and whimpered and clutched each other like children. Five bullets left. But they didn't know that. For all they knew he came equipped with an infinite number of death-dealing bangs.

"We'll look after you, master. Trust us."

That word again. Ha!

It had all been different back in the early days The Googlions had the upper hand then, and the Nowarts kept out of their way, intimidated by their sinew, their sharp eye-teeth, the poison they dipped their talons in.

All it had taken was the application of his most powerful weapon. More potent by far than any of the remaining bullets that rattled away in the lozenge tin in his pocket. More piercing than the sharpest arrow.

Mistrust.

A whisper here, a suggestion here, that's all it took.

Directed right, rumour could collapse bridges, topple lofty edifices.

Planted deep enough, gossip could gather with the force of a tidal wave and roll over entire communities, disintegrating them.

Mistrust enabled him to whip up enough suspicion amongst the Googlions to scatter their herd instinct. Tribe fought tribe. Family fought family. Husband fought wife … brother fought sister.

They learned his rules soon enough: trust nobody from one day to the next. Confide in nobody but me. A friend is an enemy with a smile. Get them before they get you.

At the same time he relentlessly drilled fear and suspicion into the Nowarts. One public execution was all it took, out in front of the gathered masses … after that they were his for life. That wretch he tied to a pole and shot between the eyes – well, he had it coming. Sneaking a look into his cowl like that while he slept … how dare he. If he'd been left to blab he'd have damped the powder of his other secret weapon - the unknown.

Deeper. darker into the mountain they descended, down to where the crystals rested and the sleeping thing slept. That had been a real find, that nest of ill-shaped beasts his gangs of labourers uncovered in the heart of the mountain. One glance at them and he knew. He had found watchdogs for the crystals.

There'd been no shortage of labourers to carve his castle from the mountain. No need to plaster up posters to drum up willing lackeys:

Labourers Wanted.
Back-breaking Work.
Long Hours
Paltry Rewards.

Instead, word of mouth became his best recruiting sergeant. From near and far they came, over the mountains, out of the caves, up from the valleys, all for a plate of roots twice a day and the hopes that some of his magic powers might rub off on them … death with a bang from fifty paces. They'd do anything for that.

He remembered how he had unfolded the picture of the castle.

Here.

Build me that.

Carve it out of that rock.

I want it identical in every respect.

First we build a furnace to smelt the ore in the rock. Then we forge our tools. Down on your knees, all of you. Any disobedience and you die with a bang like thunder.

They'd worked like the slaves they were. Bit by bit the castle took shape. He watched it emerge from the rock, tower and moat, window and battlement, every one identical to the picture he once fixed his eyes on as he stretched out over the desk and the birch came down with a whistle ...

Time? He had more than enough of that.

After he'd released those forces from the jar he noticed that time stopped telling on him. He ceased to age. Years passed and the same young face stared back out at him from ponds and puddles If anything he looked younger ... more naive .... even more of a schoolboy with his wire glasses and tooth-brace and bum-fluff on his upper lip. That's when he'd ambushed that pilgrim and stolen his cloak off him, sending him running for cover into the bushes screaming and sobbing, the pink pock-marked cheeks of his bottom wobbling as he ran ... how he'd laughed ...

Over the years the Nowarts aged and died ... their children rose to pick up their parents' tools and dig, to use their parents' whips on the buttocks of Googlions ... but he remained fixed in his youth.

Eternally young, he lost all track of time as the castle emerged from the rock.

Googlions were sent to find wood ... they returned with entire forests on their backs. Planks were stripped out .... doors carved and riveted ... the great drawbridge lowered into place. Below their feet other Googlions tunnelled deep into the bedrock. And still they came, lured from distant valleys, which was lucky because he lost hundreds ... maybe even thousands ... victims of clumsy footing and the bottomless abyss at the end of the world.

Deeper and deeper he strode, Xero struggling to keep up. He studied the chip-marks on the tunnel walls, every inch, foot and yard the product of Googlion sinews. He recalled the day when they'd uncovered those … things. A bug-eyed Nowart had come scrambling up … monsters, master … and he'd thought, talk about pots and black kettles, but his inquisitiveness had got the better of him and down he went, curious to see what strange creature a Nowart found ugly.

He got there just in time.

A Googlion was already raising the sharp end of its shovel over their nest. Wait! he'd cried out, stepping forward to see. And there they were, blinking in the lantern light, snuffling into each other's coats like moles.

Pets! shrieked the Nowarts, grabbing their tails and tugging them out of their huddle. But they too had a trick up their tails, those misshapen things. They reminded Podd of the lizards that once lived under the rocks in his back garden … how their tails would break off when you snatched them, leaving them free to run off to find new hideaways. Unlike the lizards, though, in this upside-down land it was the tails that grew replacement creatures.

He timed them. It seemed the creatures had exactly twenty minutes after becoming detached from their tails before they collapsed and died and identical replacements wriggled out of their tails.

Twenty minutes.

He could store his precious crystals down here, delicately balanced on the fountain of air that shot up from the crack in the ground, and set one of these … things .. to guard them.

Twenty minutes.

That was just long enough for it to scamper up the passage and tell him when harm befell any of the crystals…

Now he'd lost one of them.

He strode into the cave.

There they were, the remaining eight, quivering in the amber light from his lantern. Deep in the dark shadows the creature woke and scuttled towards him. He kicked it away. One crystal … there … on the bed of air but almost off it … he didn't dare touch it in case the movement brought the whole crashing down.

He swung towards Xero.

"Quick. Back upstairs. We must separate those Beyonderlings … now

... immediately ... before it's too late! Run, Xero ... run!"

Then, precisely at that moment, the eighth crystal fell to his feet and shattered.

*

Let's go back in time just five minutes, to where our two nervous prisoners are huddled in their cell, cold and lonely, miles from home, just a few short steps from the tip of the world. Just down the passage an overdeveloped Nowart with bug eyes is impatient to perform unspeakable acts on them. Deeper down, a hooded lunatic has even crueller plans up his sleeve – and they're big sleeves. They long to escape but there are only two routes in and out: a bolted door guarded by two armed sadists, and a tiny window high up in the wall overlooking a bottomless pit. An insurance man would have rated them 10-Minus - and gone to drum off business elsewhere.

Quite sensibly for once, Nimrod decided that their only hope was the window.

"Help me up, Lemli," he said. "If our situation really is hopeless I need to see for myself or I'll never rest."

"It's no good, Nimrod. Even if we could squeeze out of the window - which we can't - we'd only plummet off the world. Anything's better than that, even being locked up. At least here I've got you."

"Nonsense. We've got each other – and that's whether we're inside looking out or outside looking in. Come on, let's have your hand."

Lemli extended a pale arm through his curtain of hair and lowered it so that Nimrod could climb up. His hand quivered under the burden. It had been donkey's years since he'd last worked out and his son, also a stranger to the gym, wasn't in much better shape; he had to strain muscles he never knew were there to stretch an extra inch or two out of his body.

With much huffing and puffing Nimrod elongated his neck towards the sill but his eyes only just cleared the sill. "Can't you shove me up just a bit more?" he pleaded. "Another foot would do it."

"Then climb on to my shoulders. Sorry, Nimrod, I just don't have the strength anymore. Ah the indignities of age… one day you'll be in the same boat."

"If I ever get there." With a little hop Nimrod planted both his feet squarely on the old man's shoulders. He heard a little groan from beneath his soles - but the extra few inches had done the trick. Cold air fanned his face as the window hove into view.

Outside it was too dark to see much, but he could just make out the jagged face of the mountain extending below them into blackness and oblivion.

"Come on!" he said decisively, "I'm off!"

At this his step-ladder became so alarmed it almost collapsed. Nimrod hung precariously from the window as Lemli struggled to regain his balance.

"Off?" he called in a voice as unsteady as his legs. "Off? As in – out that window? You can't mean that! Why, we'd tumble to our death!"

"Not necessarily," said Nimrod. "There's a ridge of jagged rocks down there: if our feet can get a decent grip on them we might just be able to work our way round the castle and down into the village."

"Impossible," said Lemli, not very helpfully. "One slip and we're mincemeat. Two bags full."

"Well I'm going." Nimrod's legs clawed at the slippery wall. "You stay behind in your dirty, smelly cell if you like, but me, I'm out of here. Good luck with your treatment tomorrow, dear father. I'm sure you'll make a cute Nowart."

"Would you really leave me behind? At the mercy of the Nowarts? You – my own flesh and blood?"

"I've offered you your chance - it's up to you to take it or leave it. If you give up now you'll never see World's End again. Never again play Willowbats on Thistledown Green. Never … never again feast till your belly shines, or lick the last few drops of chilled Nectar off your lips. Anyway, when you're a Nowart I suppose you won't want to any more."

The Nectar bit did it. Finding one last droplet of energy in his reserve tank Lemli gave it all he had. This last shove was all Nimrod needed to clamber up over the sill. Below him Lemli rested his head against the wall and nursed his throbbing shoulders. "I suppose you're right," he said - a bit mournfully. "It may be an outside chance, but inside we've no chance. Let's go."

Nimrod heard the "let's" bit, but not the "go". By then he was already wriggling through the narrow gap, his legs kicking in the air like a sheep at dipping time. As his head penetrated the inky blackness a piercing wind directed a thousand tiny arrows into his ear. A button torn from his doublet fell and struck the mountain wall and bounced down into eternity ... it's probably still there, Nimrod's little button, careering through space like a little circular red meteorite with six holes and a scrap of thread.

"What about me?"

Nimrod's made a face: he hadn't thought this through. Lemli had helped him up all right – but who was there to do the same for him? He could hardly tap on the cell door and call out to a guard: "I say, you over there, be a pal and give me a bit of a push up, there's a good fellow."

Nimrod looked down at his father, who looked glumly back up at him. What a pathetic figure he cut. Sad eyes drained of hope ... fingers clenching and unclenching ... that tangled mass of thick grey hair blowing in the breeze ... thick grey hair! Yes!

"Listen to me, Lemli," he called out in his loudest whisper. "There is a way to get you up here, but it may hurt."

"Never mind that!" shout-whispered Lemli back, "just get me up."

"Then throw your hair towards me and leave the rest to me."

Lemli didn't look enthusiastic. But, short of an alternative – *any* alternative - he caught hold of the ends nearest his feet and tossed a hank of it up to Nimrod, who wound it round his hand and tugged with all his might.

"*Oooh!*" said Lemli, really meaning it. "*Oooh... eeeh... aaah ...* and *snftschttbktd!*" (Don't bother to look the last word up in your dictionary, not unless you own a rare first edition of the **Dictionary of Pain and Suffering, W & R Chambers and Sons, 1927.)**

"Ready?" asked Nimrod - and slithered off the sill, down into the great abyss.

Lemli zoomed up like stone from a catapult, plugging the gap in the window like something a plumber might keep in his bag. Nimrod spread his feet wide on the last mountain ledge this side of eternity and made a cradle with his arms.

"Jump!" he called out Nimrod, bracing himself against the wind.

"You're mad, Nimrod!" whimpered Lemli. "Mad, mad, mad. Oooh!" This particular howl – which emanated from Lemli, not the wind - was caused by Nimrod giving the hank of grey hair one last almighty tug, dislodging the old man from the sill down into his waiting arms. He teetered on the edge of the rocky ledge, fighting for balance against the icy forces of the wind that howled up at him from beyond the world. Slowly he lowered his burden – after years of boiled roots his father was as light as a satchel of schoolbooks – until the old man stood beside him on the ledge of rocks, clinging on for dear life.

Then the night cracked open with a rolling clap of thunder and a flash of yellow light.

They stood there, father and son, pressed close against the edge of the last mountain in the world, fingernails piercing the cracks, heels gripping the rocks below, each pretending not to be scared. Neither succeeded.

"The winds are angry!" shouted Lemli into Nimrod's ear, but even in the short distance from mouth to ear – inches, no more than that – something snatched the middle of his voice away, leaving only a thin, pale strand of whisper, his yowl reduced to a thin bleat.

"It's Podd that's angry, more like," Nimrod shouted back, just as weakly. "Look…" He jerked his chin up towards the window they had just squeezed through. Lantern light played over the edge-stones, flickering this way and that, and Podd's wail of frustration followed it out. "Just in time. Another minute and he'd have had us."

The Master of Nowhere was more than angry. When the door had crashed open … when his lantern had exposed the emptiness of the cell … his first reaction was a howl that swirled up from his most private depths and escaped like a wind trapped in a tunnel.

His mind raced this way and that, searching for explanations for the unexplainable.

They were crouching behind the door.

No they weren't.

They were huddled in a dark corner.

No they weren't.

Perhaps the Outsider had mastered the power of invisibility. Perhaps he could turn himself on and off like a lantern. He ran around the cell, waving his own lantern like a mad thing, swinging it like a weapon in every inch of the cell, hoping to strike their invisible crouching forms. The shadows of the guards shrunk and stretched on the walls.

Nothing.

Nobody.

His belly filled up with fury, like a cistern. Somebody would pay for this.

The guards. It was their fault. They should have kept watch.

"Take them," he shrieked. "They have failed me. Fling them off the edge."

At that moment there was a loud crash from the corridor outside. He rushed out. One of the guards gazed at him with pleading eyes as if to say: not my fault, guv'nor. Podd looked down. The Nowart was still holding the amber box and the crystals he had packed carefully away – but now there were only six of them. The seventh lay shattered at his feet in a thousand tiny fragments.

At first he blamed himself. He should have left them below, where they were safe. But it seemed they weren't safe anywhere, not even in their box.

"You dropped it!" he shrieked at the embarrassed guard.

"It jumped!" said the guard. "Honest it did. One moment it was in the box, the next ..." he looked down at the shards of crystal sparkling in the light.

"Give those here!" screamed Podd, snatching the amber box away. From now on they wouldn't leave his possession. "Throw him off."

Again he raised his head and howled, like a wolf at the moon.

Nimrod and Lemli pressed themselves back hard against the mountain. Lights were coming on everywhere, left, right, up, down, wherever there were windows, flickering, casting their golden hazes into the night air like dancing phantoms.

The howl became a screech ... the screech split and split again ... then one of the guards came flying headfirst out of the window followed by another and then another, their arms spinning like the propellers. Their screams of terror seemed to go on for ever, resounding in the emptiness of eternity, bouncing against the mountain, filling the air the way sausage meat fills its skin, until they were blown away by the wind.

"We'd better move," said Nimrod, "before we get struck by a falling Nowart. Slowly now; we must hold on to each other every step of the way. Our life depends on it. Go on, grab my jerkin."

Lemli did, making martyred noises to let Nimrod know his hair was still stinging.

Off they went, slowly edging along the ridge, fingers clutching and gripping at the rockface, toes curling within their boots as they inched along. Moving at a rate of about an inch a minute is hardly fast, but when there's a endless drop beneath you it's fast enough. Pebbles skittered over the edge but never struck bottom … pebbles that could have been … *them*. The icy breath of the wind puffed at them to dislodge them and shatter them into thousands of human pebbles.

"How … much … further?" huffed Lemli.

"Oh at least a million miles," puffed Nimrod back, hoping there was an element of exaggeration to his guess. "Maybe even twice that."

"Oh dear," muttered Lemli. "That far?"

A mountain eagle came fluttering down to investigate the trespassers, eyes angry, talons plucking at the wind; its great leathery wings flapped and fanned Nimrod's face.

"Don't leg go of the mountain!" he called out to Lemli. "Hold on for all you're worth!"

The eagle flew off with an derisive squawk. Nothing to fear from these ungainly creatures; they didn't belong … wouldn't last long here.

Then Lemli did an odd thing. Raising his head in the direction of the disappearing eagle he squawked back … a magnificent aria of a squawk, one that almost outdid the bird in its eagleness. Nimrod felt an awful sinking feeling. His father was going barking mad. (Or should that be *squawking* mad?) Better pick up their speed before a fresh wave of madness detached the old man from the mountain and made him believe that he could fly – as well as squawk – like an eagle.

"Faster … faster …"

Do you remember your first long distance race? When you thought you couldn't take another step, yet something inside you forced you to continue? How you got to a stage when you weren't even thinking, just setting one foot in front of the other again and again? That's the way Nimrod and Lemli proceeded, their minds blanked out completely, the only thought in their heads the next finger grip.

"I think I'm falling!" said Lemli suddenly. And to add spice to his words, Nimrod heard that rock-crumbling sound climbers have nightmares about.

"Don't say that!" said Nimrod. "And don't do it, either. I don't want to go on all alone!"

"What can I do?" asked Lemli in a wistful voice. "I don't think this rock likes my fingers."

"Then move!" said Nimrod. "Quickly!"

And they moved. Very quickly. Just as Lemli changed his grip the rock he had been holding broke away and began to bounce down the mountain. Bounce, bounce, bounce, bounce .... until the sound was so far away they couldn't hear it.

"Do you know what's worrying me, Nimrod?" asked Lemli.

"What?" said Nimrod.

"That rock..." whispered Lemli in a small voice. "It could have been me!"

The silence gaped. There they were, hanging by their fingernails above the edge of the world. A few inches further and there'd be no more world to cling to.

Nimrod heard a sad little whimper. "What's the matter, Lemli?"

"You go on, Nimrod. I think I'm glued to the mountain. My mind wants to continue, but my body's not particularly interested."

"That won't do," said Nimrod, "have you tried talking nicely to it?"

"I've pleaded and begged, shouted and screamed. All within myself, of course. But my body stubbornly refuses to obey. It does that sometimes, you know..."

Nimrod took a deep breath. "Well you do that. At least you'll have company."

"Company?"

"Yes, company. That big snake coming up behind you."

How it happened, Nimrod never know, but one moment Lemli was on his right, the next on his left.

"Where? What snake?"

163

"It worked!" announced Nimrod triumphantly. "Off we go."

And off they went. Hand over hand, ever so gently, this time Lemli leading the way.

Some twenty or thirty steps further he said to Nimrod: "Don't you think we've gone far enough? We must have gone beyond the Castle by now."

"Possibly," panted Nimrod. "But we must be sure. We'll give it another hour."

"Another *hour*!" Lemli was aghast. "My old fingers will never last that long!"

"They're going to have to," said Nimrod. "Come along."

But only for another few dozen yards. That was when Lemli made his most desperate squawk of all – and without even looking Nimrod knew they were in trouble. There was something in that squawk that smacked of desperation and defeat.

"Oh dear," said Lemli. "I do believe we've just run out of ledge."

Indeed they had. Beyond where they stood on the jutting rocks there was just wind and air and emptiness … nothing more to stand on. The only way forward was back.

"This looks bad," admitted Nimrod. "On second thoughts, don't look. It's too depressing."

Lemli squawked again. Twice.

Only it wasn't Lemli. It was the eagle. Returned. In duplicate. Hovering in the air just inches from their faces, fanning them with their great feathery wings. Their eagle-breath smelt of worm.

Was he seeing things? Had he developed double vision? Was this a dreadful hallucination, the precursor of a final burst of vertigo before surrendering to the endless chasms of space?

"Hello Akadi," said Lemli, suddenly.

No doubt about it. His father had gone over the edge … well figuratively speaking. Now he was speaking to eagles.

"Can I introduce my son Nimrod? He came all the way from World's End to take me home. Isn't that brave of him?"

The eagle squawked something back. Nimrod cast a troubled glance in his father's direction. What was going on here?

Lemli had a goofy grin on his face, showing between the long strands of hair. He caught Nimrod's eye.

"Nimrod? Say hello. This is Akadi," he said "Not sure what his friend's called, though. All those years of loneliness, locked up in my cell … Akadi was the only one to visit me, bring me a warm worm or two to munch on, sometimes a nice scrap of raw rock-rabbit. After a while he began to teach me eagle. Funny, he never got the hang of our language … hasn't got the beak for it. Words like *whistle* and *properly* … impossible without floppy lips." He squawked something back at the eagle, who reacted with what sounded like a cross between a squawk and a giggle … a *squiggle*? … before repeating it to the second bird.

"What did you ask him?" asked Nimrod, hardly believing he was taking all this seriously.

"You'll see. Just wait and see."

The klaxon of an alarm rang out from deep within the castle. Out of the corner of an eye Nimrod saw lantern lights flicker as guards sprinted past windows. There was much shouting and slamming of doors. The eagles retreated to hover high in the night sky, their feathers haloed in gold by the glow from the lanterns. Then they too flittered up into the darkness.

"Even they're scared," said Nimrod, knowing the feeling.

Lemli snorted. "Scared? Ha. They're eagles. Eagles don't panic. "

Then, out of the night came the rushing of headwinds past beaks and out of the black night they flew, perfectly synchronised, as if their entire lives had been devoted to practising just this.

The great curved nose-cone of one eagle opened and caught Nimrod's jerkin just behind his neck. He felt himself being drawn away from the mountain. He scrabbled with his hands at the rocks, gripping them for dear life, but this was eagle territory and he didn't stand a chance. His legs swung out over the Great Abyss, his precious spectacles slithering down to the very tip of his nose.

"Wheee!"

Dad?

He couldn't believe it. His father was having fun! Father's weren't meant to have fun. Their role in life was to put the dampers on yours. But there he was, at his age, arms stretched out like a bird, hair streaming in all directions and streaking back to reveal a mouth curved upwards into a delighted grin of ecstasy.

"Look at me, Nimrod. I'm flying!"

And then it got to Nimrod. Flying. Yes, he was flying too, suspended over the very end of the world, the wind whistling up one nostril and down the other and venturing into other places too private to even think about, only he didn't enjoy one measly second of it for he could hear the slow ripping of the name-tag sewn into the neck of his jerkin, the only link between himself and Akadi's golden friend.

And then ... and then he was down, secure, feet planted on solid ground, high on a plateau overlooking the courtyard of Dunroamin' Castle.

Far below, through the dark mists, the wind howled around the rocks of the castle, still angry after all these years at finding something so stubbornly standing in its way.

"We're free!" gasped Lemli.

"Free of the Castle, yes," panted Nimrod. "But I can't say I feel very liberated, up here on this cold mountain, surrounded on all sides by Nowarts. What am I going to do: that's the big problem."

"You mean what are *we* going to do," corrected Lemli. "Don't forget me."

"Any ideas?" asked Nimrod hopefully.

Lemli placed a finger into his mouth and sucked away as if he knew there was an answer in there somewhere if only he could draw it out. He sucked so furiously his body swayed backwards and forwards then, suddenly, he stopped and turned to face Nimrod, his face flushed from exertion.

"No", he said. "No, I'm afraid not." Then, as an afterthought..." I'm not much good, am I?"

Nimrod smiled and patted his hairy coat. "Of course you are," he said "You're the best, the bravest father in the world. If you hadn't learned eagle-talk we'd be dead by now. Dead – or worse. But if you insist on swaying like that you won't be in the world any longer, so beware."

Lemli's eyes began to swim, and he looked up again at Nimrod.

"There is *one* way..."

Nimrod asked quickly: "What?"

"No." Lemli shook his head. "We couldn't."

"What is it?" repeated Nimrod.

"No," said Lemli. "Silly of me. It won't do."

"For goodness sake tell me." insisted Nimrod.

"You'd only laugh at me."

"I'll never laugh at you, Lemli. What is your plan?"

Lemli tugged at Nimrod's sleeve and pointed in the distance to a small gully winding down the far side of the mountain, tinted an unearthly silver by the moon. "That path ... it leads to the Valley of the Googlions. The Nowarts never go near it. The Googlions are even more devious than them, and that's saying something. It's our only chance. If we take the main mountain path down someone is sure to spot us. Anyway, they'll have warned the gatekeeper to lock up and let nobody through."

Out of the night sky the eagles swooped, settling on a bare branch. One of them squawked something at Lemli, who squawked something back.

"What was that all about?" asked Nimrod.

"Good news," said Lemli. "But you'll need to shut your eyes and open your mouth. Trust me."

"Trust. Does that word have any meaning in these parts?"

"It does when your father speaks it. Now do as I say. Eyes shut, mouth up, tilt your head back, just as I'm doing. No cheating now."

Nimrod did as he was told. He had an intimation of what was coming, but didn't dare explore the subject.

Eyes shut.

Mouth open.

Head back.

He heard the eagle wings flutter – and a moment later felt the cold hard beak insert itself between his lips.

To his dying day he never once asked himself what it was he had for dinner that day. He remembered something soft and squishy and tasting of the earth… and he remembered that there was lots of it.

He waited till the eagles fluttered off before opening his eyes and mopping his lips with his sleeve.

"Well?" There were pinky-grey smudges of something shiny and slimy on the edges of Lemli's mouth and Nim mopped it away too.

"Well what?"

"Tasty enough?" asked Lemli.

"Filling," answered Nimrod. "Should we leave it at that? Now let's get going. I don't like the sound of those sirens in the castle, and I think I heard the main door open."

The silver pathway through the trees curled like a snake. The moon glinted through the leafless branches but the light was too pale to cast any shadows. They would have to hurry. They needed the cover of darkness to scurry down unseen, and the night wouldn't last for ever.

"Are we likely to meet up with any Googlions here?" asked Nimrod.

Lemli shook his head. "Most unlikely. They're scared of the mountain. Scared of the night too, come to that. When it gets dark they prefer to stick together. Strength in numbers, and all that. They're all down in the valley below, sleeping in their caves and their holes in the ground, those that haven't been press-ganged into working for Nowart families."

Nimrod thought about the girl Gluçilla in Xero's kitchen. What wretched lives they led, sandwiched between rocks and hard places.

"How about Googlion guards?"

Lemli shook his mane. "No Googlion ever steps away from his herd if he can help it. They're naturally timid creatures; every night, without fail, they gather to plot the downfall of the Nowarts. All talk, of course. All bravado. They'd never dream of actually doing anything about it. They're all gas and no flame, your Googlion."

Nimrod thought about it. "But if it came to the push, do you think they'd stand a chance? If they rose up against the Nowarts, I mean?"

Lemli nodded. "They're in a strong position. They breed like rabbits; there are so many of them they outnumber the Nowarts by about five to one. And they've got the muscles and teeth of a creature three times their size … your Googlion is a hairy ball of solid energy, with a little raw cunning thrown in. But they're losers. They've convinced themselves the Nowarts are superior creatures: stronger, smarter, braver. If only they knew. With a strong leader and a little planning they could tear their overlords to shreds."

Nimrod clambered down the path silently, a plan forming in his mind, one that excited him so much he began to tremble. Lemli mistook the trembling for fear. He laid his hand on Nimrod's shoulder and said:

"Don't worry, lad. Your dad's here, right behind you."

Down the mountain path they scampered, keeping to the edges where the moonlight shone palest. The trees grew sparser as they descended into the valley, having been plundered for firewood, and the moon dripped with tattered clouds. Each time the moon swam behind a cloud they used the brief darkness to dart from stump to stump, avoiding open spaces where they could. Lemli pointed across the valley to a row of black holes in the slopes.

"See those caves? That's where they live. Listen … hear that? They're having one of their meeting's right now."

Squinting his eyes, Nimrod picked out little squat shapes dotted around a fire. More of these crumpled little specks spilled out of the caves and moved down the slopes and across the plain like termites out floorboards. The cold night air was filled with the grumble of their voices.

"What language are they speaking?" whispered Nimrod. "Would they understand us?"

"You're not planning to talk to them, I hope!" shivered Lemli.

"Just answer me," pressed Nimrod, "would they?"

Lemli nodded. "You see, Googlions are such devious creatures they've developed the knack of instant interpretation. The unfamiliar frightens them; they can't bear the thought of anyone plotting secretively behind their backs. They might not be smart enough to assemble a wheelbarrow, but, well, they have this facility for language … something built in, the way babies can swim without swimming lessons. I suppose you could say it's their secret weapon."

Nimrod nodded. "Good. That could be our secret weapon too."

They crept forward, towards the campfire. Lemli tried to hold Nimrod back.

"We'd better branch off soon, Nim. We're getting too close!"

"Not yet," replied Nimrod. "Just stick with me. I know what I'm doing … I think!"

Further.

And yet further.

"We must turn!" urged Lemli. "That path there curls back towards the village – and the swamps. If we dart down it while they're all talking … well it's probably our last hope. The Googlions have incredibly acute hearing."

"Not yet," whispered Nimrod. "Leave everything to me."

They drew closer to the gathering, closer to where the flames of the fire snapped and popped and sent tiny embers soaring up into the night sky. Lemli, clutched at Nimrod. "You're mad! You don't know what you're doing! If those Googlions see us they'll tear us apart bone by bone!"

"I don't think so," muttered Nimrod cryptically. "I have a plan."

Lemli's eyes sunk. "Hark at him. Plan, he says. Plan? Death wish, more like. Plans are things people take their time over, plans are *planned*. This is just craziness on toast!"

"Just tell me one thing," whispered Nimrod urgently. "They're greedy, these Googlions?"

"The greediest."

"Hateful?"

"The hatefulest."

"Cruel?"

"The absolute cruellest!"

"Unhappy?"

"Miserable. So would you be if you relied on Nowarts for your peace of mind."

"That's all I wanted to know!" said Nimrod – and stood up.

From out of the seething mass came a strangled cry - and hundreds of heads turned their way. Their eyes were like fireflies.

"Down! Down!" Lemli tugged frantically at his jacket. He was almost mute with fear. Nimrod hardly heard him. Shrugging off the clutching hands he clambered up on to a gnarled old rock covered in moss, rising up into the full view of the massed Googlions, who were now well within smelling distance.

"Sit down!" screamed Lemli in his loudest whisper. "Oh heck, too late. They've seen us. Oh my! Oh mercy me!" In the presence of his son the old man's imprecations were mild; there's no telling how much more strongly he might have put it had he been alone.

Nimrod laid his head on the trembling mass of grey hair and raised his voice to a bellow.

"Googlions of Nowhere!" he called out. "Turn this way. Listen to me. I'm here to tell you that your time has come!"

His words had an extraordinary effect. At first the Googlions muttered and murmured and clutched each other, huddling together for protection. Had the Nowarts descended upon them? Was this a trick? Then, when they saw it was just a pipsqueak, a short hairless pipsqueak in bright clothes, they surged angrily forward.

Lemli began to whimper. "Goodbye, Nimrod. It was nice knowing you. Goodbye, my dear young son…"

But if Nimrod shared Lemli's terror (and he did, he did, with knobs on) he didn't show it. He held up his hand.

"Wait. No further. Hear me out. I have good news for you" A wind rose behind him, lifting and carrying his reedy voice far across the valley.

But the tide of Googlions flowed on. Soon they'd surround them, crashing down on them like storm-waves on a shore. If the purpose was to halt them he'd have to offer them a lot more than have a nice day.

Change of tack.

What would Podd have done?

He held up his hand.

"I told you: wait. Your restless surging is making my army of winged serpents anxious. They've slithered and flown long and hard and they're not in a good mood. Come any closer and they'll emerge from the long grass and consume you. They're starving hungry; none of them has eaten a thing since a fortnight last Thursday."

The Googlions turned to one another and muttered. Mistrustful as ever they guessed he might be bluffing … guessed, but couldn't be absolutely sure.

"You tell them, Captain!" Nimrod made a military gesture in the general direction of Lemli, half-whispering half-shouting: "Get up on a tree-truck, so they think you're taller than you are."

And Lemli, bless him, obeyed with aplomb. He rose majestically up onto the stump, shook his grey hair until he was one shapeless trembling mass - and emitted the most blood-curdling cry Nimrod had ever heard. It was so effective it even terrified its creator.

"That's him saying grace," explained Nimrod to the bewildered Googlions. "We always like to say thank-you before we tuck into our dinner. We may be ferocious, but we're also well-mannered."

Lemli entered into the spirit of things by plunging both arms through his curtain of hair and raising them to the sky; he blew a few more hairs away from the general position of his mouth and at the top of his voice began to shout out gobbledegook.

The Googlions stayed where they were, which was not exactly the hoped-for reaction … a little mild retreating would have made both Nimrod and Lemli a great deal more comfortable, even if it was just one small step at a time. Anything to indicate that they were reconsidering.

Nimrod scanned the terrain, left to right, right to left. There were Googlions everywhere: the fields were crawling with them, the hillside carpeted in them, and low mutters and snarls were billowing forward through the masses like Chinese whispers, only hissier.

"Any last words for your relatives?," asked Nimrod at the top of his voice, battling to keep out the quiver. "In a moment we begin the ceremony of Mass Roasting by Magic. Sorry, but my winged serpents aren't into raw food. A word of advice: if you shut your eyes and take a deep breath when the sizzling begins it won't hurt so much."

The mutters and snarls descended into a low blur bordering on sullen silence.

"One moment – there's a message coming through. From Beyond."

While he worked out what to do next he whipped the glasses from his nose, paused, counted to ten, and replaced them again. The terror-stricken Googlions fell into a frightened hushed. What sort of creature could vanish and appear at will?

Out of the side of his mouth Nimrod whispered down to Lemli: "Do these creatures worship any gods? A god of war, say?"

"There is one," answered Lemli, also in a whisper." But I can't remember the name…"

"Think!" urged Nimrod. "It's important..!"

Swaying backwards and forwards and still mumbling out his gobbledegook Lemli dug deep into his memory and the tours the Nowarts had taken him on. It was thee somewhere, the name, the Googlions' stupid god of war. Once he had heard the Nowart guards laughing about it, jeering, mocking. It began with a K ... or was that a W? No, more like a Z ... His mind raced. Every name he had ever heard raced through his mind, from his grandfather's cat (Alfonso) to the Oastman's mother (Yolanda). Still it evaded him.

Nimrod drew himself up and surveyed the masses The whole valley was thick with Googlions, seething like a nest of spiders. If they lost their fear now neither he nor Lemli had a chance.

"DAHOO!"

Nimrod almost fell off his rock. So delighted was Lemli at remembering the name he had shouted it out at the top of his voice.

When he looked down again, he could hardly believe his eyes: the Googlions were crouched down on the ground in a praying position, their hands splayed out before them, rocking backwards and forwards on their haunches. Once the plains had been speckled with thousands of little glowing coals, now all was black but the circle of fire. It seemed to be working. They had all shut their eyes in supplication.

"Listen, O mighty Googlions."

That shook them. The word mighty.

Immediately, all the coals were rekindled.

"Dahoo has just instructed me to delay our dinner. He says ... what's that, Dahoo? ... are they? Really? He says, Googlions, that he has a tastier meat in mind this day. Even tastier than you. "

There was a flicker and a glow as the Googlions blinked up at Nimrod, who took heart from their mass obedience and raised his voice until it had become a quivering shriek.

"For too long, Googlions, you have paid your homage to the Nowarts. For too long have they laughed at you and trampled you like insects. Now the worm's turn has come."

Still the Googlions remained silent.

Googlions?

Silent?

This was too much to believe.

"Dahoo says to tell you: the meat he has in mind is spit-roast Nowart. And - *tonight is the night!*"

This time a rousing cheer exploded from the gathered masses, so loud, Nimrod feared the Nowarts might hear them from the castle. He held up his fist and shook it.

Silence. Immediate silence.

"Be still. Do you wish the Nowarts to hear you? What sort of

Googlions are you to spoil the plans of Dahoo? You ought to be ashamed of yourselves!"

A shamed mutter passed through the stooped Googlions.

Nimrod continued: "I have come to lead you up into Nowhere. We depart immediately. Grab what you can in the way of weapons.... and if you can't find any, pick up sticks and stones on the way. You have Dahoo's promise that you will succeed. He is here with us at this moment – in spirit if not in person ..."

Then a curious thing happened. A fork of lighting cut through the sky, scribbling a jagged scar into the blackness. The Googlions fell to the ground, clutching at each other, moaning and making painful whimpers of terror. "

Nimrod seized the opportunity.

"Dahoo has spoken. We must waste no time. We march now!"

A Googlion in the front row stepped nervously forward. His grating, ugly voice curled the night.

"What about your army of winged serpents. Will they come too? Or are we expected to do all the dirty work?"

Nimrod adopted a hurt expression on the war-god's behalf.

"Take that man's name. Does he dare question Dahoo's judgement? Answer me, Googlions. Would you leave your camp unguarded? Would you have the wily Nowarts attack your valley and invade your caves and steal all your possessions? For shame, Googlions, think a little better of your war god than that. While you attack the castle, my winged serpents will render themselves invisible like this – " quick on-and-off of the spectacles – "and protect your caves. Only the Captain here – " he gestured at Lemli – "will come with us! What a stupid question that was!"

A second Googlion grabbed hold of the questioner and tossed him into the middle of a writhing mass. In moments he had been set upon by his friends and torn to pieces. Oh the life of a Googlion. Oh what sacrifices had to be made.

Nimrod felt no pity: frankly he was really quite pleased there was one less Googlion in the world to contend with.

"The time has come. Hasten off. Collect your weapons We attack now!"

The gathering broke up as the creatures slithered into the dark holes, returning with spears and lances and axes and clubs and kitchen knives and screwdrivers and pairs of pliers and marshmallow-toasting forks and chopsticks and ...

Nimrod put his arm around Lemli.

"Come. We march on Nowhere!"

And then, out of the chaos of scattered Googlions, as if some sleeping instinct had woken in each of them, they silently formed into ranks, shoulder against shoulder, row after row. Platoons grew into companies which grew into battalions. From the midst of this sudden army a voice screeched out "let's get 'em!" but even then there was no panic, they simply began to march efficiently forward as if to the beat of an unheard drum, on towards the city where the Nowarts lived.

And then a new kind of rumble emerged, the rhythmic rumble of a marching song, an anthem of war, deep voices chanting over the drum-thump of horny heels on rock. It was mesmeric; only when they were in the thick of it did Nimrod become aware that the sheer rhythm and force of the song had sucked them both in ... they were marching too, alongside the Googlion soldiers, in perfect synchronisation, *left, right, left, right,* off towards the village.

In terms of numbers, the Nowarts didn't stand a chance. But in terms of weapons... Nimrod glanced doubtfully down at a rock tied by twine to a bamboo pole one of the Googlions was swinging round his head. As he watched, the string snapped and the rock went flying off to strike another Googlion on the head, rendering him immediately unconscious.

"How far is it to Nowhere?" asked Nimrod, struggling to pitch his voice above the chanting voices.

"Straight on then left past the swamps," replied Lemli. His weary slump had lifted – he marched with strength and confidence now, why, there was even a gleam to the one visible eye. By heaven, thought Nimrod, he's licking his lips in there ... he can taste revenge!

He still couldn't believe what he had set in motion. Him, a lad from World's End had ordered an army of Googlions into war against the hateful Nowarts. He had had wild dreams in his short life – mainly about feasting - but this was beyond wild. It was ... well, there was a savage element to it, he could feel it in his blood which pulsed against his temples to the beat of the marching feet. If only he could see Podd's face when he found out, if only he could be there when the hood slipped from his head and read the terror in the eyes of the man who had dished it out for so long…

Across the bare, windswept fields the army rolled, nothing resisting for long its relentless progress. Watchtowers groaned … buckled … toppled. The fence around the Nowart's root-garden collapsed - in a matter of seconds its posts and barbed-wire fencing had been transformed into brutal clubs and vicious-looking lassos, the barbs whistling as the battle-hungry Googlions swished them round their heads. All this to the hard, determined drum-beat of an entire army marching as if one man. One long, powerful man. One angry, ruthless man.

Lemli nudged Nimrod in the ribs. "How about this then, eh? Never been so excited in my life, you know, Nimrod. They made me suffer for all those years - now it's their turn. I'd hate to be in their boots right now. These Googlions are *mad!*"

Behind them, a repetitive hissing started up… *Shwa! Shwa! Shwa! Shwa!*"

"What does that mean?" asked Nimrod.

"It's Googlion for "kill". Told you they meant business." Then, after a moment's thought he added: "Speaking for myself, I might give the fighting a miss. Never been one for sticks and stones and broken bones."

"I'm right with you there," Nimrod agreed, enthusiastically. "Give me a plate of food and a jug of nectar any day!" Then, after a sorrowful sniff, "…. I'm sorry they stole my satchel. I'd hardly touched my nectar!"

"You had *nectar?*" Lemli's eyes lit up. "Real World's End *nectar?*"

Nimrod nodded. "I can't bear to think of a Nowart mouth curled around that flask. What a waste of good nectar. I mean, *we* could be drinking it!"

"It doesn't bear thinking," agreed Lemli. "Hang on … something moved!"

Something had indeed moved. Something which looked very much like a Nowart. Hardly surprising - it *was* a Nowart. He had appeared from behind a tree to stand staring in blank-faced amazement at the advancing army. It was the last thing he ever saw. A band of Googlions sprinted up to him and severed his head with one sweep of a sharpened dustbin lid. It rolled off down the hill, eyes still popping, and sunk with a gurgle into the swamp.

"We must be extra careful now," warned Lemli. "That guard's the first of many. If the next is any wiser he'll keep himself concealed until we've passed, and take a short cut back to the village. I don't think we can expect to arrive unheralded."

The lights of Nowhere glittered on the horizon. From here on the hill it looked so still and peaceful. The clouds in the sky broke for a moment just above the central square and the moon peered out, bathing Nowhere in a soft benign glow. How deceptive moonlight can be.

A thought suddenly struck Nimrod and he scampered up on to an elevated rock to one side.

"Wait! Listen to me!"

How they heard him over the determined chanting he never knew, but almost immediately the army halted and thousands of glowing embers flickered his way. He could hear their excited breath.

"Listen closely, Googlions!" he called out. "This is Dahoo's last word to you before battle commences, so be sure to pay attention. Advance on the village as fast as you can. The Nowarts will still be groggy with sleep – hit them hard before they wake. Destroy everything in your path ... but do *not* - I repeat – *not* - go near the cave of the wizard, or the whole plan will fail. Do I make myself clear?"

A hum passed through the ranks. They seemed to understand.

"When I drop my hand, it's Goodbye Nowarts. Are you ready?"

They replied as if one loud, quivering voice.

"Ready ... ready ... ready..."

And so Nimrod dropped his hand and stood back.

The fetid breath of the advancing Googlions warmed his face as they panted past him. Already signs of activity were flickering below, a good sign, for Nimrod did not want the Nowarts taken completely by surprise. They needed time to collect their weapons together and fight back, for his plan was to get rid of Googlions as well as Nowarts – the more the merrier.

They stood and watched as the army passed.

"It's lucky you moved so fast," Lemli told Nimrod. "The Googlions would never have gone through with this if you'd given them time to think. They're naturally doubting creatures, and don't trust anyone, not even each other. But it's too late now."

The last of the Googlions passed them by. These were the oldest of the creatures, limping behind their young leaders, brandishing heavy sticks and calling out evil curses. Nimrod and Lemli followed them at a soft trot.

"We'd better stay close to them until we reach the village," said Nimrod. "I'd hate to be left out here all alone. At least, for the moment, the Googlions are on our side!"

Then the chanting stopped. There was a loud sigh in reverse as the army - like one man - drew in its breath … and everything went a deathly quiet. Then … crash … everything was shrieks and yells and the thump of running feet and … yes, the first alarmed cry of a surprised Nowart.

Out of their tumbledown houses they poured … big Nowarts and small … naked Nowarts clutching filthy cloths to their bellies pursued by Googlion servants who had realised that finally the tables were turned. Nimrod watched as a rope lassoed itself round one of the sleeping vultures … it shook its head and screeched in anger then rose up into the morning sky in the direction of the castle, two Googlions clinging desperately to the end of the rope.

Down in the village of Nowhere the sting of sword against sword and the rattle of rock on shield could be heard. The square was alive with fighting. Nimrod and Lemli stood back in the doorway of a building, watching through partly opened fingers: the savagery was nauseating, and death almost as painful to watch as it was to experience. Through a break in the masses Nimrod saw Xero fighting for his life with three angry Googlions, an expression of evil joy dominating his features as the second great vulture of Podd hovered above, squawking excitedly and flapping its great leathery black wings. It screeched something out to the other bird who was now well on its way to pass the disastrous news on to its master, the Googlions still dangling from the end of the rope.

"He's right there!" said Lemli. "That vulture spoke the truth!"

Nimrod tugged at Lemli's hair. "Come on ... this way. We've done what we can ... now it's over to Kabil!"

They began to run.

"Which way?" gasped Lemli. An arrow narrowly missed his head.

"I'm not sure," admitted Nimrod darting down what looked like a familiar alley. "But I know it's not that far!"

Down the they ran, dodging swords and arrows and skirting the battle areas. The Nowarts were too busy defending themselves to take any notice of unarmed men, and the Googlions were so far still on their side, so - for the time being - they were safe.

"This street doesn't look familiar," said Nimrod. "Let's try the next one. Stay close to me."

"This one?"

"Not yet! Keep running!"

"Maybe it's the next one!" wheezed Nimrod. "It must be here somewhere. I know – it's the next one! Follow me!"

Lemli did. But it wasn't.

Either it was a new trick Kabil had just learned, or .... Whatever it was Nimrod didn't like this one bit.

The cave – and all who dwelt in her – had clean gone and vanished.

*

He slid the stone forward and reached in. Still there. Gently his fingers closed round it and he drew it out, careful not to let the surface scrape against the harsh edges of the rock. He held it up, turning it in the pale light: inside small objects slid from one side to the other and clinked against the near edge. Four bullets. And ... his fingers closed around it, protectively.

The words were faded but he could still read them, the pastel-pink letters curling round the countryside scene. Three sheep and a white-bearded old man leaning on his crook.

DR. SHEPHERDS LIQUORICE THROAT LOZENGES.
EXTRA STRONG.
PLACE UNDER THE TONGUE AND SUCK.

Alarms were ringing all over the castle. Doors slammed. Footsteps echoed in the corridors below where he crouched. A fusillade of knocking drummed on the door but he said nothing. Best nobody knew where he was. If he had to beat a retreat – and it looked that way, now – better there was no trail to trace.

Rage boiled in his belly like bile and rose up into his throat, the bitterness almost causing him to gag. He couldn't remember when last he'd been this angry. But was it anger – or was it frustration? Alone he had caused those stupid creatures of the nether world to raise up a town, no, more than that, an entire kingdom, castle and all, a kingdom where he held sway – and that ludicrous Beyonderling had stumbled in with that idiotic grin on his face, not two lobes of a brain to rub together, and suddenly it was all threatened.

He raised his face to the ceiling and opened his mouth. A howl of pain burst out from it, embittered by the bile in his belly. The knocking stopped. A voice called out: "Master? Are You there? Are you safe?"

He said nothing, allowing the howl to tail away into nothing.

The vulture on the window sill cocked its head to one side. He smelt weakness. Was this indeed the Lord of Nowhere, the All-Powerful, skulking down there on the floor like a rodent? Howling like injured prey? He watched as his Master rose from the floor and dusted himself off. He lowered his head, turning his ear cavity into the room, in case there was something he needed to hear. A command. A secret. Below him he could hear the grappling of Googlion claws on the ridge jutting from the castle wall; the first of those ugly freaks had dropped to his death over the valley, the other had clung to the rope all the way up, slithering off only when he landed on the sill. Now he was clutching at the stones, his strength growing weaker by the minute. He gave him two minutes, three if he was lucky.

From the distance came the clash of cold steel and the battle-cries of the Googlions. Flames licked at the sky. Through its needle-sharp eyes the vulture watched as the silhouettes fought to the death against the scarlet ball of the rising sun. The path was crawling with escaping Nowarts – women and children and carts laden with possessions, crawling desperately up towards the castle.

There was a noise back in the room … a scrape … a scratch … a low heavy thump. His swung his head back to investigate, his blood-red dewlap flapping against his breast.

Empty.

The room was empty.

Where he had gone? How had Podd vanished like that?

He fluttered into the room, his flapping wings kicking clouds of dust up off the floor, disturbing the footsteps that led across to the far wall and then … just … ran out.

Gone.

Nowhere had no Master.

Now even he was scared.

*

In his cave Kabil crouched over the cloud, speaking to it.

"Come on now … you can do it … one nice icy-cold teardrop …then another, if you can spare it … just for me…"

The cloud trembled a little. Something small and glistening dripped from its grey mass. Its edges seemed to focus into a harder edge, and there was a low scraping sound deep within.

"Yes! That's the way! Firm up! Chill down! Go – go – *go!*"

He leaned in closer until his nose was almost buried in the fluff of the cloud, and added a trickle of something from an eye-dropper held above the little cloud. "Firmer yet … still harder … colder … go on …*push!*"

From a distance there came a loud crash then a frantic rattling and a voice calling out his name … his *other* name … his *alter ego* …

"Balik! Balik! Let us in! Quick!"

He turned from the cloud and reached for a little switch set into the wall.

"Enter!" he said, and his voice lowered an octave and boomed through the cave, magnified by loudspeakers hidden behind cardboard rocks.

"Damn! he thought (in his secret, inner, unmagnified voice). Damn visitors. Always pitch up at the worst of times.

He wiggled the switch a second time and the circuit-breaker inside the switch made contact with its other half and sent the signal to open along the wires buried in the wall.

He shook his head sadly. Not magic. Just good old-fashioned Science. Common or Garden Physics. Just like the trick with the cloud. If only he could have summoned up *real* magic to make his voice billow out like that. Or – even better – to make his cloud weep icy tears. Then they'd look up to him with wide, adoring eyes…

They came swinging round the corner, the two refugees, and Nimrod flung his arms around the wizard and squeezed hard.

"Sit down, Kabil, we've got so much to tell you!"

"What's … that?"

The wizard pointed to the large ball of fluff shaking and shuddering in a grey heap next to Nimrod. "Well I'm … it isn't Lemli, is it?"

The hair-ball nodded.

He was overjoyed. He hugged both in turn, spending a little longer on Lemli, whom he hadn't seen in years.

"The revolt has begun!" Nimrod gabbled so fast he had to start all over again. "You see, they locked us up in a cell in the castle, and I decided … that is to say *we* decided, my father and me decided …"

"There's time enough for explanation later," said Kabil quickly. "First we must get you out of here."

"No hurry," said Nimrod. "Well, not too much, anyway. They won't touch your cave. The Nowarts are scared of it, and the Googlions have orders not to come near it. What's that you're doing there? Surely it can wait? There's a war going on outside. This is no time for weather."

Kabil gave him an odd sort of look, and turned back to his cloud. His voice came floating over his shoulder.

"What did I tell you? I told you my plan of escape would work." He tapped his head. "There's more than fluff in this head of mine, you know. Deep, mysterious thoughts, that's what this is full of.!"

"Your plan of escape?!" But Nimrod was in no mood for arguing.

"Can you transport us magically back to World's End? I don't fancy that forest path again."

Kabil turned. Behind him the cloud-drips were become firmer as they fell into the waiting bowl, starting as wet plops of water and growing progressively tinnier. He shook his head. "Afraid not, Nimrod. But don't worry, you should both be safe. As long as you stick to the path this time. By jings, one of you needs a good haircut and it's not Nimrod."

Lemli made an ambiguous sound deep within his forest of hair. Kabil broke in.

"But I haven't congratulated you yet, Nimrod. I couldn't have plotted it better if I'd thought of it myself!"

"Were you here when the fighting began?" asked Nimrod.

"Goodness me, no. I was in my cottage in the Lower Valley Forest. Can you picture my surprise when I looked into my crystal ball and saw the Googlions swarming over the hill? *That's Nimrod's work*, I said to myself, *Nimrod's behind all this, the clever lad.* I wasted no time getting myself here. I knew you'd need help."

Ka-*boom*.

Ker-*rash*.

It came from the end of the passage. From the gates. They were either battering them down or very, very impatient. Nimrod looked at Lemli, Lemli looked at Kabil, and Kabil studied his fingernails.

"I knew it was only a matter of time."

The voices of a dozen Nowarts speaking all at once panicked up the corridor.

"Balik! Are you there?"

"Quick!"

"Help!"

"We need your spells – and we need them *now!*

"Podd has decreed it!"

"Stay here," whispered Kabil. "Don't show your faces. I'll sort it all out."

Down the corridor he strode, his cloak flapping behind him.

*Plip … plop … clink … clack …*went the cloud.

Lemli flung himself on the floor, and adopted a sleeping posture, his legs tucked up beneath his chin, his hair curling round him in a cocoon of snug warmth.

"Sssh!" he said., "I'm going to grab forty winks. It's not over yet, and we need all the rest we can get. I wonder if Kabil keeps a snack-fridge?"

Nimrod nudged him with his foot. He too longed to crash out, but now wasn't the time for that. Not with angry Nowarts banging on the gates.

"I hope I'll be able to see again when we get back." Lemli's voice wound its way through the hairy undergrowth. "I mean, now that I've accustomed myself to the darkness of Nowhere."

"I'm sure you will," said Nimrod. "Me, I'm longing to get these spectacles off my nose. This furrow is itching like a mad thing. I'm sure it's affected my sense of smell."

Kabil returned. He was shaking his head in amazement.

"I can hardly believe it. It's gone,"

"What?" said Nimrod. "The gate?"

"The visitor?" asked Lemli, rising unwillingly to his feet.

"The *town!*" said Kabil. "The whole *town*. Nowhere's nowhere. Parts of it are up in flames, the rest flattened. Was this your doing, Nimrod? Or am I dreaming? No, don't tell me now, that can wait, this business isn't over yet. It seems the Nowarts are fleeing to the castle. It seems they still have an almost childlike faith in Podd, even as their houses fall about their feet and their families run off in all directions, screaming and sobbing. Poor deluded wretches."

Poor? Poor in the sense of no possessions left, or …. but Nimrod didn't wait to explore the concept. As he turned, Kabil thrust a large domestic bucket into his hands then grabbed a bow and two arrows off a hook and shoved them Lemli's way. "Here. Grab these. I'd have liked another day or two … a year would have allowed me to refine it … a decade or two more would certainly have made me famous, oh dear where is time when you need it most …"

He snatched up a beaker from his laboratory bench and disconnected the rubber pipe from what seemed like the very heart of the cloud. It made a loud plop – and clinked. Muttering, he sloshed the contents into the bucket in Nimrod's hand. "Careful now. Don't spill." Then off he strode, down the corridor, all vestiges of a silly, bumbling old wizard replaced by quiet, steely determination. Nimrod arched an eyebrow at

Lemli, shrugged, and trotted down the passage to catch up.

Outside, the scarlet from the flames devouring Nowhere were melting into the streaks of dawn from the rising sun. Around them the village had sunk to its knees. Rats scurried through the tumbled blocks of mud, darting on tiptoe over burning embers, gnawing on splinters of furniture, dragging scraps of matting over to the nests they were constructing in the debris. Nowarts and Googlions alike sprawled out where they had been felled, their dead eyes fixing them with grotesque stares as they picked their way through the wreckage.

Schwa ... schwa ... schwa.

Kill ... kill ... kill.

They turned a corner, to see a band of chanting Googlions pursuing a Nowart family up the hill, waving their weapons. One of the Nowart children, a snotty-nosed girl with selfish eyes, was clutching a rag-doll to her chest and blubbing uncontrollably.

What have I done! thought Nimrod. So many lives wasted ... so much destruction.

Overhearing his thoughts Kabil turned on him, his face a battleground where weariness struggled against stamina. "You've done well, Nimrod. You haven't taken lives ... you've saved them. Anyway, it was a massacre waiting to happen. You were the flint, not the flame. You sparked it off but you never raised a hand in anger. This ..." - he made a broad gesture encompassing the devastation - "... this was all their work, evil destroying evil. But we haven't won yet."

Nimrod looked up at him gratefully. More. Tell me more. I need your reassurance.

"Thank you, Kabil. But what's left to do? The village has been flattened. The Nowarts are on the run."

"And the Googlions are in control. That's like cheering on a tidal wave after an earthquake ... both are equally destructive forces. Both need reining in. No, the Nowarts will lock themselves away in the castle and regroup, the Googlions will take heart from their victory and who knows what they'll do next ... World's End is only a two day march from here, and they'll be wanting food and fresh water and new homes to live in. No, we haven't won, Nimrod, not by a long chalk. Watch that bucket ... you're spilling my precious concoction. Oh for pity's sake, Lemli, what do you think you're doing there?"

The old man had raised the bow up to where his face hid behind the cataract of air, and was drawing back an arrow.

"See that Googlion with the flaming torch? He's got five seconds … count them!"

With an angry gesture Kabil snatched the bow from his hand.

"Don't waste it. I've got other plans for this. Come on. We haven't a moment to lose.

He strode quickly up the path, sidestepping the bodies of the fallen combatants. Though the sun was up it had been devoured by the dark chocolate rainclouds that gathered menacingly in the sky above them.

"Storm," said Lemli, stopping to study the dark canopy. "Not long now. Oh dear."

"What's the matter?" Nimrod grabbed a handful of hair and tugged him up behind him.

"All this hair." The old man shook himself and the curtain of grey hair shuddered like a bush in the wind. "I was just thinking. You know how heavy your head gets after a good hair-wash? Well, when the rain saturates me I'll be too heavy to move."

"Nonsense," said Kabil as they stumbled to catch up. "Not if my plans work."

The gatehouse was deserted. The gatekeeper's last act had been to open the trap that exposed the great abyss over the river roaring deep below. From below they had watched as the Googlions took running leaps and sprang over the gap … some made it, some missed and went spiralling down into the emptiness. With their makeshift weapons the enraged creatures had hacked at the huge gates, toppling them so that they fell and formed a drawbridge over the chasm then over they scrambled, trampling the rats running in the opposite direction, their hisses and chants filling the air.

It trembled as they crossed it, first Kabil then Nimrod who led Lemli on by the hair.

The courtyard in front of the castle gates was a seething mass of Googlions, like maggots on rotten meat, shaking their weapons at the guards looking down from the parapet who in turned waved their lances and screamed abuse.

"There's a good place," said Kabil, indicating a tall rock on top of which lay a Nowart sentry, an axe cleaving his helmet.

It was set aside from the courtyard and the seething mass of Googlions by a hundred or so paces, standing at the head of a hill carpeted in stinging nettles. On top the rock was flat from years of pacing by the horny feet of a Nowart sentry; steps had been chipped out of the rock just deep enough for three tentacles to get a toe-hold.

"Hurry! Before the rain!"

Kabil clambered up with the agility of someone half his age and extended a hand to pull Nimrod and Lemli up after him.

"Careful with that bucket. I should have made more of the mixture, but it shouldn't need more than a cupful. One small cupful. If it works…"

They surveyed the scene below and before them. The castle rose up out of the clambering mob, joined at the foundations as if both were accretions of each other, its windows darkened by Nowart faces. The Googlions were struggling to shin up the castle walls but the stones were too smooth, too sheer, and they fell back onto the spears of others who were jostling to take their place, producing a row of kicking and squealing Googlion kebabs.

"They're all here," said Kabil. "Every last Nowart … every remaining Googlion." A quiet smile tugged up the corners of his mouth. "Hand me up that bucket, will you."

Nimrod passed it up as asked. Kabil held both arrows up to his eyes and selected the straighter of the two. "Either of you any good at archery?"

Now Nimrod was thoroughly baffled. Thousands of seething Googlions, a castle full of Nowarts, and one small arrow … what was he on about?

The chocolate clouds had darkened into a deep mahogany. There was a flash of purple light and, seconds later, a low rumble as the clouds collided. A fat blob of rain struck Nimrod on the forehead, dissolving the compacted mud and send a thick earthy rivulet streaming down into his eyes.

"Yes!" he exclaimed proudly. "My Dad!"

He remembered with pride the annual sports days back in World's End. They were special days … days when his family were local heroes. Not because of his paltry attempts at the long jump … those were best forgotten, particularly that shameful incident during the egg and spoon race when he had skidded and the egg had dropped and all the other contestants had slipped and fallen causing him to win by default … no, because of his mother's soup - which attracted even longer queues than the Oastman's cookies - and because of his father's prowess with the bow and arrow.

Thwack … thwack … thwack … three bull's eyes. Every time. He just had a knack for it. Once he had even split the Mayor's arrow – which stuck proudly out of the innermost ring of the target – clean in two. So good was he at it the archery event became a solo performance, the crowds gathering to cheer him on and stand in awe of his skill. Nobody else bothered to enter.

But Lemli looked anything but confident now.

"Not any more," he said. "That was then – this is now. Many a long year has passed … my old eyes aren't what they were."

But Kabil wasn't having any of this false modesty.

"Here!" he said. "You've got two go's. Only two. Do your best."

He handed the bow over to the stack of hair – and dipped the chosen arrow into the bucket.

"Straight through the middle of that dark cloud right in the centre. Think you can manage that?"

Some resourceful Googlions had jerry-built a battering ram out of the door to the gatekeeper's office and a tree-trunk sliced into wheels. Basic as it was it rolled forward now with a rumble in its throat, on towards the great castle door, picking up speed and momentum as it trundled forward. With a crash it struck the door, shaking off clouds of dust. But it was as if a fly had settled on a giant's nose.

Back it rolled to first position. More Googlions lowered their heads and set their shoulders against it, adding their muscle-power, forcing it forward, faster, faster, aiming at the spot in the door where the last attempt had grazed the wood. The second crash was louder, but it might as well have been a tap from an injured finger. The door hardly budged.

Backwards … forwards … again and again … more Nowarts each time … uselessly it crashed into a force ten times greater than itself. Jeers and catcalls streamed down from the parapets. The frustrated Googlions let go of the battering ram and shook their fists towards the sky, which had thickened into a solid mass of brown-black rain clouds, dark with menace; it rolled crookedly back down the hill like a market trolley with a squiff wheel, striking the rock they were standing on and dislodging thousands of tiny angry insects who scrambled up Lemli's hair, prospecting for food. He recoiled in horror.

Schwa … schwa … schwa…

The mantra of death.

"Never mind the creepy-crawlies," shouted Kabil over the Googlion mantra. "Now! Go! Fire!"

Nervously Lemli fitted the arrow into the bow. Nimrod was puzzled. Why was Kabil so eager to stab that particular cloud? What did he hope to achieve by puncturing it? Certainly it was a sitting duck to someone who could pierce a ring the size of a goose's eye at fifty paces.

"Watch out! He's aiming at Glwgyg!"

Who Glwgyg was and why the Googlions should care more about him than the others skewered on their swords was a question for another time, another day. What mattered was that the Googlions had turned malicious eyes on them and were advancing on their rock.

"Hurry!" shouted Kabil. "Fire! The middle of the cloud!"

Lemli pulled the bow-string back … just as a sharp rock struck him on the shoulder. The cord twanged and the bow slipped and the arrow spiralled uselessly into the thick of the blitz of Googlions.

"Damn!" said Lemli, or words to that effect.

"Wha-hey!" cheered the Nowarts from the parapets.

"Quick!" yelled Kabil. "The other one! It's our last chance!" Grabbing the second – and last – arrow and swirling its head of in what was left of the brew he passed it over. Again Lemli fitted it to the bow-string … again he draw it unhurriedly back, valiantly dodging the barrage of rocks … further and further .. tighter … tighter … until Nimrod was sure the cord would snap.

Clunk.

Twang.

Oof!

A rock shaped like a pineapple struck Lemli in his stomach. An entire tummy-full of air escaped and he doubled up, letting go of the bow-string. The arrow shot forward with a hiss, twirling in the air.

A sudden silence descended.

The guards on the parapet craned their heads to look up as the arrow coiled through the sky.

En masse, the Googlions turned their heads to follow its trajectory.

The jeering stopped. Nobody said a word. There was a loud gasp of air from Nowart and Googlion alike.

This time there was no mistake about it. The arrow, still dripping with Kabil's potion, sailed up into the sky and vanished into the cloud like a spoon into Brown Windsor Soup.

The Googlions drew closer together for support and comfort. It was like the split second before a storm broke. There was something electric in the air. They didn't like it.

Then one of the Nowarts laughed like a drain, and all his cronies joined in, the air ringing with their jeers.

"Oh dear!" shouted one. "We're in trouble now! Mercy be! We're all going to get damp!"

The laughter billowed. The Googlions joined in. The jeering had created a truce as they turned their contempt on the common enemy – them!

"Listen!" hissed Kabil, dancing with excitement. "Can you hear that?"

From the heart of the cloud came a rolling, cracking sound and the cloud seemed to draw in on itself, the chocolate brown colour leeching out until it loomed overhead massive and black and transparent, all at the same time. Then the same happened to the next cloud and the next, until the sky above them was one huge black ice-block.

Kabil began to jump up and down on his rock. "Yes! The biggest ice block in the history of the world! And I made it!"

A split appeared in the cloud. The pale light caught its silver lining which flashed like a huge bolt of sheet lightening, filling the sky with a sudden momentary blinding flash.

One of the Googlions screamed.

The rumble became deafening. A network of splits and cracks zigzagged across the clouds, giving them the crinkly wisdom of a very old man's face. The immense weight of the ice-block - now the size of a small planet - turned the sky icy-blue. And then...

"Jump!" yelled Kabil. "Run for it!"

They jumped all right. But there was no running for it. Almost simultaneously they landed on the make-shift battering ram, slewing it round so that it pointed downhill, and off they spun on a wild roller-coaster ride down the mountain path. Nimrod, who had landed in the front, used his feet to steer it like a skateboard, negotiating the corners at accelerating speeds which caused their stomachs to lurch.

"Wheee!" went Lemli, regressing into childhood.

"Careful," cautioned Kabil, ever the adult.

"Hold tight!" said Nimrod, hanging a sharp left.

Over the door-bridge they sailed, whilst behind them the cracking and rumbling filled the air.

And then … and then came the biggest crash in living history, possibly the loudest since the big bang created the world we stand on. It was so thunderous, so positively ear-splitting, Nimrod lost concentration and put all his weight into his left foot when he should have used the right. Their vehicle slewed to the left, struck a Nowart sprawled out on the path, wobbled, spun, and crashed into a rock big enough to halt it in its track but small enough to rip out its undercarriage.

They picked themselves up, dusted themselves off, and turned to look back up at the castle.

Or what was left of it.

The vast block of ice had toppled out of the sky and crushed the castle into pebbles. Huge chunks of ice still rained down from the shreds of the clouds, flattening what few recognizable bits of the castle remained standing, the U of a battlement here, the gaping mouth of a carved gargoyle there.

There was not a Nowart nor a Googlion to be seen, although dark flat shapes could be seen through the partial transparency of the ice-block. All was silent but the rolling of the upended tree-trunk wheels of their trolley.

"Brilliant magic" crowed Nimrod.

"Fantastic archery!" said Kabil, slapping Lemli on where he thought his back was most likely to be.

"What driving!" swanked Lemli, his voice quivering with pride. "That was my son, that was. My very own flesh and blood!"

Flesh and blood. The words sucked the celebration out of them. They looked at each other, saying nothing, then turned away. Yes, the Nowarts were nasty, evil and despicable, certainly there was nothing quite as appalling as a Googlion, but, well, death was a stranger to them, and its shadow chilled them.

Eventually it was Kabil who broke the silence.

"Time we were on our way. We've done what we can; Podd's kingdom is destroyed, and its inhabitants won't be coming back for more of the same. Gloating won't achieve anything. They're history now. We've got our life to live and it's waiting for us over the brow of that hill and sixty-five miles down the road.

Below them the charred remains of Nowhere smoked and sighed; ravens swooped down to peck scraps from the rubble.

"Come," said Kabil, "come with me. There's food in my cave, food and a shower – though only a cold one. I may even have a bottle of nectar stashed away somewhere safe. You both need a sleep before you head back home. While you catch forty winks I'll try my new spell out on your dirty clothes – I call it Wizard Biological Washing Powder – and rustle up a picnic basket. We'll meet this time Friday in the main square of World's End."

"You bet," said a weary Nimrod.

"Did you say nectar?" asked Lemli.

And Kabil, well Kabil reached both arms out and tucked both father and son into the folds of his lofty frame, one each side, and down they walked, stepping over the scattered flotsam and jetsam of Nowhere, falling into the same rhythm of footfalls until they were like one single six-footed creature with an abundance of hair on one side, a wryful expression on the other and an elevated tall wizardly bump in the middle, down past the swamps and the town square and the toppled statue of Podd, down to the gates of the last remaining edifice in all Nowhere which Kabil opened and in the went, into the warmth and out of our story.

*

Every squeak and creak of rope over flywheel was like a snigger, every shudder of the cradle a mocking belly-laugh. How the Beyonderlings must be scoffing. How they would pay for it one day, when he had rallied his strength.

Deeper into the pit he sank, down to the dark river where a boat waited, moored against the jetty, pointing towards the rapids and ... what? He wasn't sure, but he welcomed its strangeness as he'd always sought the shadows of the unknown.

They'd never dream of looking for him here. Over the "edge of the world". Or so they thought. He'd like to have taken credit for that rumour but the pilgrims had set it in motion. Fleeing from the strife of the real world ... his world once, too ... they had travelled as far as they dared. Here, they said, here we will settle and meditate and count our blessings. Let us, they said, let us call it World's End. And the myth had stuck.

It had served him well. If others believed the world came to a sudden stop at his feet, well, let them. If they believed his castle stood on the brink of eternity, well, that myth would guard his final escape route better than a thousand platoons of Nowar warriors.

Deeper. Lower.

He thought no more of the Nowarts, of his companions of all these years, of lives lost, of Nowhere shattered behind and above him, the end of his dream. He'd built it up once. He'd do it again. A rock skittered down from his tumbled castle, striking the cradle, but that was yesterday's rock, that was a chapter closed.

The Beyonderling, Nimrod, he was another story. He'd pay, oh how he'd pay. Podd slid the lozenge tin out from where he'd tucked it, between the cold barrel of his pistol and his belly, and prised it open. Rust fell away, staining his fingers.

Four fresh bullets.

A faded, creased print of The Pilgrim's Rest, the prototype of his castle. He stared at it for a while then, in a fit of temper, tore it up into confetti. Gone. Both of them – print and castle. They had served their purposes. Those parts of his life was over ... miserable childhood, then victory.

He unfolded another sheet of paper. A clipping from a long defunct local newspaper. It was faded almost into illegibility now, but that hardly mattered, he knew it off by heart. And those two dark eyes, staring out of the page from a face so paled by time it could no longer be recognized. Father pleads for son's return. Were they still waiting for him, him and his silent, martyred woman, he with his birch, she with her hoard of hidden bottles? Did they still keep an ember of hope alive, fanned into the belief that one day there'd be a rap on the door and a hug and old scores forgotten?

He flicked through the last remaining objects in the tin. A wooden soldier. Cigarette cards of war heroes. A spill of itching powder which he'd only ever tried once. His grandfather's watch, the strap long worn and gone. The detritus of childhood. Well if ever he needed it here was proof that the simple faith of the young could be turned and subverted and transmuted into strength.

He shut the tin and replaced it back where it could once again print its shape into his belly. Next to the pistol.

The Beyonderling had tasted power. He had sent creatures to their death. He had lost his innocence. Give him a month … a year … give him three, four or more … but one day the craving would resurface. One day he'd want to travel back to a world empty of pathetic daydreams and neighbours you automatically trusted … to where the sword ruled and you hankered after more complex tastes, the way children brought up on sweet cakes and fizzy drinks are all one day weaned on to hot spices that burn your mouth, and bitter drinks that made your mouth curl and your stomach lurch and your lips beg for more.

One day, Beyonderling, we'll face each other again.

You can bet on it.

Printed in the United Kingdom
by Lightning Source UK Ltd.
124474UK00002B/3/A